Evenings at Mongini's

AND OTHER STORIES
• • •

RUSSELL LUCAS

SUMMIT BOOKS

New York   London   Toronto   Sydney   Tokyo   Singapore

Summit Books
Simon & Schuster Building
Rockefeller Center
1230 Avenue of the Americas
New York, New York 10020

Originally published in Great Britain
by William Heinemann Limited
SUMMIT BOOKS and colophon are trademarks
of Simon & Schuster
Display by Eric Ziman
Manufactured in the United States of America

1   3   5   7   9   10   8   6   4   2

Library of Congress Cataloging in Publication Data

Lucas, Russell.
Evenings at Mongini's, and other stories / by Russell Lucas.
p.   cm.
"Originally published in Great Britain
by William Heinemann
Limited"—T.p. verso.
Contents: Beautiful Billimoria—The massage parlour—An
afternoon's pleasure—The vulnerable Mede—Evenings at Mongini's—
The Pathan's girl—Moving targets—Keep smiling—Nets—
Bismarck.
1. Bombay (India)—Fiction.   I. Title.
PR6062.U154E9   1991
823'.914—dc20   90-44923
CIP

ISBN 0-671-72746-X

For June

Acknowledgments
• • •

I would like to thank Des Hogan
and Shena Mackay for their encouragement;
Toby Eady, my agent; Helena Petrovna for her inspiration;
and Nadia Lawrence, to whom my particular gratitude for
her invaluable help and many creative suggestions.

Contents

• • •

Beautiful Billimoria

· · ·

When Bomanji Billimoria was twelve, he had a turbulent time. He became seriously infatuated with Miss Dorothy Lamour, an actress who swayed and sang her way into his scrotum from the cinema screens of Bombay. He secreted dozens of glossy photographs of her sarong-clad flesh under his semen-stiff mattress. And he penned dangerously suggestive letters to the sultry and sinuous object of his improbable ambitions. He crouched in the four-anna seats during the 3.30, 6.30, and 9.30 shows, hollow eyed and breathless, practising self-abuse through a hole in his trousers as he mentally fornicated with his dream girl on distant atolls or walked proudly, arm in arm with her, along Colaba Causeway, through profound swells of heavy breathing from envious multitudes of priapic onlookers.

On more than one occasion, his mother dragged him out of cinemas where Miss Lamour's films were showing. He was gripped by the windpipe, shaken, slapped and struck on his bare arse with a whippy cane. His mattress was ripped open and the glossy photographs burnt. And in a desperate attempt to stem the defluxion of his precious seed during the hours of darkness, his hands were secured in boxing gloves and chained to the opposite sides of his bed. Finally, while he was pinioned by two powerful uncles, his mother, in an awesome act of maternal devotion, charred the screaming Bomanji's testicles with the red-hot tip of a Burmah cheroot. That did it. He grew up to be a tractable and loving human being.

At twenty-one he was considered by his mother to be the most beautiful man on earth. He was exactly six feet tall, which is regarded by many experts to be the perfect height for a man, and weighed one hundred and fifty pounds, with a well-muscled torso and thighs that were sturdy but unbulging. His body hair was well distributed but not so thick that one could not see the contours of his pectorals or the quality of an almond-shaped navel embedded in a flat stomach. But Billimoria's strong point was his face. Not only did he have a classical nose and large brown eyes set just the right distance apart, but his lips were naturally cherry pink and he possessed a complete and symmetrical set of glistening white teeth. His ears were neither too large nor too small, and each fortnightly visit to the barber evoked much praise for the perfect conformation of his head.

Billimoria, or Billy, as his friends called him, was, however, concerned that his personal beauty had not brought him the rich rewards this attribute probably deserved. Being a thoughtful fellow, he concluded that, although God had blessed him with physical excellence, what he now needed was to sharpen up his mental side. This had never been a conspicuous endowment, although his mother felt that passing Standard Seven was something not to be sniffed at. So every morning, Billy, who was unemployed, visited the David Sassoon Mechanics Library near Elphinstone Circle and studied the 1929 edition of the *Encyclopaedia Britannica*. After six months, he had reached BONHEUR, *Rosa* (1822–99), and had so improved his reading technique that he was able to skim down columns of words without the assistance of his right index finger. There were moments, particularly after teasing out the meat from an article that interested him, when he experienced an exaltation of the mind; a state, he was convinced, permanently enjoyed by all educated people. Yet he was often dispirited, when flicking back over the 'A' Section, for he discovered that he could remember hardly anything of what he had so diligently studied.

'It's quite impossible to store everything in one's head,' his mother said.

'But there's nothing in mine,' Billy fretted, 'literally

4

nothing. If I could remember ten per cent of what I read, I'd be happy.'

Mrs Billimoria smoothed every wrinkle in her son's life. She shopped, cooked, cleaned and ironed for him. And she never stopped giving him valuable advice. Each morning, she would enquire about the consistency of his stools, the colour of his water and the texture of his tongue. She inspected his eyes and never failed to smell his breath. When he complained of a headache, she rubbed his forehead with Oriental Balm; when he cut his skin, she was ready with the Zam Buk. She was not above giving him enemas or bathing his body with French brandy when he had an excessively high temperature. No son could want for more.

'Perhaps you should study mathematics on the side, to strengthen your brain muscles,' she suggested. Her uncle was a mathematician who, before the Great War, had won an open trigonometry competition in Surat and district.

Billy stared at her gloomily. 'Numbers have always depressed me,' he said. But he took his mother's advice to heart. After a morning at the David Sassoon Mechanics Library, he started to practise simple arithmetic. By the end of his first year of self-improvement, Billy had reached DRYOPITHECUS and had broken the back of long division.

Now despite Billy's extraordinary beauty, he was not significantly successful with girls. Far uglier chaps – guys with big noses and bad teeth, short fat fellows with dandruff and pimples, men with speech impediments and twitches – attracted the most glorious women. But Billy just didn't interest females. He even mugged up stanzas of his favourite poet, Sir Walter Scott, and learned a dozen tricky quotations from a book on Victorian wisdom. It made little difference. After ten minutes in Billy's company, girls would make some excuse and disappear. Even worse, employers were not disposed to take a chance with him. At twenty-five, Billy was still beautiful and unemployed. He was now working his way through the *Encyclopaedia Britannica* for the second time and was capable of solving quadratic equations.

It was his mother who suggested that he needed some social skills.

'Why not music?' she asked.

'Music?'

'People like nothing better than a man who can play an instrument or sing.'

She showed him an advertisement in an American magazine. It depicted a fat jolly man with a bobbed Mozartian haircut, playing the piano. He was surrounded by several large-breasted female admirers. One of these even posed cheek to the pianist's jowl, laughing rapturously at the artist.

'It would take me years to learn the piano. By the time I was any good I'd be too decrepit, anyway.'

'It says here', his mother said, 'that you could be playing Beethoven's "Moonlight Sonata" after seven days.'

Billy read the advertisement several times.

'No,' he decided at last. 'I don't think I could play anybody's sonata after seven days.'

'What you need', his mother said, 'is confidence. Remember, anyone is capable of anything.'

He looked at her doubtfully. 'Who told you that?'

She stroked his handsome face with a wrinkled hand. 'That's a fact, my son.'

Billy decided that the development of his voice was the safest musical option. He purchased a record of Richard Crooks singing 'Song of Songs' and listened to it carefully several times each evening. Then he tried very hard to replicate the sound that came out of his HMV gramophone.

'You've got the sobs off wonderfully well,' his mother said, 'but the higher notes need a little more attention.'

Night after night, Billy practised 'Song of Songs'. Eventually he mastered the phrasing, the vocal flourishes and the volume. His mother said that when she was waiting for a tram fifty yards down the road from the apartment block where they lived, he sounded, despite background traffic noises, remarkably like a real tenor.

It was shortly after this, just before his thirtieth birthday, that Billy's luck changed. It all happened in one week. On Sunday he discovered Émile Coué; on Monday he learned to swim the American crawl; on Tuesday he mastered 'Macushla'; on Wednesday he managed 'Ah, Sweet Mystery of Life'; 'Thora' and 'Because' became part of his growing repertoire on Thursday; and on the Friday morning Billy found employment in Arbuthnot Crombie's shipping office at Ballard Estate. He was overjoyed.

'I understand calculus,' he told the old chief clerk who interviewed him.

The man looked at him suspiciously. 'We don't want any trouble here, my boy. All you've got to do is to enter the names of passengers in this Sailings Register. That is what you will be doing all day. Arbuthnot Crombie want nothing more from you. Do you understand?'

'Yes, sir,' said Billy respectfully.

Arbuthnot Crombie was acknowledged to be one of the most prestigious shipping firms in the city. It occupied a spacious nineteenth-century building that could be described as moghul-gothic, a fusion of islamic rococo and imperial swagger not untypical in mercantile Bombay. It faced the sea, not far from the old East India Company premises. Billy felt that he was now part of the romance of a great port. *Urbs primus in Indus*, as his maternal Uncle Pestonji boasted. The Pestonji family had worked for ship chandlers for one hundred and fifty years. It was a responsibility his blood could not easily deny.

He was stimulated by his new environment. Uniformed chaprassies, in brightly coloured turbans and belts with

7

brass plates bearing the crests and names of great companies; strawberry-pink Scotsmen, with their feet up in vast air-conditioned offices; clever men in black coats negotiating berths, crewing, insurances, victualling and the maintenance of giant liners; wizened clerks, sweating over huge ledgers; mysterious bells rung throughout the day in accordance with maritime custom and practice; red-sashed peons running bills of lading and shipping manifests along vaulted colonnades from company to company; important ladies and gentlemen streaming in throughout the day to enquire about passengers, luggage or goods transported between the Far East and European ports. He was even excited by the smells of glue, sealing wax, marking ink, damp hessian, methylated spirits and freshly planed deal whenever he passed through the Small Parcels room. Billy worked diligently at inscribing the names of passengers in the Sailings Register. He scarcely looked up or spoke to anyone around him. In the drawer of his desk he kept a little card. This he glanced at once every hour, by sliding the drawer open as though he was searching for a nib or a piece of blotting paper. On the card was written in his best handwriting: *Day by day, in every way, I'm getting better and better.* And although there were times when he missed spending his mornings in the David Sassoon Mechanics Library reading the *Encyclopaedia Britannica*, he was confident that he had now embarked upon a path to happiness and success.

At lunch he was conscious of a young female watching him. It was a measure of his growing awareness that he recognised the signals. On reflection, he was certain that nobody of the opposite sex had ever before watched him in quite the same manner. He felt elevated and flattered. The girl was, by most standards, plain: small, with big ears, close-set eyes and a receding chin. Billy found, however, that if he stared at her long enough her features seemed to blend into a more prepossessing composite impression. He wondered why this should be. After several minutes'

8

consideration he realised that the answer was that she was lively. She had the alertness of a small bird. That was it. Her vitality made her modestly attractive. He was convinced that she was a nice person.

It was Billy who spoke first. She responded without any fuss. Her name was Amy Engineer and she lived not far from him along Colaba Causeway. They had several friends and acquaintances in common. Indeed, on the second day of their lunchtime conversations they discovered that Amy's maternal great-aunt had married a Pestonji. This man was Billy's great-grandfather's second cousin, or so they believed. The consanguinity amused them, although their conclusion was at that point speculative and resided upon the circumstance that this link was a bone-setter in Navsari during the eighteen-eighties. The reason they had not encountered each other before was explained by the fact that the Engineers had only moved to Colaba Causeway in the last six months. They were originally a Gowalia Tank family, Amy explained, with strong Navsari affiliations.

On the third day, they travelled home together on the tram and shared a seat. They each purchased their own ticket. Amy insisted on this. As she was fairly small, Billy was rewarded with rather more of the seat than he would usually have had. Even with his thighs expanded he barely touched Amy's leg. But she did not seem to mind the occasional pressure of his knee. Indeed, as the days went by she maintained the contact by moving her knee sideways to meet his. After about ten days they sat knee to knee, with intent.

One Saturday Billy took Amy to the Prince of Wales Museum. He had always loved the natural history section which, his mother had assured him was the finest in the world. As a boy he had spent hours gazing at the wild buffalo, which looked as though it was ready to charge through the plate glass, the tiger at the watering hole, and crocodiles in a tableau on a river bank. But it was the hamadryad, with its hood as large as a soup plate, that filled him with pleasurable horror. He told Amy of his mother's cousin who, when cycling down a jungle path, had accidentally run over and enmeshed a female hamadryad in the rear wheel of his bicycle. The male, who happened to be coupling with the female at the moment of this accident, chased the bicyclist. Spattered in the mangled female's blood, the rider reached the main road, still pursued by the enraged mate. He rode as fast as his legs would propel him but the male drew closer. Finally, when fatigue made it likely he would be caught, he leapt from the bicycle and ran for his life. Looking back, he saw the vengeful hamadryad wrapping itself around the cycle frame and striking the saddle with its envenomed fangs again and again. It was a story that never failed to chill Billy's heart. But Amy expressed profound concern about the snakes.

'Poor creatures,' she said wistfully.

Amy had an aversion to stuffed animals and was more interested in the archeological rooms, particularly in the artefacts from Mohenjandaro and the carved stonework of the Mauryan period. Billy considered that some of the exhibits were excessively salacious and quite unfit for a woman's eyes. He tried to hurry Amy through, but she stared in wonder at effigies of male and female forms frozen in frenzies of sexual union.

'The size of the lingams', she declared, 'appears to be out of all proportion to the rest of their bodies. Why, in this one the lingam is larger than his leg.'

'That does appear to be unrealistic,' Billy admitted wryly.

After their tour of the building they sat in the garden and ate pistachios while Billy talked. He never stopped talking for two hours. She giggled when his voice cracked.

'You've gone quite hoarse,' she said.

'I've talked too much,' he apologised.

'Not at all,' Amy said, 'I found everything you said very interesting. You appear to be so well informed about many things.'

'I haven't bored you?' he asked huskily.

'It was quite the nicest afternoon I have ever had,' she said, her eyes lighting up with admiration. Billy did not tell her that he had spent nine years of his life mugging up the *Encyclopaedia Britannica*.

His mother was delighted when he confessed to her that he was seeing a girl.

'It's about time you settled down,' she said.

'Nothing of the sort,' Billy said. 'Amy is just a good friend.'

'What does she do for a living?'

'She writes up the Arrivals Register at Arbuthnot Crombie.'

'Oh! Where does she live?'

'Up the road. At Cushrow Baug.'

'Oh! How old is she?'

'Twenty-nine.'

'Then she must be plain.'

'So-so.'

'Has she got wide hips?'

'She's small and thin.'

'She could have trouble giving birth.'

'Who's giving birth?'

Billy's mother smiled. 'You must bring her to dinner.'

'She's asked me to her place, to meet her people.'

'When are you going?'

'Sunday.'

Mrs Billimoria got up from her chair and came to her son. He was trying to read *Marmion*. She ran her fingers through his thick black hair. 'I'm proud of you,' she whispered.

Billy did not reply.

'Bring her here next week,' she said.

Before Mrs Billimoria left the room to go to bed, she turned to Billy.

11

'Sing them a song on Sunday. Give them "Ah, Sweet Mystery of Life".'

'Don't be silly, Mama.'

Mrs Billimoria smiled. 'They'll like that. Mark my words.'

Billy was a great success at the Engineers. Mr Engineer poured him brandy after brandy.

'I'm not used to this,' Billy giggled.

And Mrs Engineer could hardly believe her eyes. She took Amy into the kitchen.

'My God, isn't he a handsome man?' she whispered.

'I told you he was quite good-looking.'

Amy glowed with pride as her father, mother, grand-mother and aunt made a great fuss of Billy. Mrs Engineer senior, who was seventy, played the piano.

'Can you sing?' she asked, rumbling through a few preliminary chords.

'A little,' admitted Billy.

'Sing, sing!' everybody shouted.

Amy came quickly to Billy's side. 'Can you really sing?' she asked nervously. 'I'm not too bad,' laughed Billy, blushing.

'And what are you going to give us?' Mrs Engineer senior demanded. She was a former member of the Navsari Madrigal Society and an acknowledged authority on the human voice.

'"Ah, Sweet Mystery of Life"', Billy suggested.

'I say, that's semi-classical,' Mrs Engineer senior said, winking at Amy. Billy's choice had impressed her.

The Engineers settled into their seats as the introduction was played. Mrs Engineer senior muted the boom of the old piano by keeping the soft pedal depressed. She apologised for her left hand, holding it up for Billy's inspection. The third and fourth fingers had been severed from the first joints.

'A mongoose bit my grandmother's fingers off at Lonavla several years ago,' Amy whispered.

Billy looked troubled. Mutilations made him ill. Mrs Engineer senior resumed playing. She was fudging the bass quite cleverly.

'The mongoose got her at Lonavla,' laughed Amy's father, who found the subject of his mother-in-law's missing fingers extremely amusing.

Billy felt queasy. But he shut his eyes and thought of Émile Coué. It was his first public performance. He began.

They sat enthralled as the liquid sounds issued from his throat. He sensed that he had never sung so well, and gained in confidence with every note. When he finished, they rose and acclaimed him noisily. Billy blushed. Amy was tearful. She ran to him and squeezed his hand.

And then he sang 'Song of Songs', and 'Because', glorying in the vibrancy of his new-found power. It was only when Mrs Engineer senior handed him a plate of liver vol-au-vents with her left hand that he vomited over a bronze of Annie Besant, splashing an acquarelle of Bassein Fort and a monkey-skin skimmer. But he had no need to worry. He was the hero of the evening and could do no wrong.

'It was the brandy,' cried Amy angrily.

'Hair of the dog,' shouted her father, filling another glass for the tenor. And while the ladies tidied up the mess, Mr Engineer and Billy saw the bottle out.

Mrs Billimoria opened the door to her son just after midnight. She made a wry face when she smelled his breath.

'It must have been a successful evening.'

Billy beamed stupidly. 'I enjoyed myself.'

The wedding took place on Amy's thirtieth birthday. Mrs Engineer was very concerned about her daughter's size.

'I had to use ghee on my wedding night,' she warned.

Amy looked anxious. 'I must admit, I'm a little appre-hensive,' she said.

But the honeymoon at Mount Abu was clouded by a problem that neither of them had envisaged. Billy was unable to consummate the marriage.

'Perhaps you require a prettier woman,' said Amy sadly.

'Is sex that important?' demanded Billy. 'Why can't we be friends?'

Amy put her arm around him. 'Have you ever had an erection?'

Billy looked gloomy. 'Many years ago.'

'When?'

'I was twelve.'

'My God.'

'I'm sorry I caused you all this trouble.'

She kissed him on the cheek. 'There are far worse problems in marriage than impotence,' she declared bravely.

'You could divorce me.'

'Don't be stupid. Anyway, my mother's second cousin's uncle couldn't do it for the first five years of his marriage.'

'And then?'

'He discovered that he was not ingesting enough starch. Once he stepped up the amount of rice he consumed, everything was fine.'

'Rice?'

She lowered her head and looked at him playfully.

'Why do you think China and India have the largest populations on earth?'

But the couple returned to Bombay disconsolate and grim.

After a few days, old Mrs Billimoria took Amy aside.

'What's the matter, my dear?' she asked.

'What do you mean?'

'The bed that Billy and you sleep on is usually a real creaker. Every night I lie awake listening for a creak, but nothing. Only silence. In the first year of any worthwhile

14

marriage I would expect at least three sessions of high-speed creaking a night.'

Amy burst into tears and told her everything.

Old Mrs Billimoria considered the problem with her usual thoroughness. She asked Amy a great many questions.

'I'm surprised', she said, 'that you appear to be ignorant about the state of his bowels, bladder or breath. Does he have flatulence? Bleeding gums? Are his underpants too tight? Is there any evidence of nocturnal emissions? Or excessive perspiration?'

'These are details', Amy replied, 'that do not concern a modern wife. As far as I can tell, Billy is perfectly healthy.'

Old Mrs Billimoria frowned.

'Let me give you some advice. A man is like a sarangi. He needs a bow rubbed artfully against him to make frisky music.'

But Amy, who was a matriculate with passes in General Science and Physiology, was not impressed by old Mrs Billimoria's ideas. She had tried to read a paperback on psychiatry and half understood some of the more exotic concepts.

'Can you', she asked, 'think of any traumatic experience Billy had in his pubertal years?'

Old Mrs Billimoria's brows furrowed in deep thought. 'Yes,' she said at last, 'I can.'

'What?'

'When he was twelve, I scorched his testicles with the end of a cheroot.'

Amy uttered an involuntary shriek of repugnance.

'My God!'

'He had a crazy infatuation for a Hollywood actress.'

'That's no excuse', Amy reproved, 'for such filthy barbarity.'

Old Mrs Billimoria looked contrite. 'I admit I was wrong. But his constant masturbation terrified me. My brother Ardeshir wasted away through the evil practice. He died at

15

seventeen, infirm, insane and drained of all the vital fluids that sustain life.'

But Amy was convinced that she was now close to a solution.

'Who was this actress that excited my Billy?' she asked.

'Miss Dorothy Lamour,' old Mrs Billimoria replied in a whisper, scarcely daring to articulate the dreaded name.

The next evening, Amy returned with a photograph of Miss Lamour clad in a sarong and wearing a moonflower in her hair. She hoped that the picture might prove to be the catalyst that would restore Billy's potency. What trepidation she had originally felt about the ordeal of consummation had long since evaporated. She pinned the photograph to Billy's pillow and climbed into bed. She watched Billy with some apprehension when he followed her into the room. He undressed, whistling an air from *Manon Lescaut*, noticed the photograph and smiled, not immediately recognising the subject. But then he screamed and bent double, holding himself between the thighs.

'What's the matter?' Amy asked, terrified by her husband's twisting, turning and cries of agony.

Old Mrs Billimoria, listening for creaks, was alarmed by the screams of her son. She ran breathlessly into the room. Billy's eyes were clouded with pain. He threw Amy to the floor and thrust away his mother's restraining arms. With tears streaming down his cheeks, still clutching his genitals, he ran through the living room to the balcony. The two women followed him.

'He's going to kill himself,' old Mrs Billimoria warned.

Amy reached her husband first and clung to him, her arms around his waist. Old Mrs Billimoria threw herself around her son's neck.

'You have to give me grandchildren, my son,' she wailed, wrestling with Billy. At that point, Billy escaped from Amy's grasp. He turned quickly around, spinning his mother, who was hanging from his neck, up in the air. He lifted the old lady above his head with the demonic

16

strength of madness. Amy tried to hold him, mesmerised with horror at what she knew would follow. Old Mrs Billimoria whimpered helplessly as her son launched her like a bundle of rags over the balcony into the starlit night.

'What have you done?' sobbed Amy, rushing to the balcony rail.

Billy turned and grasped Amy. He raised her frail body before him, bearing her like a marionette back into the apartment. He tripped and fell with her across an ebony card table that splintered beneath them. They lay dazed on the imitation Shirazi carpet, among pieces of wood and fragments of glass.

'Oh Billy, Billy,' Amy cried, dimly conscious of a head injury as he tore desperately at her clothes.

'My pain has gone,' he shouted, closing her mouth with dozens of wet kisses. She clung to him in disbelief as he mounted her and consummated their union with authority.

Mrs Billimoria's body, which lay in the rear courtyard of the building, was not discovered until dawn. She was taken away in an ambulance to the morgue. The police made enquiries, took false statements from Billy and Amy, and the coroner returned a verdict of suicide.

From that moment, the young Billimorias never looked back. Amy was pregnant three times in the next four years, producing sturdy and beautiful sons on each occasion. Billy eventually became a senior manager with Arbuthnot Crombie, secretary of the Richard Crooks Appreciation Society of Bombay, and a regular member of the Parsee quiz team on All India Radio. His Uncle Pestonji died, leaving them a villa with a walled garden that was filled with cashew trees.

And there, on Cumballa Hill, they live to this day. In the living room, above an illuminated cocktail cabinet that plays 'Moonlight Serenade' when the door is opened, is an enlarged photo-portrait, tinted by a local water-colourist, of old Mrs Billimoria. It depicts a smiling silver-haired matriarch beaming a benediction on her family. Her three grandchildren have been taught to respect and revere her memory. Their father frequently reminds them of her love and wisdom. On a bedside table by Billy's head is a simple picture of a moonflower. It is Billy's only reminder of his jungle princess. One matter Billy and Amy never discuss is the events of that climacteric night when Mrs Billimoria fell to her unfortunate end. It has become a family secret. And they both hope that in time the truth will recede into a comforting blur, like a strange misremembered dream.

The Massage Parlour

• • •

Chiao was beautiful. She looked as fragile as porcelain. But she had the steel for the tiring work expected from the girls at the Happy Times Massage Parlour. This was an establishment which, by and large, serviced the needs of seafarers but also welcomed other gentlemen who were hot for a really pleasurable time. Chiao had a ten-year-old son called Lu Fong. His best friend was Seamus Caunce whose father was the Deputy Fire Chief. Seamus spent more time at the Happy Times than he did at home, and this was not something of which his parents approved.

Chiao used to fry salted fish in a big black wok over a charcoal fire, incandescent with heat. The clay furnace on which the wok sizzled almost filled the kitchen alcove that was never free of acrid smoke when Chiao was cooking. But if Seamus was around when Chiao cooked Lu Fong his meal, there was always a bowl of boiled rice and some salted fish for him.

Lu Fong taught and showed Seamus many interesting things, like how to smoke, get pleasure from himself and catch farts in his fist. He spoke knowledgeably about the effects of bhang, Spanish fly and dried goat's testicles. He explained the meaning of flies stuck together, dogs joined tail to tail and birds balanced on other birds' backs. He showed him the alley where bearded stevedores humped one another, the café where men painted their faces and dressed like women, and the crazy woman who pushed refuse up herself. He pointed out the restaurant owner who paid for the services of young boys, the fat English-woman who slept with both her Gurkha watchmen, and the sad girl who exposed herself for half a cigarette.

21

It was Lu Fong's ambition to be a pimp, to devote his life to the procuration of foreign sailors for the girls of the Happy Times. Seamus, on the other hand, had always imagined that he would like to be a ship's engineer. He wanted to sail to distant ports. He dreamed of drinking whisky in dockside bars, dancing tangos with lascivious ladies, playing *fan-tan* with desperate men, smoking big cigars, returning home with tattoos on his arms and a grey parrot in a brass cage. In these dreams of the future, Seamus's parents were always happily dead and he lived at the Happy Times with Lu Fong and Chiao.

Lu Fong had a tiny cubicle next to his mother's room, in which there was barely space for his narrow string bed. It was dark, even in the day. When Seamus visited him in the afternoons, they lay in bed together, smoking and listening to the squeaking of Chiao's bed as she entertained her customers. Seamus often dreamed of being one of Chiao's customers. But this was something he did not discuss with anyone.

Despite his many amoral concerns, Seamus had inherited a streak of Irish holiness from his mother, Trilby. He cherished wild birds. He fed feral pigeons, encouraged sparrows to nest along the beams of his vaulted bedroom and attracted carrion crows to the balconies facing the road, with strips of raw meat. His father tried to thump this Franciscan virtue out of his son but had little success. The Deputy Chief knew that when a flock of flapping crows suddenly appeared to spatter his shining red Mereweather Turntables with their corrosive investments, Seamus was exciting them with gamey tit-bits.

'Seamus, you crazy bastard,' he'd scream, squinting up at his son's window.

He complained to his wife that his executive duty to maintain the property of the Fire Service was being made more difficult because of feathers, grain-husks, straw and shit. So Seamus's mother dutifully slippered her boy on his bare arse, again and again.

A sharp-featured, ginger-haired woman, Trilby hated the dust, the heat and the location of the fire station. She longed for the moist cool benediction of a Galway breeze, a clean autumnal frost nipping her slim pink thighs, and the perfume of wet leaves down quiet country lanes. She was haunted by Seamus's wild birds, by the grinding shudder of solid-tyred lorries, rattling bullock carts and clanking metal-wheeled handcarts. The Pathan stevedores pissed up the stone wall of the Prince's Dock that faced the fire station. Jesus, what a dreadful place. She slouched around the hot dusty rooms in which they lived with a handkerchief drenched in *eau de violet* to mask the stench of asafetida, fermented toddy and stale urine, and she sniffed with alarm whenever her son came in.

'And where the blazes have you been?' she'd ask. 'You're stinking of rotten fish.'

'Nowhere.' That was Seamus's usual answer.

'You haven't been up to that dirty massage parlour, have you?'

'Of course not.' He had learned to edge his voice with the right tremor of pious indignation.

Trilby looked at her solemn blue-eyed son with his close-cropped yellow hair, and feared for his innocence.

'The massage parlour is a wicked place.'

'Why?'

'Because it bloody well is.'

Seamus's father was a red-faced bull of a man, tattooed and hairy, with bushy eyebrows above intense blue eyes and an imperious nose. His snuff-trump, he called it. An ex-quartermaster-sergeant in the Loyals, he could whistle 'The Lincolnshire Poacher', his old regimental march, accompany himself with six tablespoons and demonstrate an eccentric walk, simultaneously. His acknowledged skills included strumming on biscuit tins, playing the Jew's harp, reciting funny monologues, singing comic songs and drinking a bottle of Johnny Walker at one sitting.

He had met Trilby Finnegan at a camp dance in Preston.

He had first beguiled her with his orange-peel teeth and a comb-and-tissue version of 'Galway Bay', then overwhelmed her with his ardency in a dark gymnasium. She lay panting on a vaulting mat, her skirt above her navel, as he bore down on her.

An eighteen-year-old hotel cleaner, she had arrived only six weeks ago from the west of Ireland, to stay with her aunt. She had come to the dance armed with pious advice, sound Catholic scruples and a native decency which, until that night, had allowed no male to interfere with her underclothing. None of this was proof against the lunatic persuasion of Charlie Caunce, who subverted her most sacred assumptions. There was nonsense verse before he set about her and a bawdy version of *The Wreck of the Hesperus* after he'd broken in; she was tailed by a clown who found hard-boiled eggs in her brassière and a sticky King of Hearts between her thighs. In retrospect, Trilby found it difficult to determine whether Corporal Caunce's entry into her body was solicited, reasonable, an act of extreme amiability, or brutish assault. And she had only drunk three shandies. Corporal Caunce had bitten Trilby's breasts, torn the lace edging to her chartreuse-green knickers, and kissed her lips sore.

Her closest friend Eudora advised her that had she complained to the Provost Marshal on her return from the dark gymnasium, Corporal Caunce might have faced serious charges. However, the subsequent acceptance of a fourth shandy, the dancing of the last waltz in subdued lighting, and a stroll back to the Whittaker Albion Inn at one o'clock in the morning, arm in arm with Corporal Caunce, amounted to a brazen mitigation few juries could conscientiously refute.

'And did he snatch your virginity?' Eudora demanded.

She was an older woman, twenty-four and thrice seriously engaged. Eudora lived the perilous life of a room maid, highly skilled at evading the lightning gropes of horny motor-car salesmen, the sly fondling of vicars and the silky invitations of paunchy businessmen in slack three-piece suits. She felt responsible for young Trilby.

'Oh dear Jesus,' Trilby sniffed miserably.

Ever since the incident in the dark gymnasium, Trilby had prayed that if she could efface the memory of what she had allowed Charlie Caunce to do to her, in the end things would be as they had been before she met him.

'Well did he or didn't he?'

Trilby felt dazed as she tried to forget the previous night. It seemed a blur of lips, exploring hands and bared flesh. The regimental dance band was playing 'Alice Blue Gown' when he mounted her. She suddenly recalled the penetration with dismal clarity. She remembered sobbing, 'Oh Mother of God,' as he rode deep into her.

'I think he did,' she confessed to Eudora, white faced and foolish.

Then Eudora gave Trilby the worst possible advice.

'Don't let the dirty sod get away, my girl.'

Corporal Caunce did not attempt to get away. They married on his next leave and honeymooned at his mother's boarding house in Bispham. Seamus was two months on the way when they embarked at Liverpool for Bombay. Charlie Caunce, now Acting Sergeant, had been posted to Mhow.

Trilby had never been sure whether she loved her husband or even liked her son. She knew that she hated Bombay and wished that Charlie had taken his demobilisation at home instead of India. But he was rather proud of landing the fire brigade job. He never tired of telling her about the seventy-five unsuccessful applicants, one of whom was a regimental sergeant-major. Charlie was now in charge of eighty men and a Parsee junior officer. He was particularly pleased that the officer, Damania, was a graduate.

'Education doesn't mean a pig's fart in this country,'

he'd tell Trilby. 'What is important is *this*.' And he'd pinch his forearm to exhibit his pink skin.

'Then it's all wrong,' Trilby would brood, watching two sparrows copulating on a beam at the far end of the bedroom.

'Of course it is,' Charlie laughed, 'but hells bells and little onions, thank God, that's the way matters are fixed out here.'

Then he'd sing a mushy song to her, tugging gently at her nipples to simulate the ringing of chapel bells in the valley.

'For mercy's sake, Charlie,' she'd protest, escaping naked to the immense stone-flagged bathroom to take a cold shower. She shuddered at the lizards and cockroaches on the wall. Trilby showered six times a day. At Wadi Bunder she imagined that her body was always sweating, prickly and covered in dust.

Trilby often dreamed that she was a virgin again in Galway. She had never given boys much room in her life in those days, and planned at one point to become a nun. But her mother caught her looking at herself between the thighs with a hand mirror. She said that Jesus and all the blessed saints were watching her doing that filthy thing, so how could she possibly aspire to be a bride of God's only begotten son. And so Trilby was persuaded that she did not have a religious vocation and found a job working in a laundry in Galway City. But her heart pined for her lost girlhood at the convent school and the beautiful people that she knew there. Oh, how she loved the smell of Sister Rosemary Clare and the fat chubby comfort of her hands. Sister Rosemary's hands on her head, her arm cool against her face and moving tenderly along the arch of her back.

'Pray for me, Sister Rosemary,' she pleaded, before leaving Galway. And when Sister Rosemary kissed her on the forehead, Trilby smelled the fragrance of wild thyme and warm starch, mingled with the sour intimacy of sweat on linen garments.

Trilby soon discovered that Charlie Caunce was not a person whom she could endure for long periods. She was happiest when he was on duty. Charlie was an amiable lunatic who meant no harm but whom she found increasingly incomprehensible. His dreams were of pier and pierrot shows, dancing, singing and ukelele playing. He was the life and soul of parties past and parties to come. She could not understand his endless joking. She began to believe that all his patter was part of one awesome joke that went on for years and years. She strained her mind waiting for the laugh-line that never came. Mother of God. Where had that silly half-hour in the dark gymnasium brought her? To a hot and dusty fire station in Wadi Bunder, overlooking a twenty-foot-high pissing wall. Pathans, sailors, pimps, whores and smokers of bhang passed her balconies everyday. Young children were corrupted and victims of vendettas were left eviscerated in dirty gutters. Even Seamus seemed a stranger; him and his precocious Chinese friend who lived in a brothel and taught her boy to pick up butt ends from the street.

Across the way was The Evergreen Bar where Charlie played billiards most Sunday mornings.

'They've got an unofficial "whites only" policy that keeps out the local riff-raff,' Charlie remarked, tapping one side of his nose with a knowing finger.

The billiard tables were in an inner room, behind the peeling paint of the white venetian doors. Most of the seamen played in their vests. Other customers drank iced lager at black metal tables, below whining ceiling fans. The mirror wall-panels, set in red plush and framed in scrolled gilt, gave the place a seedy glitz. It reminded Trilby of a fearsome dance hall Eudora had once taken her to in Liverpool. All the men appeared to be drunk and all the girls wore torn black stockings. They escaped after five minutes and walked coatless through the cold and wet night to Lime Street Station. Eudora with a broken shoulder strap and she with sore heels, as the sequinned black

27

dancing shoes, one size too large, she had borrowed from the receptionist rubbed her skin away. Eudora always referred to that night as a 'good time'. And Trilby tried to pretend that it had been. But Trilby found it difficult to remember a 'good time' in her life that she would really want to relive.

Their next-door neighbours at the fire station were the Damanias. When Mrs Damania first responded to Trilby's invitation to call and see her, she never sat down until she was invited to and, when she did, she preferred to balance on the edge of a hard wooden chair rather than relax in the comfort of the rexine chesterfield on which Trilby reclined.

Schéhérazade Damania was a short solid girl with big breasts, large buttocks and thick legs. She had black eyes, an arched nose and a strong jaw, and raven hair which fell to below her hips when it was released from its large chignon.

'For God's sake, don't tell her that you were once a hotel cleaner,' Charlie warned Trilby.

'Why not?'

'Our position would be prejudiced.'

'What position?'

Charlie wiggled his bushy eyebrows in reproof. 'Didn't you know that I am fifty-seven thousand and twenty-sixth in succession to the Viceroy?'

'Don't be an arse, Charlie.'

'Surely you feel an occasional twinge across your shoulder blades?'

'What the blazes are you talking about?'

'The twinge that comes with bearing the white woman's burden; not as painful as the white man's burden, but one of the penalties of racial superiority and our imperial responsibilities.'

Trilby was never sure whether he was serious or not. Charlie had a way of wrapping everything up in a joke. Despite his cautionary advice, on Schéhérazade Damania's

28

second visit Trilby confessed that she had been a laundry girl in Galway and a hotel cleaner in Preston. And as they relaxed, side by side on the chesterfield, Trilby told her about the dark gymnasium in Fulwood Barracks and even the hand mirror she used to hold between her legs. And Schéhérazade confided many of her secrets to Trilby, even those she had never disclosed to anyone, like how a Maisie Robinson used to suck her nipples in the changing room of the Victoria swimming baths at Back Bay.

'I'm jealous,' murmured Trilby, squeezing Schéhérazade's hand.

'You may call me Sherry,' she said.

'I prefer Schéhérazade, like the princess in the "Arabian Nights".'

Trilby had not felt so happy since the old days in Galway. She smiled at Schéhérazade. And Schéhérazade, who understood the smile, laid her head on Trilby's shoulder.

Seamus often dreamed of Chiao. In these dreams Chiao and he were birds. In one particular dream they flew together to a nest at the top of the clock tower that stood at the entrance of the Prince's Dock. This was a dream of snuggling together and looking down at Wadi Bunder. Sometimes he would find himself pressing down on her rump and smooth hollow of her back. It was always dark when this happened. One bird upon another. Often the pleasure was too exquisite to bear and Seamus awoke, unable to sleep again. One night he dreamed that he was alone, soaring over a landscape of death and destruction. There was silence, darkness and sadness. The next morning, Seamus told his parents about this dream.

'I believe,' Trilby decided, 'that the boy has a gift, being born as he was with a caul around his head.'

Charlie laughed. 'I thought that prevented him from drowning.'

'And often it is a sign of second sight,' Trilby insisted.

'And when are we all going to die?'

'I don't know,' Seamus replied.

'Well we all have to go sometime,' Trilby said.

'I have heard', said Charlie, 'that dreams about death mean good luck.'

After Seamus had gone to school, Charlie said, 'The trouble with our Seamus is that he's bird mad. He even flies about in his dreams.'

But a few nights later, Seamus had a nightmare. He found himself on the dark wooden stairs that led to the first floor of the Happy Times. Two of the Chinese massage girls sat by the window. They smelled of lotus blossom and wore ornamental combs in their hair. In his sleep, Seamus drew his pillow between his legs and floated down the narrow corridor of the massage parlour, inhaling the smells of the evening cooking and looking out at the red lights of the whorehouses above the Evergreen Bar. He saw Chiao floating towards him. She was naked, her black hair loose over her shoulders. As she passed over him, Seamus held her. Her short plump thighs clamped around his body like a vice. He found it difficult to breathe. Then her impassive face, dusted with rice powder, loomed against his. He saw her violet-shadowed eyes closed and her mouth puffed and smudged with red. She wore a circlet of jasmine on her head. Her wax-smooth breasts swung as she pivoted above him. Seamus gripped the pillow. He watched Chiao's eyes open and swell like white balloons. They got bigger and bigger, until they were the size of ostrich eggs. Suddenly they burst and he was drenched in blood and the shimmering pink-and-grey porridge of her exploded skull. Seamus woke up screaming.

'What did you dream?' his mother demanded of her shaking son.

'I can't remember,' Seamus lied.

While she went out to make him a cup of cocoa, his father came in.

'More flying, eh?'

30

Seamus nodded. His father took down a tin drum from the shelf.

'How would you like me to cheer you up?'

Seamus stared at the beefy man in striped shorts strumming on the drum. He knew that he could not escape a song.

Charlie sang to Seamus in a light fruity tenor. When Seamus recalled the song, many years later, it came to him like an old-fashioned record. A voice, tremulous, metallic and full of vim.

> *I've got a pill,*
> *For every ill,*
> *They're guaranteed to cure or kill,*
> *Or give your money back,*
> *A cut or bruise,*
> *The pip or blues,*
> *I'm sure to cure you, in two twos,*
> *I'm Oojah, Oojah, quack . . . quack.*

Charlie finished with a jaunty camel-dance around his son's bed. But as the boy watched him, he saw his father's head change into smoke. He buried his head in the pillow.

'What's the matter?' Trilby asked, giving Seamus the cocoa. He waited until his father had returned to bed then told his mother about the smoke.

'I'll leave the night-light on,' she said. She looked pensive and troubled.

When Trilby got back to her room, she told Charlie that it might be prudent to let Seamus board at the school for the remainder of the term.

'I don't want him mixing with the Chinese boy,' she said. 'There's evidence on his sheet that he's been having impure dreams.'

'Eleven is early for that,' Charlie said.

31

They lay in silence, thinking about Seamus for some time. Then Charlie spoke.

'I'll poison the birds while he's away.'

Charlie Caunce returned unexpectedly one morning to find Trilby sharing a soapy tub with Schéhérazade Damania. He was stunned. He could not comprehend the strange relationship. To Charlie, sexual encounters were very much like jigsaw puzzles: one bit had to fit into another bit. That made sense. But in a bath tub with another woman? As a two-minute cold-shower man, Charlie could not understand aquatic sensuality. And with an Indian – a junior officer's wife. He wondered bleakly, as he waited in the lounge for Trilby to dress and provide him with an explanation, how he could survive the ignominy of his wife's eccentric behaviour if the story ever got out. What would he say to poor Damania? Or to his chief, Peter Plunkett, who was a pukka sahib? But Trilby's confrontation with Charlie was not protracted.

'Schéhérazade and I are going away together.'

'Where?'

'Pondicherry probably. To Aurobindo's ashram.'

'Who the fuck is he?'

'An enlightened man.'

'What will you do for money?'

'Beg.'

'Jesus Christ. How can an Englishwoman beg in India?'

'I'm Irish.'

'It's the same bloody thing.'

'Are you offering to support us?'

Charlie Caunce would have sung a comic song or tried an eccentric walk if it would have helped. He drifted across the room and looked out of the window.

'I've always done my duty,' he brooded, 'so I'm unlikely to stop now. I'll fix you up with an allowance of some sort.'

He looked genuinely sad. She offered him a friendly hand. Charlie took it and held it for some moments, then squeezed it affectionately.

'How about a nice hot poultice for the once-eyed fiddler?' he suggested archly. 'You never know . . . eh?'

Trilby evaded his clumsy attempt to kiss her. She held up a restraining hand.

'Charlie, please. I'm in love with Schéhérazade.'

'Don't be fucking stupid.' His face clouded with hurt anger.

'This is the real thing,' she said fervently.

Charlie found it difficult to articulate a reasonable response. He turned away and went down the stairs. She looked over the balustrade at his head. And at that moment, Trilby felt gloomy.

'Goodbye, Charlie,' she called.

He did not bother to look up. 'Bugger off,' he cursed.

One night at boarding school, Seamus dreamed he saw his father in bed with Chiao. He got up with a start. The dream confused him and disturbed him for several nights. Seamus spoke to Martin, his best friend.

'Tell me, Martin, have you ever wished your father dead?'

Martin stared at him curiously. 'That's a terrible thing, Seamus. It's a terrible thing to wish.'

'I know,' Seamus said softly, 'I am cursed with wishes I can't control. Will you pray for me?'

Martin nodded solemnly. 'Of course,' he promised.

Dr Mascarenhas, the Headmaster, summoned Seamus to his study after prep one evening in April.

'Your mother will be coming to see you tomorrow, Seamus,' he said.

'My mother?' Seamus stared at him.

The headmaster fiddled with some papers. He looked miserable and Seamus sensed something was up.

'Is it about those explosions we heard this afternoon, sir?'

'In a way, Seamus. A great number of people have been hurt, my boy. Some have died. And it's been particularly bad around Wadi Bunder. You can imagine what that means. Such a crowded part of the city. Chaos . . . absolute chaos.'

Seamus bit his lower lip. Tears came to his eyes. He thought of Chiao and Lu Fong, and visualised them entombed in the rubble of the Happy Times Massage Parlour. He saw fire engines turned turtle and the great stone wall of the dockyard flattened, with not one stone left standing upon another. He tried not to think about his father.

'There are times, Seamus, when one must be brave. Your mother will need your strength and support.'

He waited for the Headmaster to tell him the news, to confirm what he suspected. But Dr Mascarenhas took his time, coughed and rubbed his tired eyes.

'I have arranged for you to sleep in the infirmary tonight. In the next room to Matron. You know, Seamus, I lost my own father when I was about your age. He was carried off in the great Hooghly bore. Do you know what a bore is, boy?'

Seamus shook his head.

'It's a gigantic tidal wave, often caused by the rushing of the tide up a narrow river estuary. Yes, I know what it is for a boy to lose his father.'

'Lose him, sir?' Seamus whispered, suddenly abased by a sense of dreadful deprivation.

The headmaster coughed lightly before he spoke. 'Your father died this afternoon, Seamus. I understand it was the second explosion.'

Seamus did not speak. He felt a constriction in his chest and throat. There was a light tap at the door.

'Come in,' ordered Dr Mascarenhas.

It was Mrs Adcock, the matron. She was a small plump woman, cream complexioned with grey shingled hair and bright dark eyes, one of which had an eccentric turn to it as though she was playing a silly game. The boys nicknamed her Wobble Eye. She professed she came from Tasmania but nobody really believed that as there was abundant evidence that she had spent her early years in Jhansi, where her father had been a driver on the Great Indian Peninsula Railway.

'I'd like you to look after Seamus tonight,' the Headmaster said quietly.

Mrs Adcock walked across to Seamus and appropriated his hand in hers. She smelled of disinfectant, aniseed and stale cabbage soup.

'How would you like a chocolate bar?' she asked Seamus, as they made their way along the corridor.

She talked to Seamus in her tweety little-girl voice, of her late husband, Major Kilroy Adcock, who not only had once strangled a fully grown Himalayan bear but had memorised the square root of every number up to one thousand.

'To ten decimal places, Seamus,' she declared with pride.

Mrs Adcock was well known for her strange stories. She even attributed her defective eye to a spell cast by a fish she had once eaten.

'You see,' she explained, 'the fish was a yogi in disguise.'

Seamus told her that he would like to pick up his night clothes and toilet bag from the dormitory on the way. She waited for him as he ran in.

'What's up?' asked Martin as Seamus rummaged in his locker.

'I've lost my father,' Seamus whispered.

'Gosh.'

'The second explosion,' he added solemnly.

'Gosh.'

He felt vaguely important as he marched away to rejoin

35

Mrs Adcock. She gripped his hand again and led him to the sanctuary of the infirmary. The chocolate she had promised him turned out to be rather less than he'd expected. Three good bites saw it off. Later, when he was alone in bed, he cried a little. But not too much. He heard a laugh uncommonly like his father's and was momentarily excited by the thought that he had arrived bloodied but alive from Wadi Bunder. And even when he realised that this was not the case, he was comforted by the mad prospect that his father would probably turn up in the morning. He dozed off and awoke in the small hours. He padded off to the lavatory. When he returned, he sat on his bed in the darkness, conscious for the first time of the ghostly unreality of the world outside him but assured of his own self-sufficiency.

'My father is dead,' he said to himself, loudly.

He repeated the phrase several times, like a mantra. It gave him an inner peace and he knew that being without a father was something he would be able to endure.

Trilby saw Seamus in the junior library. The Headmaster had placed the room at her disposal. A prefect stood sentry outside to stop anyone disturbing the Caunces during the darkness of their tribulation.

'I know Daddy's dead,' Seamus said, before his mother could speak.

Trilby was solemn. She was thankful that Seamus was dry eyed. He appeared to be coping with the tragic news extremely well.

'Have you any idea what happened to Lu Fong?' Seamus asked.

'That Chinese boy from the massage parlour? I'm sure he's gone. There were few survivors in that area. Even the fire station has disappeared. Mr Plunkett told me that Daddy died heroically. He was actually on the munition ship that exploded. Supporting his men to the end. You should be very proud of your father. He might be recommended for a George Cross.'

Seamus couldn't imagine his father in tiny pieces. He

saw him, in his mind, doing a funny walk on the deck of the blazing ship. His mother was weeping, but with dignity and restraint.

'You saw all these terrible things in your dreams, Seamus. Remember?'

Seamus nodded gravely. He made an effort to empathise with her sadness.

She wiped her eyes. 'After the war, you will go to England to live with Nana Caunce in her hotel at Blackpool. You'll love Blackpool. Pier shows, miles of golden sands, donkeys, illuminations, the big Dipper, peppermint rock and the Tower.'

'And you?' he asked.

'Schéhérazade and I will probably spend the rest of this incarnation on the Path.'

'What path?'

'The Path to Enlightenment, my son.' She smiled beatifically, placing a hand on her son's shoulder.

'Many wonderful things have happened to me, Seamus. I can now generate ectoplasm.'

She searched his face for the slightest evidence of scepticism. 'You understand what that is?'

Seamus nodded. 'You explained what it was in your letters.'

His mother got up and arranged five chairs side by side. Then she put her black bead handbag on the floor. She lay face upwards across the five chairs, her hands folded, eyes closed and inhaled deeply. After a few moments, she exhaled noisily.

'I want you to look at my navel,' she instructed Seamus.

He bent dutifully over his mother, staring at the gilt buckle on her blue plastic belt. She was making singing respiratory sounds. Seamus noticed what he concluded was a trickle of saliva issuing from the corner of her mouth. He peered under the chairs. His mother opened one eye.

'From my navel, Seamus,' she directed. 'Did you see that wisp of smoke?'

He placed his face close enough to identify the tiny floral patterns on his mother's black-and-blue voile dress. Then Seamus tapped her on the shoulder.

'May I leave the room for a moment, Mummy? I'm dying for a pee.'

By the time Seamus had returned, his mother had joined the temporal world. She had even replaced the chairs.

'I'd like you to write to Nana Caunce. Tell her how upset you are about Daddy's death. Write her a nice sad letter.'

Seamus nodded. His mother prepared to depart.

'Would you care to walk me to the gate? I've promised to meet Schéhérazade at five.'

They walked down the path slowly together. The Headmaster watched the mother and son furtively from his office on the first floor. He thought that Mrs Caunce had lovely legs with a strength in the calves he suspected had come from dancing. He was something of a dancer too, and saw himself doing a foxtrot, skimming across the French-chalked parquet of the Assembly Hall with the red-haired widow in his arms. She would, he reflected, be delicious to hold against him at a school social. He resolved to ask her to the next one and hummed '*Nuages*', a favourite tune, slitting his eyes as he drew her closer, sliding on the imagined turn, a questing knee deep into her yoke. A young red-haired widow. What could be sweeter? He licked his lips. She was almost edible.

It would be prudent to be pleasant to Seamus. The odd packet of cream crackers, an occasional mango fool topped with buffalo cream, custard apples, chickoos and jambools from his private garden. The idea of inviting the Caunces to his family villa in Panjim suddenly excited him. He mentally despatched Seamus on a day-long boat trip with some local fishermen and danced Mrs Caunce into his cool bedroom overlooking the harbour. He took her to bed, dreaming of titian hair spread out on a coverlet of blue, Catalonian silk, her slim legs locked urgently around him and her vibrant face regarding him with grateful acuity.

'Ah, Dr Mascarenhas. What an absolute bounder you are.'

'Call me Boaz.'

'Ah. Ah.'

Yes, it was important to keep a fatherly eye on the Caunce boy, he decided, restless hands scrotum deep in his trouser pockets.

Trilby bent down to kiss her son. She pressed her lips against the side of his mouth. Tears welled up in her eyes. She sniffed, reaching for a handkerchief.

'You're a brave fellow, Seamus, like your father. I'm very proud of you.'

He looked at her calmly. She patted his head.

'After the funeral, I'll let you know where Schéhérazade and I will be staying. You'll spend the holidays with us, of course. Everything will be arranged with Dr Mascarenhas.'

Trilby turned away, then stopped. She sensed there was something incomprehensible about her son. But it did not seem an appropriate time to probe too deeply.

'Seamus,' she murmured tearfully, 'I want you always to remember that you are the beloved fruit of my womb.'

'Mummy?'

She wiped her face before using a little finger to gently part the adhesion between wet lashes.

'I'll get a black tie for you to wear on Tuesday. Is there anything else you need?'

He shook his head, managing a reassuring smile for her. And there she left him, at the gate. She walked quickly away, sorting out the immediate problems in her mind, like the silly mourning dress, hat and gloves she would need. Why not a khaddar sari? Schéhérazade had asked. She was right, of course. Trilby was doing the expected thing for little Seamus. And although she had almost decided to donate Charlie's insurance money to the ashram, just a shameful doubt or two remained. God, she felt such an unworthy bitch at times. Trilby turned to wave. Seamus waved back. Finally, she made the corner.

And unknown to them both, Dr Mascarenhas stood behind the shutters of an upper window, contemplating unlikely strategies.

When his mother had passed from view, Seamus jigged back towards the school. He sang nasally to himself, an impressionistic parody of his father, as he hurried in for tea, recalling that it was guava jelly on Sundays.

> *My father was a navvy,*
> *Working on the line,*
> *Twenty-four and sixpence,*
> *And his overtime,*
> *He gave a guinea to a lady,*
> *And a golden ring besides,*
> *The cheeky lady asked him,*
> *For his overtime.*

As Seamus skipped, singing happily, below the cloisters to the refectory, he contrived a crazy goat-shuffle, a manic exultation that would have warmed the cockles of Charlie Caunce's heart.

An Afternoon's Pleasure

• • •

Miriam Gulbelkian had known Colette Gascoigne since she was a little girl. Every now and again, when she was bored by the heat, couldn't be bothered to read another romantic paperback, wanted to hear the latest gossip or be spoiled in a special way, she would phone her old friend.

'Drop in for tea,' Mrs Gascoigne said.

'Darling, I'm so busy just now,' Miriam yawned, scratching herself inside her plump thighs, where her prickly heat was particularly troublesome.

'Don't tell lies, Miriam Gulbelkian,' Mrs Gascoigne reproved with a disbelieving laugh.

'Tomorrow, then,' Miriam suggested, regarding herself critically in the hall mirror. She licked her lips, admiring the wet sheen on their fullness. But the hint of a double chin depressed her. She lifted her head and smacked her jaw irritably with the flat of her hand.

'Come at two,' Mrs Gascoigne entreated.

'I'll do my best,' Mirian replied, hissing softly at the reflection of her small, white teeth, imagining herself to be a predatory animal.

Miriam Gulbelkian was a short rounded woman, with black curly hair and the smouldering features of a Circassian beauty. She had sloe-black eyes, thick brows, long lashes and the merest suspicion of down along her upper cheek and ·top lip. Corsetted and dressed for the street, Miriam looked as succulent as a laying hen. Unclothed, she was madly vain about her firm, papaya-shaped breasts but concerned that the folded roll of her belly and fleshiness of her short thighs were signs of irretrievable decay. She had bought herself a rowing machine, a stomach trimmer and

43

an elastic vibrator. Every morning, as she lay, moist with perspiration, among the tangled sheets, she resolved to commence her programme to eradicate the unwanted fat. Miriam was twenty-nine, with a weakness for duck pâté, black olives and baqlava.

Miriam Gulbelkian always dressed up for a visit to Mrs Gascoigne. She knew exactly what was needed to evoke her friend's compliments. Then she did more. Just a little over the top. She sprayed herself with *Vénerie*, Colette's favourite perfume, and wore all her rings, especially the large amethyst, the sapphire cluster, and the diamond eternity circlet.

'Sweetheart, you look almost edible,' Colette Gascoigne said, embracing her with unconcealed delight and kissing her on the mouth. Colette's breath always smelled of aniseed pastilles. She was from Goa, a quarter Portuguese, with a creamy, mottled complexion. She had hennaed hair, slightly frizzed, cut severely in an old-fashioned shingle, and a fine long face, mocking and intelligent. Her eyes were light brown, hazel perhaps, and she angled her head in an attractive manner when she spoke. She was undeniably toothy. In repose, she had the serenity of a beautiful giraffe. One sensed that she did not admire men. She had been, since the dissolution of her only marriage, twenty-five years previously, the mistress of a French jockey, the lover of a Punjabi actress, and a professional procuress. She lived a comfortable life in her large terracotta house, set in an acre of garden along the fashionable Neapean Sea road. She was forty-nine.

'And how is Gory?' Colette asked, over a tray of blehat samak. She sipped a glass of iced tea from a silver holder.

'Bigger and uglier than ever,' grumbled Miriam, dipping a fish-stick in a bowl of tamarind sauce, then bringing it to her mouth above the small blue plate, to catch the falling breadcrumbs.

Gory Gulbelkian was an all-in wrestler. He was seven feet tall, bald, bearded, with several gold-capped teeth, and weighed three hundred and twenty pounds. Although at the end of his career – he was forty-eight – his name on any wrestling promotion was guaranteed to increase the gate. Since leaving his native Azerbaijan, Gory had wrestled in the USA, South America, Europe and the Far East. He had settled in Bombay, where he met and married Miriam, whose mother was Armenian and whose father was a Turkish dry-fruit and nuts wholesaler. Like many large and prodigiously powerful men, Gory had a sweet and gentle nature. He was one of the few men Colette Gascoigne liked. In the old days, before he met Miriam, Colette would supply him with women. He preferred short plump girls with large breasts. To earn their fee, they had to ride him three times on each afternoon engagement. The girls always found Gory to be a perfect gentleman. He had no esoteric vices, except a proclivity for sucking their toes when not actually coupling. This, Colette Gascoigne knew. She instructed the girls on the importance of well-maintained feet and unpainted toenails. The girls seemed surprised that Gory was not inconveniently large.

'I've had bigger ones,' they used to laugh, but there was no malice in the observation, only relief.

Few of the girls Colette Gascoigne supplied, were full-time professionals. Most of them were shop girls, office workers, minor actresses, dancers or housewives. One of her regulars was the wife of a wealthy surgeon, and at least two were married to successful barristers. Everything was arranged with the utmost discretion. Colette used two or three small hotels behind Marine Lines for the business. The owners were pleased with the additional income they got for the rental of their rooms. One of these hotels, the Philadelphia, permanently allocated part of a ground-floor cluster of four bedrooms to Mrs Gascoigne. It had a pleasant approach screened by flowering shrubbery at the rear of the building. The proprietor, an astute Sindhi, had bidets, twin showers and ceiling mirrors installed in each room. And he was particularly proud of the security bolts provided on the bedroom doors and additional exits that allowed the occupiers to escape into the central plaza of the hotel in emergencies. Since most of the senior officers of the Bombay City Police and many of the stipendiary magistrates were Colette Gascoigne's customers, neither she, nor her hotelier clients, ever had problems with the law.

'I would like', Miriam confessed to Colette Gascoigne, 'to lie below a man for a change. I am tired of straddling Gory like a bloody jockey. My thighs get chafed and my back aches. It is no joke.'

Colette did not reply at once. She rose, then went to the sideboard, returning with a brass tray on which there were a napkin, a knife and a covered glass dish.

'Oh, you darling,' cried Miriam, lifting the lid of the dish.

'I know how you love baqlava,' said Colette, kissing Miriam on the cheek. She sat down on the sofa beside her friend, stroking her thigh with affection.

'Don't tell me,' laughed Miriam, filling her mouth with a portion of baqlava; 'I'm too fat.'

'You are just right,' said Colette. Miriam allowed her to move her hand further up her skirt.

'I've got prickly heat on the inside of my thighs,' Miriam complained, pouting like a little girl.

'My poor sweetheart,' Colette whispered, brushing Miriam's facial fluff with her lips. 'Would you like Colette to powder your thighs?' Miriam looked sideways at her, smiling, as she munched the baqlava.

'Of course,' she whispered, resting her head against Colette's shoulder. Colette put her arm around Miriam, cupping her right breast lightly in her hand.

'You were telling me about wanting a man on top of you,' Colette murmured.

Miriam growled contentedly as she was caressed.

'I've never had a normal-sized man. Somebody who could make love to me properly. Sometimes I wake at night, wet with desire for a partner whose face was above my face, whose lips covered my lips when we were making love.'

'It must be a problem,' said Colette, kissing Miriam again. They rose and went, arm in arm, into Colette's bedroom.

'It might be necessary', reflected Colette, reclining beneath a red parasol with golden tassels on the terrace that overlooked an emerald-green lawn, 'to use a gigolo.'

Miriam giggled. She tinkled the last ice cube in a tall glass that had once contained lime juice. She put a black Russian cigarette in her mouth, then lit it.

'Will I have to pay him?'

Colette Gascoigne nodded. 'It's a trade just like any other.'

'Perhaps I prefer that,' Miriam said. 'At least I can instruct him what to do.'

'Leave that to me, sweetheart,' Colette replied. 'It'll be easier for me to settle those kinds of details.' She wondered whether Gory sucked Miriam's toes and whether she enjoyed it. It was something she hoped Miriam would disclose when she took her instructions.

'Have you any man in mind?' asked Miriam.

'Of course,' Colette smiled, crunching her unmelted ice before setting the glass down on the white enamelled table. Miriam's rounded face was alive with curiosity. She blew a grey plume of smoke towards the cockatoo stand at the end of the terrace. The ancient white bird shuffled its crinkled, grey feet and eyed her reproachfully, below one lidded eye.

'The gigolo I was thinking of is George Labouchère,' she said. 'He's from the Seychelles. He is known to the world as Raper George.'

Colette gave a brittle laugh at the astonishment on Miriam's face.

'What an appalling nickname,' Miriam said.

'It's all a rather poor joke,' Colette explained. 'Some years ago, he was acquitted of indecently assaulting a young schoolgirl. Since then, he has been called Raper George by all his friends.'

'Doesn't he mind?'

'I suspect he quite enjoys the notoriety. He really is a very simple and foolish young man. But then, you are not paying for his mind.'

'How old is he?'

'Thirty-five, perhaps. Past his best, of course, but excellent value for the money he receives. He has few complaints.'

'How tall is he?'

'About five feet seven, slim, with a pencil-thin moustache. He appears to enjoy his work enormously.'

'Does he have many women?'

'He has his regulars. A wealthy Parsee lady has him twice a week. And George doesn't like to work more than four afternoons every eight days. I'll have to book him, of course. It could be some time before he has an afternoon free.'

Miriam looked doubtful. 'It sounds dreadfully cold blooded.'

'I'm confident you'll change your mind once you're in bed with him.'

'I'll have to think seriously about going ahead with the affair.'

Miriam stretched her feet, placing them on the side of the garden seat on which Colette reclined. Colette dropped a hand over Miriam's open-toed shoes.

'That tickles,' Miriam said.

'Don't you like your toes being touched?' asked Colette, moving her head flirtatiously to one side.

'Not too much,' Miriam smiled ruefully. She drew her

48

chair closer to Colette's and clasped her hand tightly, conscious that the movement away of her foot could have been construed as rejection.

'I thought you knew my feet were ticklish,' said Miriam softly.

'I'd forgotten,' replied Colette.

'You've probably got me confused with another girlfriend.'

Colette Gascoigne made a face. 'Ooh là là,' she said, 'you're making me feel like a woman of easy virtue.' And they both laughed good naturedly at that.

Miriam Gulbelkian was surprised when she found Raper George lying on the bed in a Chinese dressing-gown, reading a paperback. She squinted at the title through her sunglasses when he placed it on the table beside him. It was called *The Kid from Montez*, and had a picture of an advancing Mexican wearing shaggy chaps and a sombrero, firing both his six-guns. She also noticed an open tin of giant bullseyes on the bedside table. Miriam had sniffed the strong peppermint smell outside the door. She now saw that Raper George had a bulge below one cheek. She suspected it was a giant bullseye.

'Oh hallo,' he said, in a flat, tuneless voice. He was evidently as surprised as she was. 'I didn't expect you until two.' He swung his feet over the bed and stood up. She estimated that he was probably shorter than the advertised five feet seven inches. She looked at her watch.

'It's three minutes to,' she said.

'Oh, is it?' he cried. 'Mine says one-thirty. I expect it must have stopped. I'm terribly sorry.' He whinnied vacuously, then placed a half-sucked bullseye in the ashtray.

'I'll have to use the bathroom,' she said, edging through the door with her leatherette overnight bag. It really was Gory's wrestling bag but she did borrow it occasionally. She locked the door and looked at herself in the mirror.

49

What a disgusting business. It was quite ridiculous. At first sight she hated the little man. She thought about the matter for several minutes, then decided not to undress. She placed the overnight bag on the bathroom floor and switched on the mirror light. She lifted her pink shantung skirt, parted her lace-trimmed French knickers and peed as silently as possible against the porcelain. Miriam washed her hands and returned, fully dressed, into the room.

'I don't really think I can go through with this,' she said, twisting her mouth apologetically. Raper George was leaning against the wardrobe, looking like a parody of a professional lover. All he needed was an ivory cigarette-holder and a spotted silk scarf.

'I've got butterflies myself,' he said, grinning mischievously.

'I would have thought that you were inured to this kind of encounter.'

He advanced a cautious pace towards her, standing with his hands stretched out and clasped before him. He looked small and vulnerable. What a rotten job, thought Miriam. She felt intensely sorry for him, and wondered how often he encountered indifference, dislike and even revulsion.

'As a matter of fact,' he said slowly, 'I usually have much older women, and rarely attractive ones. Why do you need me? A woman of your class and appearance could have as many lovers as she wants.'

'As I said,' Miriam said, 'it was a mistake.'

'A strange mistake to make,' he said. 'You must be extremely unhappy with your husband.'

She remembered that she had left Gory's wrestling bag in the bathroom and went back to collect it. She returned to the bedroom. He was still standing gloomily in the same position.

'It's none of my business,' Miriam advised him, as she prepared to leave, 'but I would have expected someone with rather more enthusiasm for his work.' Raper George did not reply. He just nodded sadly. A man, Miriam

50

thought, conditioned to unkindness and abuse. She brushed past him and, opening the door, walked out into the courtyard to her car.

She let down the window-glass. It was searing hot and she started to perspire the moment she settled on the seat. Sweat trickled down the inside of her legs. She blew an imaginary wisp of hair off her forehead and inserted the key in the ignition. Miriam glanced down at the clock on the dashboard and saw that it was twenty minutes past two. She had paid for Raper George's services until five o'clock. She thought of the strange little man, probably lying on the bed, sucking his bullseye and reading *The Kid from Montez*. She started the engine and reversed several yards so she could steer past the car in front. It was at that moment that the image of herself astride Gory came to her. She switched the ignition off and considered why she had come to the bedroom in the Philadelphia Hotel in the first place. Miriam wound the window up again. She got out of the car and, collecting the overnight bag, went back to get her money's worth.

A strange thing happened to Miriam Gulbelkian after Raper George had made love to her for the first time. Or perhaps it was *while* he was making love to her, she was not sure. The experience was hallucinatory. She remembered floating, falling, hearing symphonic music, the pounding sea, feeling her breasts and bowels melting away into a torrent of hot buttermilk, smelling roses, hearing Colette calling to her, then screaming as a huge engine raced into her crimson tunnel.

'You have', Raper George assured her, 'been in continuous orgasm for forty-five minutes.'

Drenched in sweat, Miriam sat up. And trembled.

'Have you', she enquired solicitously, 'come?'

Raper George grinned.

'Not yet.'

Miriam bit her lip. She realised that what she had been doing with Gory had as much relevance to the sexual act

51

as having her teeth pulled. She looked down at Raper George's cock.

'How can that piece of tissue change consciousness to such an alarming extent?'

'It's my dream-stick,' he said, proudly.

Miriam, despite her transcendental fizzle, brooded. She reflected sadly on the mechanistic source of ecstasy. Raper George lay beside her. A little hairy man with an extravagant talent to please. She wondered about him. She noticed for the first time that he was not unhandsome, and thought about the terrible nature of his life.

'Have you ever', she asked, gazing at him in awe, 'been in love?'

Raper George was not surprised by the question. Every woman he had slept with — he estimated that there had been about two thousand — was interested in the answer to that one. And, like the excellent professional he was, he had prepared an answer, many years ago.

'Once.'

'What was she like?'

'Something like you.'

'In what way?'

He put his fingers against Miriam's wet slit.

'Down here,' he whispered, 'the way you grip me when I move inside you.'

'Am I okay?'

Raper George bent over her and kissed her eyelids, softly.

'You're marvellous, darling, just marvellous.'

At five o'clock, after their shower together, Miriam embraced Raper George tenderly. She laid her head against him.

'Can I see you every week?' she asked quietly.

'I'm busy for the next two weeks,' he replied, fixing his quiff in the mirror. She felt abysmal and cheap, like a bitch on heat, waggling its posterior in the street.

'I'll pay you more. I simply must see you next week.'

He looked at her and smiled wanly. Then kissed her on the nose.

'Okay, but it will have to be after seven.'

Miriam knew that he was fitting her in after some other dreadful woman. Suddenly she hated all the women with whom he slept. How could he do it, she thought bitterly. How could he degrade himself in such a way? Some of the women were probably sixty or seventy. The idea of him sleeping with old decaying females filled her with nausea.

'It will be in the same room,' Raper George reminded Miriam, as she hurried through the door to her car. She peered at her watch. Shit, she thought, she had to pick up Gory at the stadium in ten minutes.

Miriam phoned Colette Gascoigne when Gory was having his shower.

'Didn't I tell you he was good?' Colette laughed. 'He's a freak. A priapic wonder. In France he would earn a fortune. But he is shallow and quite content with his lot in Bombay. Ten years ago, he could satisfy six women a day, five days a week.'

'I like him,' Miriam admitted.

'It always helps, if you're going to sleep with a man.'

'I mean, I have a deep feeling for him. I suspect that he's a sad man way down inside. I'd like to do something to ease that sadness.'

Miriam heard Colette Gascoigne's bell-like laughter at the end of the line.

'What's the matter?'

'I love you, my little honeypot. I love you.'

'But why are you laughing?'

'Raper George is not a man, darling. He's just a walking prick.'

Miriam Gulbelkian booked Raper George three afternoons a week. One of his conditions was that on the third afternoon they only talked. He told her that it would be imprudent for him to make love more than twelve times a week.

'Who is this other bitch you're sleeping with?' she snarled.

He covered her angry mouth with kisses. She bought him gold chains, rings, a wristwatch, a radio, silk shirts and a Raleigh racing cycle with five gears.

'Tell me about your mother,' she said, lying on his shoulder.

'She was a hunchback.'

'Where is she now?'

'Dead. She drowned in the harbour at Saint-Denis. That's in Réunion.'

'How?'

'A drunken English sailor pushed her off the quay.'

'The English are bastards. And your father?'

'I don't know who he was. You see, my mother was taken when she was barely thirteen.'

'Raped?'

He twisted a hand enigmatically. 'No, taken . . . in the doorway of a carpet shop. There were three of them. A Frenchman, an African and a Spaniard.'

'Well, you're not African looking. I wouldn't mind betting that you're French, or maybe Spanish, like the flies.' She giggled.

'Who knows?' He was pensive.

'Your mother . . . did she consent to these men . . . taking her?'

Raper George looked at her curiously.

'She was paid.'

Gory Gulbelkian had noticed a change in Miriam. She now weighed twenty pounds less and was spending considerably more money than she ever had before.

'You drew three thousand last month,' he remarked, checking their bank statement.

'So what?'

He regarded her solemnly over his reading glasses.

'It seems rather a lot, that's all.' He laid a hand gently on her shoulder. 'Are you well?'

'I'm fine, thank you.'

Gory Gulbelkian lifted her high in the air, as easily as a normal man could lift a baby.

'Put me down, you crazy bastard!' she raged, losing a shoe, as her head brushed the ceiling. He moved her down a foot and tried to kiss her. She turned her head away.

'What's the matter?'

'Put me down,' she screamed.

He set her on the floor.

'I'm going to sleep in the guest bedroom,' she said.

Gory Gulbelkian caught her hand as she tried to leave him.

'We haven't made love for a month,' he murmured, in a voice thick with emotion.

'I don't feel like being a bloody jockey any longer,' she said, running out of the room. The taunt wounded the big man. He did not understand why he had suddenly made her so unhappy. He was blinded by tears welling up in his eyes. He sat down and thought about Miriam, terrified at the prospect of losing her. And as he wept silently, Gory realised for the first time what an important part of his life Miriam had become.

Colette Gascoigne was also concerned about Miriam. The fact that she was spending three afternoons a week with Raper George alarmed her.

'You are just one among two thousand,' she said.

'I love him,' Miriam replied.

'Consider one important fact, my darling,' Colette said. 'Will he sleep with you if you don't pay him?'

'He has to earn a living, the same as everybody else,' Miriam said.

Colette sniggered derisively. She was certain that Miriam had taken leave of her senses.

'Gory and I are finished anyway,' Miriam said.

'But you're paying Raper George with Gory's money,

my darling. How will you be able to maintain your prick once you have parted from Gory?'

'I'll find a way,' sniffed Miriam.

'Darling, come and see me. We must talk together. What you are doing is madness. It is contrary to your true nature. Do you really believe that prick loves you?'

'In his own way,' Miriam sighed. She knew that there were many ways for people to love one another, but felt that Colette could never appreciate that Raper George was capable of higher feelings.

It was a week before Christmas. Colette Gascoigne had just written a Christmas card for the Gulbelkians. It was a picture of three black shepherds standing in a pale green field, looking up at a star made of silver glitter in a bright orange sky. Over the *Merrie Christmas*, she inscribed a greeting to her friends. To Gory and Miriam, with much love, Colette. She placed three crosses above her name. One for Gory, she thought, one for Miriam, and the third for . . . She remembered with bitterness the other person in the triad.

As a matter of professional etiquette, Colette Gascoigne never discussed her clients' business with others. And as a matter of personal conduct, she did not interfere in the private affairs of her friends. She was now confronted by a situation that threatened the happiness of two people of whom she was extremely fond. Colette knew that she should not have facilitated the relationship between Raper George and Miriam. A significant part of the responsibility for the mess in which the Gulbelkians now found themselves was undoubtedly hers. The solution that suggested itself to Colette was extreme. It might, she suspected, lead to the end of her friendship with Gory and Miriam. And yet, in her own complicated way, she saw a possible conclusion that was not too distant from her own contentment. But first things first. Colette phoned Gory and told him the whole story.

It was fortunate for Miriam that she was not at home when Gory heard from Colette Gascoigne. She was lying in bed two miles away, under Raper George. For a matter of fifteen minutes, the giant wrestler lost his mind. He smashed all the furniture in the house to matchwood. He broke the crockery, ripped the curtains and bed linen to shreds, then tore five doors off their hinges. He threw Miriam's jewellery, perfume and clothes out of the window, and bellowed like a bull elephant suffering a terrible hurt until he lost his voice. Finally, he lay among the debris of their possessions, and wept.

Gory's neighbours heard the dreadful noise, but nobody had the courage to approach him. Although they knew that he was a pacific man in his private life, his strength was so legendary (he had once tossed the great Bert Assirati from one corner of the ring to the other) that people feared he might damage them accidentally in his grief.

Eventually, he rose and, red eyed, snotty nosed and swollen faced, he set out to walk to the Philadelphia Hotel. Gory Gulbelkian was so well known in the city of Bombay that crowds followed him, marvelling at his prodigious size, wherever he walked. The fact that he was so obviously distressed excited people even more than usual. They were determined to have a close view of whatever mischief the strong man was resolved to perpetrate. And if he was about to inflict serious damage on another human being, so much the better. By the time he had travelled a hundred yards from his front door, fifty people were walking behind and beside him. Halfway to the Philadelphia Hotel the crowd had increased to at least two hundred. When he marched through the hotel foyer there were probably five hundred spectators gathered outside the entrance, spilling out onto the paved concourse and road, climbing the ornamental palms, even hanging from the lamp-posts more effectively to witness what Gory was about. The police were informed, but decided not to inhibit officiously the freedom of a famous and much-loved public figure. Two sergeants turned their motor-bikes in the opposite direction, an inspector decided to keep a semi-official eye on proceedings from behind the curtains of his brother's apartment across the way, while several constables decided it would be advisable for them to engage in more pressing duties in other parts of the city.

Gory pushed the bedroom door open with a nudge. The security bolts bent like plasticine. Miriam saw him first. She drew Raper George up by the hair from between her parted thighs. There he crouched, like a small, snuffling beast. He glanced back apprehensively. Being a relatively timid man, he suffered a coronary palpitation so sudden and severe that his vision blurred in the few moments before he was engulfed by an uncontrollable palsy. It was probably inconsiderate of Miriam not to have warned Raper George of her husband's extraordinary dimensions, but the thought had never seriously occurred to her. And her dilatory introduction did little to repair this negligence.

'It's my husband,' she screamed, as the bald and bearded giant towered over the wretched Raper George, now wholly incapacitated by terror. When Gory bent down and lifted her naked paramour up by the neck, Miriam aimed valiant but ineffectual blows at her husband's knee.

'Don't hurt him, Gory,' she implored.

Gory Gulbelkian placed his left hand below Raper George's arse, like a saddle, securing him around the back of his neck with his right hand. Then, ducking under the door, he bore Raper George out through the hotel lobby to the waiting crowd. There was a loud cheer when they saw Gory's trophy. Gory passed through, holding Raper George in the air.

'It's Raper George,' somebody shouted, for although the diminutive gigolo was not as well known as Gory Gulbelkian, he was hardly a nonentity. Gory marched down Marine Lines towards Churchgate Reclamation. The crowd now exceeded a thousand. It had grown with the rapidity with which crowds in Bombay miraculously increase. By the time he passed the bandstand and headed in the direction of the Cowasji Jehangir Hall, traffic in the roads around Gory's procession could not move. Gory was now drenched in sweat and Raper Geoge's eyes were closed. He could not endure the humiliation of his exposure, feigning unconsciousness, as he babbled importunations to the Blessed Virgin.

By now the crowds had guessed at Gory's destination. He was making for the Gateway of India. People thronged in front of Green's Hotel and covered the area between the Royal Yacht Club and the Taj Mahal Hotel. Gory went through the Gateway and down the steps into the sea. He set the naked Raper George down on the steps. The sea lapped around their feet.

'Can you swim?' Gory asked in a whisper.

'A little,' Raper George replied, still trembling. He was now shivering with the cold as well. The spectators nearest Gory had wondered whether he would smash the little man on the stone steps, as Hindus sometimes smashed coconuts to propitiate the gods. But once Gory was sure that he was not endangering Raper George's life, he tossed him into the Arabian Sea. A great cheer went up from the onlookers at the water's edge.

'Is he dead?' people asked from the back.

'No. Gory just chucked him in the sea.'

And when the crowd were satisfied that there was no flowing blood or scrambled brains to be seen, they drifted away, disappointed that so dramatic a progress had come to such a peaceful end.

And then what? Well, Raper George left Bombay shortly afterwards. He was last heard of in Palm Springs, living quietly with the widow of a tobacco baron whose name is instantly recognised throughout the cigarette-smoking world. Gory and Miriam are divorced. He has resumed his former arrangement with Colette, who sends him short plump girls with large breasts and well-scrubbed feet.

Miriam also made it up with Colette, and now lives with her. Her official title is 'companion'. Miriam rarely fails to be astonished at how she never recognised her authentic sexual tendencies before. As for Colette, she has never been happier. Particularly when she wakes up in the morning and sees her beloved Miriam asleep on the pillow beside her.

The Vulnerable Mede

• • •

Apart from Zubin's tenor saxophone, they allowed him three pencil stubs (not longer than two inches, the regulations stated), a sharpener, six blank sheets of paper at a time, and two books, one of which was a dictionary. He decided on *Robinson Crusoe* as the second book, because at the time he had been having a friendly discussion with Meehan about identity. Zubin was not sure whether he was Crusoe or Friday; Meehan thought he should aspire to being the island. This search for identity was something Zubin dreamed about, lying on his narrow bed, drugged by the summer heat, listening to the throbbing spaces between the noises of insects and birds. Sometimes, beyond the layers of silence, he could sense somebody playing 'Out of Nowhere'. When he held his breath, the melody merged with the beating of his heart. When he breathed again, the sound returned, like music from a scarcely audible radio station.

After the last attempt, they took away his sheets, pillow cases and shoe-laces. The bed, table and chair were all secured to the floor with steel bolts. However, the oak beam that traversed his cell eight feet above ground level, fascinated him. He saw it as a raft on which to escape. All he needed was a sail, in the shape of a good rope. If he stood on the table (Zubin was five feet in his socks), he calculated that he could manage with a sail about four and a half feet in length. He offered Meehan a thousand pounds and promised that he would not try anything for a month, until the fuss from the last bit of nonsense had quietened down. Meehan looked doubtful and talked portentously about his professional reputation.

Zubin laughed derisively. 'But you're only a psychiatrist.'

'I've been in trouble before, you know,' Meehan confessed sadly.

'I'll wait until St Patrick's Day, if that pleases you,' Zubin offered.

That was six weeks off. Meehan seemed puzzled.

'Why? You're not an Irishman.'

'I'll do it for you,' Zubin said, 'as a sort of Irish farewell present.'

'You're bloody mad,' Meehan said, pointing to the bars on Zubin's window.

They both laughed at that.

'Any old washing-line will do,' Zubin said. 'There's not much of me. I'll hide the rope in my saxophone and work out the technical details when it's dark. I want to make sure it'll support my one hundred and twenty pounds. Perhaps I'll make myself a swing for a start.'

'Now that does sound fun,' Meehan said, picking his teeth.

'Wish me *bon voyage*.'

'There's no need for you to go,' Meehan brooded with a shiver. 'You'd make a grand mate. We could traipse around Dublin together, getting gloriously smashed.'

'Come sailing with me,' Zubin invited.

'What? At the end of a fucking noose?'

'Two thousand pounds for a bit of old rope. What do you say?'

Meehan contemplated Zubin's offer in lugubrious silence.

Zubin fined the end of the longest pencil stub and told Meehan that he was going to write his testament. Meehan seemed very interested.

'Perhaps I could sell it to the papers after you've gone,' he said, 'for your estate, of course.'

'Only distant cousins survive, and they have little need of money.'

'You could leave it to the Society of Jesus, or I could manage a Trust Fund in your memory.'

Zubin laughed. 'My style is a little too flowery for publication.'

'We'll tone it down a bit. I'll edit out the filthy parts and any lies about me. Remember, we could have impressionable young convent girls reading your stuff. Virgins are easily inflamed by salacity.'

'Do you seriously think that we have a responsibility to them?' Zubin asked.

'Of course.'

'And what do you see as the object of the testament?'

'Contrition.'

'That's not my style.'

'Listen Zubin,' Meehan warned, 'you don't want to appear before your Maker unshriven.'

'Why not? Unshaven and unwashed as well, if needs be . . . with muddy boots, piss-stained underwear, soiled shirt, crumpled suit and a snot-stiff handkerchief.'

'Now that's blasphemy for a start,' Meehan said, 'and what is more, God would throw a bloody fit.'

'You carry on as though Heaven was a cross between a Bournemouth hotel and a launderette.'

'I can see why they had you in a fucking straitjacket,' Meehan sniffed.

'I'll need some more paper and a reasonable typewriter, if that's possible.'

'It's against the regulations.'

'Don't be a fart, Meehan.'

He looked pained.

'Go on, you greedy sod. I'll give you another thousand, right away.'

Meehan licked his lips uneasily. Then he disappeared, returning ten minutes later with an elderly Imperial portable and an unbroken pack of A4.

'You'll get me shot,' he grumbled.

Zubin borrowed Meehan's Parker and scrawled out a cheque in emerald-green ink. It was in French francs, drawn on an account in Nîmes. Meehan stared at it suspiciously.

'I've given you the best of the exchange rate,' Zubin said.

But Meehan did not appear to be entirely convinced.

ZUBIN'S TESTAMENT

I, Zubin Gagrat, being a Mede, a reputed descendant of Hvovi, mother of Zarathustra, and Kaikobad Khush, Vistushpa's chamberlain and cockscourer, am naturally inclined to arrogance. Meehan, the psychiatrist here, who has a face like a pig's arse, tells me that this is a response to English indifference. But then he is a drunken Dubliner, festering with ancient hatreds and terminal cirrhosis. The arrogance is deep rooted and was evident long before my arrival in England. An early photograph, taken outside the refectory of the Ardeshir Jeejeebhoy Academy (the Parsee Eton), records my sardonic smile. And in the studio portrait, marking the occasion of my string ceremony, the curled lip and heavy-lidded stare of disdain is clearly visible. As I write this, I am being observed by Jackson, the night nurse. A section of his stupid Saxon face has appeared at the grille. A marble-blue eye, below the silver-fibred brow; just the shadow of a curious nose. Jackson? He does not reply. It is impossible not to despise a creature who has never heard of Chishpish, and unable to distinguish a genuine Mede from other quite ordinary wogs.

The genuine Mede has good teeth, a sound intellect and a large organ of generation. Mede's sperm, not to be confused with Persian spunk, is a nutrient, and in its cockfresh state may be safely ingested by females of any age. Many enlightened physicians prescibe fellation with an adult Mede as a remedy for pernicious anaemia, thrush

66

and even halitosis. Dido of Carthage, for example, retained an old Mede as a general elixir. The remarkably preserved state of the Queen's oesophagus has been ascribed to her practice of taking the Mede before every meal. In more recent times, Saint Thecla of Iconium used the scrotum of a Median slave called Kashtar to accomplish the miraculous cures of Seleucia.

Jackson has gone. I am quite alone. Somewhere, somebody appears to be playing 'Lady Be Good'. I shall take my saxophone out of its case, put out the light, climb onto the table, crouch in the darkness, close my eyes, and dream myself into a duet.

I was born in 1930 at Thana, although my birth certificate states Bombay. This documentary deception was procured by my venal Uncle Rustam, who bribed the clerk at the municipal office with a ten-rupee note. The truth would have been irretrievably lost had it not been for the cruel taunts of my elder sister Sophie, who informed me, during an unhappy quarrel over money, that I was born in a madhouse. The madhouse was in Thana.

My beautiful mama, who was half French, died of puerperal fever when I was twelve days old. There is no substance to the report that she was a suicide. I am assured that the bottle of phenol she inadvertently consumed was mistaken for toddy, an alcoholic drink, particularly relished by her and milked from the palms of our estate. It should be on record that Mama was never certified but was a voluntary patient (depression) at Thana, rarely spending more than two successive nights on the premises. During the periods of her attendance, she profoundly demonstrated her sanity by driving the family Marmon, riding at several gymkhanas and playing the piano with her inimitable facility. Nor did she entirely give up bridge or badminton. She also wrote a number of quite lucid letters to her cousin David in Vence (unposted), one of which I include in refutation of the untruths that have clouded her memory.

Sans Souci
Malabar Hill
Bombay
2.1.1929

Dearest David

It is very kind of Uncle to invite us to visit you in
September. Everything depends on Sohrab. He is very
busy at present, but has threatened to take me away
for the hot season. He may be disposed to allow me to
come by myself. On condition, he says, that I am
better. I don't really feel unwell, and am treated with
more solicitude than I require. The general opinion is
that I have shown some improvement, but fatter than
in the last photograph. Crocuses in the house again
and I am reminded of you. Dare I brush the 'gilded
phalloi' with my lips? It would be wonderful to have
two or three months in Vence without medical
supervision. Tomorrow I will speak to Rustam. He
may intercede for me. Although my brother-in-law
suspects that I am spoiled, he is capable of great
indulgence himself, when treated nicely. Have those
green eyes of yours settled on any young girl yet?
Please tell me about your plans. Possess me, as they
say. I am, as you know, incorrigibly inquisitive.
    As ever,
    Fierté.

My papa, Sohrab, was a cultured man with musical inclinations. Like myself, a former student of the Ardeshir
Jeejeebhoy Academy, he was an amateur flautist of some
distinction. During his travels in Europe (1911–1913), he
was even complimented by Irina Djugashvili (Tiflis Philharmonic) when persuaded to play at a soirée at Nizhny
Novgorod. He was also a celebrated bicyclist (Jamshed
Wheelers), taxation specialist (Anklesaria and Gagrat), and
an expert phrenologist. My earliest recollections are of a

cool dark study, filled with sectional craniums and wall charts illustrating cephalic indices. He was morbidly shy of women; it is rumoured that my mama was blindfolded during the coital act. There is no evidence of his intimate association with any other female but his wife. Indeed, apart from my sister Sophie, and the nurses who attended him during that final illness (d.1940 Filaria Sanguinis hominis), he never addressed a member of the opposite sex in the ten years following Mama's death.

My Uncle Rustam however, was a bugger, and is still remembered at Ardeshir Jeejeebhoy as an accomplished sod. He directed in later years the practice of this art on barely pubescent servant girls, an appetite that became so well advertised that prospective candidates were despatched to him from every corner of the sub-continent. Rustam never married. For forty years he devoted himself to the family business, the nature of which enterprise caused Papa great distress.

Sophie was persuaded that it induced his premature end. I am ashamed to admit that an income from this source supported me for thirteen years (1940–1953), until my conversion to socialism (see Finchley Labour Party Membership Files, 1953).

My career as a jazz musician was not as unrewarding as it deserved to be. My most unmusical composition, 'Pink Whiskers', acquired for reasons quite beyond me a vogue in France and Germany during the early sixties, moving finally into the upper regions of the British and American charts. (It was Number One in South Korea for three months.) I appeared on television, was invited to retail my world view on the radio, and became a familiar figure in the colour supplements. A postcard of my bewildered, nut-brown face became an icon in androgynous bedsitter land, with inexplicable resonances of integrity, innocence and truth. The postcard, now a collector's item can still be procured from Camden Market (two pounds, if you haggle). I made a fortune playing the execrable 'Pink

Whiskers' wherever I went, hiding from real musicians and myself.

Sophie became the sole beneficiary of Uncle Rustam's dividends, which accrued mainly from the licenced cages of the red-light district of Bombay. But despite my socialism I have nothing against my Uncle Rustam, who was always kind to me. Although Papa despised him as a worthless libertine, Rustam regarded my father with easy tolerance. But he was not above shocking his brother.

'It's no use waiting for me at the front gates of Heaven, Sohrab,' he teased, as Papa lay dying. 'I will probably slip in through a back passage.'

My mama, daughter of one of the well-known Surat Kakas and Francine Fanon of Vence, was married at sixteen (February 1920), nine months before the birth of Sophie. The match was arranged by the families. It was considered that the couple's mutual interest in music was sufficient to sustain an enduring relationship. Alas, Mama, a bright gregarious girl, found Papa's introspection tedious. Shortly after her first confinement, she developed a propensity to disappear for days at a time. She would usually be found playing bridge or badminton, a game she particularly loved, at the homes of friends. Fearing for my mama's safety, however, Papa provided her with two Pathan houseboys, who accompanied her on these peregrinations. Finally, after an absence of three months (she had motored to Cape Comorin), Papa sought medical advice. The treatment prescribed changed her personality. She became, Sophie told me, irritable and uncongenial. The bouts of depression with which she suffered until her death, commenced during the hot season of 1927. It was not an ideal marriage.

I grew, a lonely child, in a large old house overlooking the Arabian Sea. *Sans Souci* has dark cupboards filled with anatomical models, medical books and bottles (Grandfather practised medicine) labelled Colocynth, Gamboge, Male-fern and Dill. There were tropical plants, brass ornaments, chiming clocks and small framed photographs of dead relatives. Nearly all the Gagrats were dead. Three times a week, Papa instructed me on the flute, with the exhortation that Djugashvili had given a public recital at three. By the time I was five I could manage simple airs, but Papa was disappointed with my wet mouth.

'You must not', he reproved, 'fill the instrument with spit.'

When I went to school, life changed for the better. But the year Papa died marked the beginning of my independence. I have always regarded 1940 as the year of my true birth.

ANALYSIS

The porcine Meehan was almost the perfect host. He never failed to provide a supply of Gauloises during Zubin's visits to his consulting room and, on occasion, stiffened the institutional tea with a liberal infusion of Irish. At first, Zubin was irritated by the psychiatrist's incessant scribbling, pausing in mid-sentence to demand of him, 'Why the hell do you write twice as much as I say?' Meehan invariably defused the situation with a self-conscious laugh. 'Psychiatry, Zubin, is a sort of art form. One would never take exception to the number of brush strokes a painter made when the poor bugger was dabbing away at something central to his vision.'

Meehan had confided to Zubin his desire to be an artist. Zubin suspected that this was not a genuine ambition. He considered that Meehan had ulterior motives. The truth, Zubin felt, was that the psychiatrist wanted to get his hands on naked women. When Zubin inadvertently showed him a blurred photograph of his ex-wife Helen, naked on Pampelonne Beach (it was tucked away in a packet of tax demands), Meehan's left eye twitched. The Irishman had three framed prints in his office. They were Gaugin's *L'Or de leurs corps*, Renoir's *La Dormeuse* and Matisse's *Carmelina*.

When Zubin indiscreetly observed that they were all 'tit' pictures, Meehan was put out.

'You'll never understand art,' he complained. Then hardly ten minutes later, he asked Zubin in a husky whisper, 'What were Nadine's breasts like?'

'Is that relevant?'

'Who's the fucking therapist here?' Meehan shouted indignantly.

So they spent a great deal of analysis time discussing Nadine's breasts. But Meehan was never satisfied with Zubin's offhand replies.

'No bigger than duck eggs, eh?'

'Perhaps goose eggs.'

'And Helen's?'

'Bigger . . . like large pomegranates, I suppose.'

'Zuleeba's?'

'They were very substantial indeed, like melons.'

Meehan scribbled furiously to conceal his excitement. Once, when he went for a piss, Zubin found drawings of breasts under his blotter. Also some rather sensitive studies of female arses among his notes. But Meehan insisted that the arses were purchased from a dealer in Frith Street, as a long-term investment.

When he had too much to drink, Meehan entertained Zubin with a song. Zubin found his thin fluting voice at least one octave too high for his heavy red face. But he always applauded, stamped his feet and whistled, much to the annoyance of Jackson, who marched angrily about in the corridor outside. When Jackson returned Zubin to his cell, he often made oblique references to the noise from Meehan's office. Zubin ignored him. Neither Meehan nor Zubin had much time for Jackson. Sometimes Zubin imagined that Meehan was an escaped patient who was there to help him to subvert the system. Indeed, in Zubin's dreams of escape, Meehan was always the trusted collaborator and fellow fugitive. Zubin had come to believe in the Irishman's good intentions.

72

'Let's talk through the early voyeurism again,' Meehan mumbled, shuffling through his notes.

'Zuleeba?'

'Yes.'

'I watched her through the ceiling.'

'With this big Polish guy?'

'Sam Grabski, yes.'

'I am particularly interested in your observations of her preparations for this man's visit.'

Zubin raised himself on the couch and asked Meehan for a cigarette. Meehan lit two, passing one to Zubin. Zubin sucked at the Gauloise reflectively, leaning forward, elbows on knees. He closed his eyes and remembered. And was disturbed by a thin sad sound in the distance.

'Somebody is playing "At Sundown".'

'I can't hear anything,' Meehan grunted.

Zubin took another drag at the cigarette, then started to talk quickly to blot out the spooky tenor saxophone in his head.

'Zuleeba Talyarkhan was delicious. She wore imported hats, patronised the Theosophical Society, played Scarlatti on the sitar, translated Goethe into Gujerati and was reputed to have danced the maxixe with a vice-president of Coca Cola.'

Meehan interrupted Zubin. 'Don't horseshit around. Get down to business,' he said. There were times when Meehan could be very impatient.

'During the monsoon season of 1944, while I was convalescing after an attack of para-typhoid, I spent my afternoons peering through a hole I had bored in her bedroom ceiling.'

Meehan breathed irregularly. Zubin raised his head and watched him out of one eye.

'You okay, Meehan?'

'Sure.'

Zubin continued. 'I watched Zuleeba dressing and undressing, combing her long black hair, powdering her face, greasing her breasts with Bustofine, practising yoga, lying on her back and using her Cutie douchette, smoking cigarettes through a tortoiseshell holder and humming plaintively to the hissing bravura of a slightly warped Caruso twelve-inch. On the days Sam Grabski was expected, she loaded her electric gramophone with a selection of mazurkas, filled the vases with sunflowers, lifted her left leg onto a chair so she could insert her diaphragm, wiggled into a pair of pink lace knickers, put on a dragon kimono, plaited her hair, painted her toenails chartreuse, and set a bottle of barleywater, two glasses and a sliced lemon on a silver tray beside the bed.'

'And all this used to excite you?' Meehan asked.

'Immeasurably.'

'Go on.'

'Grabski was a well-fleshed man with a hairy back and a bald head. The director of a chain of health food stores, he travelled in a blue Lincoln Continental, flying the Jordanian pennant and bearing a *corps diplomatique* sign. He usually wore baggy trousers, a wild Aloha shirt, a baseball cap and espadrilles. On the fourteen occasions I saw them together –'

'You kept an account of the visits?'

Zubin nodded. 'I wrote everything up in an exercise book.'

'That demonstrates self-discipline of a most unusual kind.' Meehan tapped his teeth with a pencil for some moments. 'You witnessed the penetration?'

'It was presumed. Evidenced by the position, behaviour, noise, and post-coital condition of Sam's organ. It had, so to speak, been somewhere.'

'Wet?'

'Gleaming.'

74

'I'm sorry I interrupted you.'

'On the fourteen occasions I saw them together, the longest time he spent with her was twenty-two minutes, and the shortest, nine. I recorded that he kissed her on the lips once and addressed her audibly twice . . .'

'Remarkable.'

'I sensed that a fear of discovery inhibited his more inventive propensities. Grabski started at every sound; stopped, listened, eyed the door and looked continually at his watch, slyly, through Zuleeba's hair.'

'There was, of course, a Mr Talyarkhan.'

'A small, evil-tempered man.'

'The worst kind.'

'Apart from one occasion, when he lost his balance as he whimsically tickled her pussy with an outstretched toe, Grabski's investments were remarkably expeditious, wasting little time in the titillations I was convinced Zuleeba desired.'

'You practised self-abuse?'

'Immoderately.'

'And the tenor saxophone?'

'That took second place. I played with myself when I should have been squeezing harmonic subtleties and tonal beauty out of my brains.'

'Guilt?' Meehan lit Zubin another cigarette. They smoked in silence for several minutes. 'You never met her?'

Zubin shook his head, then continued. 'Ah, Zuleeba, I used to sigh, pressing a bulging eye against the hole and gripping my swollen cock. Here is a young stag who would appreciate hot mazurkas, savour the fragrance of your Cutie douchette, stroke with eager hands that slender waist, those swelling hips and seed your pulsing flesh with Medean cream. I was chained to the memory of those silken breasts, burning Byzantine eyes, slightly protuberant teeth and the soft whisper of down along her arms and legs. I was fourteen and she thirty-seven, my Zuleeba, swirling ahead of me in the tide of time, beyond my desperate reach.'

'Did you see her again when you were adult?'

'Yes. In Naples. At the Filangieri Museum. She was in a portrait by Barocci.'

'Ah.'

'The Duchess of Urbino. I went crazy standing before it. Three days, from when the museum opened until it closed, without food or water. The carabinieri dragged me away. They thought I was planning to rob something. So I stood outside and played "I Can't Get Started" on my saxophone until I was arrested and ordered to leave Italy.'

Meehan laughed. 'I like that, getting horny over a four-hundred-year-old woman.'

'It wasn't funny.'

'I suppose not. But you can't fuck dust.'

HELEN

'Would you like to talk about your wife?'

'Helen?'

'That's right.'

'It was a mistake.'

'We all make them. She was beautiful, you once told me.'

'It was all in my head, her beauty. I realised after we'd married that I couldn't get Helen's beauty out of my skull.'

'Like the music?' Meehan asked.

Zubin smiled crookedly.

'Things didn't work out then?' Meehan asked. He doodled segmented circles at the bottom of his notes, and a banded snake.

'She brought a lot of psychic furniture to bed with her. There was hardly any room in there for me as well.'

Meehan got up and crept to the door. He opened it cautiously and looked out. Jackson was not there.

'Would you care for a finger or three of Jameson's?' he asked.

Zubin sipped the whiskey appreciatively.

'Helen', he reflected, 'was not happy with my sexuality. She felt my behaviour was unworthy of a successful middle-aged composer.

' "I'm not a composer," I protested.

' "What about 'Pink Whiskers'?"

' "That's pure shit," I said. But she was unconvinced.

' "Get that dreadful thing away from my back," she once screamed. "I'm sure you've damaged my kidneys."

' "It belongs to you, my dove," I reminded her.

' "I don't want it," she snarled.

' "It goes with the detached house, landscaped gardens, two cars, speedboat, Swedish furniture, daily cleaning woman and holidays in Crete."

' "Are you threatening me?"

' "You Kandinskys are too sensitive," I said.

' "Keep to your side of the bed," she warned.

'Helen was not the kind of woman to understand my artistic problems. Although she had few equals when it came to making material decisions, she was totally inadequate when dealing with my inner fears. Sometimes, when she hadn't got a period or had just received the housekeeping cheque, or had lost five pounds in weight, or had not been troubled by her kidneys, her womb or her head, she was really good fun. But the Kandinsky and Levin blood had been enervated by a long struggle for respectability. Judging by the family album, even Grandfather Levin, who had emigrated pig-poor from Odessa, looked as though he used a laundered napkin to wipe the bortsch from his beard. And his wife, originally a Riga Jewess called Lara Muronzeff, wore ten rings on her fingers and used an ornamental cruet when there was company. Lara also trained a grey parrot to whistle "Black Eyes", and a white mongrel called Garibaldi, whom she adorned with a black sash and a feathered cap, to follow her down the road on its hind legs. This interference with brute creation illustrated a potent need to impose a respectable status on all living things.

'Helen's mother, who had married a Kandinsky, was predictably disciplined in the polite arts. She not only played the piano well, but understood bezique, astronomy and ballroom dancing. Helen's father, Kandinsky, was the son of a shirt manufacturer who owned a factory in Canning Town, a house in Brighton and a flat in Streatham, where he accommodated an Irish mistress and a handsome Mucha screen which, on his demise, became the subject of a protracted and scandalous litigation. It passed, incidentally, to his bastard, who was now a world-famous American film producer. This man, for some strange reason, never failed to send Mrs Kandinsky a card at Christmas, referring to her as "Mother", although she was ten years his junior and merely the daughter-in-law of his lost father. Nobody in the family had ever met him and, although Mrs Kandinsky wrote him several letters before the war, none were acknowledged. Helen, however, had a snapshot of him, received when she was five years old. Inscribed *"Ma petite chère*, from Uncle Bobo, Spring 1937"*, it depicted a lithe Italianate man in dark glasses and white flannels, standing beside some palms at Cap d'Antibes. There was also present a plump anonymous lady holding a lemur, and a peripheral waiter, looking like an adolescent Valentino, who lit the shadows cast by an *eau de vie* advertisement with an unbelievably glittering smile.

'Helen's father, who had been a director of a firm specialising in reproduction furniture, had never been seen in public without a hard collar, hat and polished boots. He became, during his lifetime, an acknowledged authority on marquetry, contributing many articles on the subject to trade journals and magazines. He is chiefly remembered for an extremely fine Dutch escritoire, exhibited at the Birmingham Wood Festival of 1922, and a teak liqueur tray that earned a commendation at Liège during the summer of 1938. By the time Helen arrived, there were serviettes for dinner, hot and cold water in the bedrooms, a pink flush toilet with a mother-of-pearl seat in the cloakroom, books by Galsworthy, Montherlant, Scott and Trollope in the study, a small Signac on the stairs, and a chiming electric bell by the front door. It was a heritage from which, I knew, Helen would find it difficult to escape. The Gagrats, on the other hand, secure in the certainty of their distinction, had never given a withered tit for the icons of respectability. As Uncle Rustam used to say: eat, shit, fuck and sleep well. All the rest is politics, madness or bloody lies.'

Meehan rose and went out to the toilet. Zubin looked around. He waited until he heard Meehan streaming noisily into the lavatory bowl, then strode quickly to what he thought was a broom cupboard and poked his head inside. Behind a nest of empty whiskey bottles, wine demijohns, brooms and fishing rods, he spied a skein of white rope, approximately half an inch in diameter. Zubin stretched out a hand and retrieved it carefully, taking care not to disturb anything. Then he darted back to his cell. He pushed the skein of rope between the bars of his window and heard it fall with a thud on the floor inside. When he got back, his heart was pounding painfully in his chest. He lit a cigarette, then rested his trembling and perspiring palms against the couch. When Meehan returned, adjusting his flies, Zubin managed a tricky smile.

Meehan poured Zubin another whiskey. It was a large one. He poured one for himself.

'I listened to you last night,' Meehan said. 'You were playing "Body and Soul". It was really terrific.'

'I'm spooked,' Zubin said sadly.

'I read an article about you once. It said that you were the Indian Coleman Hawkins.'

'Bastards,' cursed Zubin.

'That's a compliment,' Meehan assured him.

'You see, Meehan,' said Zubin, 'the real music stays in

79

my head. Only the shit comes out. It swirls around in my skull, driving me crazy with its arcane possibilities; subtle, thrusting, lurking in the shadows of my brain, leaking away inside my mouth, down my throat, into my legs, guts and scrotum. I blow and blow, drugged by the magic of the sounds that vibrate through my body. But only the shit comes out.'

'It sounds terrific to me.'

NADINE

'And then you fell in love,' said Meehan. He was beginning to like Zubin a lot.

Zubin stared at him bleakly. 'I've always been in love,' he explained, 'but it was like the music in my head. I couldn't get it out. I knew it was there, inside me.'

'And Nadine was the key,' the psychiatrist suggested.

'When I first saw her,' Zubin said, 'it was in the Snaffle Club on Brewer Street. I was fiddling my way through "Ain't Misbehavin'", a little wearily perhaps, aware that I was playing reasonably well without setting the place alight. I sensed that I was pushing out fairly comfortable background music but didn't feel juiced up enough to try to impose myself on the proceedings. It was cool without being questing or sharp . . . the edge was missing and I wasn't going anywhere. She came in with this black guy. It was all very strange. I knew it was Nadine, she was my second cousin's daughter, because she'd promised to drop into the club with this character, Ike Varanas, who was a jazz critic, to hear me play. I hadn't seen her since she was twelve, but knew her from photographs, and had spoken to her several times on the phone. She had sleek black hair and big dark eyes. There was nothing much to her, just a slim, leggy, fairly good-looking girl in red.'

'What happened?'

Zubin screwed up his eyes.

'At first, I started showing off. I felt a big crazy bird, the size of an eagle, flapping away in my chest. I knew that I could do anything and just closed my eyes and sailed away. Even with my eyes shut, I could see Nadine looking up at me. I sensed that I was going too far. I tried to hold on to myself and hand out the punishment slowly. Then it happened.'

Meehan raised his eyebrows expectantly. He enjoyed hearing the next bit.

'I played tenor sax for the first time in my life. The tears rolled down my cheeks and everybody rose to their feet. They were clapping like mad. I went again and again. Everybody went crazy. I thought they'd have to shoot me to get me off the stage, but I stepped back after my solo and let the horn in. When the number ended, I went across to Nadine and kissed her on the mouth. Your face is wet, she said. We clung to each other and kissed again. Let's get the fuck out of here, I said. Both of us knew that something had happened. Both of us were out of control. We booked into a hotel in the Strand. And everything seemed right for the first time in my life.'

'You have been fortunate in being close to so many beautiful women,' Meehan said. 'That is something I have never achieved.'

'I could never get close to women,' Zubin murmured, 'not really close. I dream of closeness. To know what it must be like to have a womb with a foetus curled fluttering inside me, breasts heavy and swollen with milk, a deep cleft men lusted after. My life has been wasted in trying to penetrate and defile. I have been a user of women, an abuser of women, but what I really wanted was to move into their secret core. I remember Nadine's eyes in the night, calm yet as mysterious as stars in a distant galaxy. Between us was a space I could not traverse, as inviolate as the black velvet continuum of the universe, beyond the crippled imagination of man. God, how I loved women. A snuffling pig, pressing my snout against dark mirrors that

81

curved into nothingness, engulfing me with cold despair. All I could see was the reflection of myself, the predator, the ugly predator, who knew nothing.'

'You expect too much,' Meehan suggested gently.

'No man expects more than he needs,' Zubin said.

'Well,' said Meehan, peering at his notes, 'we've nearly got to the place where we stuck last time.' He poured Zubin the last of the Jameson's, then, unlocking the bottom drawer of his desk, drew out another. He unscrewed the cap.

'You'll get me pissed,' said Zubin.

'Not you,' Meehan declared, 'never you.' The psychiatrist tilted a ridiculous amount of whiskey into his own glass. Then he shut his notebook and slumped back in his chair. He promised himself that he would write up the session in the morning.

'Are you going to tell me about Alex this time?'

'It hurts,' Zubin said.

'My partner, Mr Jameson, might help.'

Zubin shivered. Meehan looked at his watch.

'It's one o'clock in the morning. Just the time to finish a story.'

'You're not taking notes?' asked Zubin.

Meehan waved a fat, despairing hand over his head. 'I'll tell you the truth, Zubin my son. This psychiatry lark is a load of bollocks. I was thinking of getting an honest job as a hod carrier, anyway.'

Zubin lit a cigarette and drew the smoke swiftly into his lungs. They sat listening to the frogs in a distant pond. Meehan lit up. He turned to Zubin, waiting for him to continue. Zubin rose. He walked a little unsteadily to the toilet. Meehan closed his eyes and hummed a catchy rebel air he often sang for a lark, usually to outrage Jackson. Zubin returned. Meehan opened his eyes and, leaning across, poured another shot into Zubin's glass. Zubin sipped it with slow deliberation. He stubbed out his cigarette, yawned, then started to speak again.

'Nadine told me that she was working as a secretary for a Greek called Alex, at his place in Le Rayol. She invited me down as soon as I'd finished my London engagements, which took care of the next twelve weeks. At first, we exchanged postcards on a daily basis. And we phoned each other several times a week. Then, without any warning, I received a strange letter from Aix, where she had gone with Alex. She said that she was incapable of the sort of emotional commitment I required. When I examine my character, she wrote, I am profoundly ashamed of the shallowness I find. I had always dreamed of being needed by a man, but have now awoken to the realisation that I am not prepared to make the sacrifices such needs entail. The little tricks of being physically pleasing to a lover, of being bright and gay, are not enough. I have no womb for domesticity, no stomach for exclusive relationships or heart for the life-denying situation of an ordered existence.'

'Fairly conclusive,' declared Meehan. 'Enough to see off an ordinary bugger like me.'

'I refused to believe that she meant what the letter stated. I knew that Nadine was as much in love with me as I with her. One just knows certain things.'

'Not even the slightest doubt?'

'No.' Zubin sucked air noisily through his lips. 'I phoned her and told her that I wanted to marry her as soon as my divorce was completed. We spoke for three hours.'

'Everything was fine again?'

'Wonderful. From that point, we talked every night. I flew out to Nice a few weeks later. We spent five golden days at a hotel in Bormes les Mimosas. It was a honeymoon. Nothing had changed. We devoured each other.'

ALEX

Nadine promised to return to England with me as soon as she could sort out her work arrangements with Alex. We both agreed that her business could delay our departure for another two or three days. I knew that I was being selfish, rushing everything, but I couldn't bear the thought of living without her again. At lunch, on our third day at Bormes, Nadine told me that Alex had invited us both down to Le Rayol. I behaved badly. I was unreasonable and jealous. She attempted to placate me by saying that Alex knew all about our decision to leave for England and had given his blessing. I had no stomach for a confrontation with the Greek whom I instinctively feared. I shivered with dark forebodings. I even asked her a coarse and unforgivable question, which she refused to answer. Nadine wept and so did I. Then we embraced and made love. Later that afternoon, she drove me out to Alex's place.

When we got to Le Rayol, Nadine turned down a steep and twisty road that led to the sea. As we rolled down the wooded slopes of the Maures hills, she directed the vehicle along a narrow private track where the luxuriant cane hedges brushed against the sides of the white Mercedes. Now and again, as we swished past ragged gaps in the foliage, I saw the still, barely wrinkled sea. It shimmered with a metallic turquoise gleam. The track began to wind upwards very steeply for a short distance, until we emerged into open maquis. We drove under a strange asymmetrical archway, like an outcrop of pink coral. Between an arc of plane trees, which rose to a lawned plateau with fountains, stood the Villa Clare. The terracotta house, draped in purple bougainvillea, was shuttered and silent. I realised that we had arrived at the rear of the villa, looking up towards the woodland, rising to the main coast road. A barking Dalmatian ran to us from a cool grove of cork oaks on the upper slope, throwing itself wildly at Nadine as she stepped out. I noticed a young blonde woman lying on a towel under the glazed cloisters skirting the rear wall. When she raised herself briefly to wave to Nadine, I saw her sun-brown body was unclothed. We walked through wrought-iron gates set in the garden wall. Nadine informed me that the nudist was Alex's secretary, Gris.

'I thought *you* were his secretary.'

Nadine stared at me owlishly. 'Gris understands short-hand, book-keeping, and stuff like that. My work is more on the public relations side.' She sounded sufficiently vague to make me feel despondent again.

'What's the matter?' she asked.

'Nothing.'

I knew that I would not be happy at the Villa Clare.

We ambled past the swimming pool in which a tiny black man was floating on his back.

'Hallo, Hafiz,' Nadine called brightly.

'Hallo, darling,' the man cried.

'He's a Sudanese poet,' Nadine informed me. 'Alex allows him to use the pool. He works as a dishwasher at the big hotel on the beach and rides up here on his *vélomoteur* every afternoon.'

'Does he call everybody darling?'

Nadine giggled. 'He's incredibly successful with women. He's been in the village a year and he has five bastards.'

'Is he a dwarf?'

'No. He's a midget. Hafiz is perfectly proportioned.'

I heard a deep gurgling noise from the pool and suggested to Nadine that the black man was probably drowning. She laughed.

'That's a fertility song. It has over a hundred verses. He's probably made another conquest in the village.'

When we arrived at a huge Moorish door, Nadine used her key. We found ourselves in a vast red-tiled hallway with a curved staircase sweeping onto the upper galleries. The area was lit by the evening sun filtering through a pink glass cupola and tinted ports placed at intervals along the outer walls. As we walked along the lower gallery towards a brass grille that led to the living quarters, the luminous geometry of the Vasarelys, set in shaded alcoves behind

85

pointed lancets, burned like separate fires within the bare primrose of the walls.

She led me into the room. A thick-set brown man, dressed in a flowered shirt and yellow shorts, rose and extended his palm.

'This is Alex,' Nadine announced.

'The young lovers,' he cried, in a deep hoarse voice, almost fracturing my fingers in a friendly grip. As he stepped out from behind the card table where he had been amusing himself, I noticed that his feet were bare. Alex turned to Nadine and kissed her tenderly on the brow. I could see that he was very fond of her. Then, grasping me by the arm, he propelled me around the room.

'Come and see my Mondrians,' he cried with childlike joy. 'And forgive the pride I have in my possessions. You see, I have not yet mastered the restraint that is proper in the very rich, on account of my father being a clown, a professional clown you understand, whose business it was to communicate happiness. I am descended from seven generations of clowns, all poor but full of sunshine. Yet my father once told me that I was the greatest clown of them all, because I found beauty only in things and not in people. That made me very sad and, until I met my little Nadine, I never understood what he meant. Isn't she the most beautiful woman you have ever seen?'

I agreed politely and noticed that Nadine was watching us with amusement from the sofa. Alex leaned towards me and whispered confidentially, man to man, 'Whenever I see her, I want to kiss her. Do you understand that?'

I nodded. But I wondered how I could curb Alex's demonic zest for my girlfriend without appearing boorish. I found the Greek very likeable and was taken by his charm and candour.

Alex continued. 'I am terribly jealous of you. So young and virile and, what is worse, beloved by my lovely Nadine. Life is not fair. Twenty years ago, there would have been no contest, but now, pish, Alex has no hope. She told me

86

all about you from the start. Zubin is the only man for me, she said. Where is the scoundrel? I shouted. I did not believe that any man my Nadine loved would leave her side for even ten minutes – would abandon her.'

'She abandoned me,' I complained.

'The prerogative of divine creatures,' smiled Alex. 'But even if you were abandoned a thousand times, you should have returned to her window with flowers in your hand and a smile in your heart. The pursuit of happiness is without end.' He nudged me painfully in the ribs.

'See this painting in the corner? It is a Modigliani. When I was sixteen, I wanted that picture more than life itself. It belonged to a Jewish musician who lived in Piraeus, about a hundred miles from our home. At that time I was learning the piano, but instead of taking lessons in our own town, I cycled two hundred miles a week so I could practise my instrument in the same room as that picture. One day, I was astonished to find that it was not there. My teacher informed me that he had sold it to a Swiss banker from Como. I immediately gave up all musical ambitions, left home and cycled the thousand miles to Como. I called on the Swiss banker and offered to work free as his gardener for two afternoons a week, provided he allowed me to look at his picture after work. He was a silly suspicious man and called the police. After several hours of interrogation, they accepted that my intentions were honest but advised me to leave Como, unless I was pre-pared to risk arrest. I moved on to Lugano, where I was determined to make enough money to buy the painting. I took three jobs. I worked day and night, denying myself the ordinary pleasures that most young men expect. By the time that I was nineteen I owned a small hotel, two cafés and several cabin-cruisers that I hired out to tourists. I visited Como and called on the Swiss banker. To my horror, he informed me that the painting had been sold to a Paris dealer. I caught a train to Paris that night, but found that it had been disposed of to an elderly widow who lived

87

at St-Cloud. I telephoned her and offered to purchase the Modigliani. She informed me that she was a collector of the painter's works and was not prepared to sell. I sold my business interests in Lugano and invested my money in Paris. I made friends with the elderly widow, who allowed me to visit her from time to time to see the picture. When I was twenty-three, I was a multi-millionaire with interests in property, insurance, bloodstock and banking. The elderly widow agreed to let me purchase the picture from her estate on her death. The daughter, however, resented my association with her mother. She suspected that I was trying to deprive her of her inheritance. When the old lady died, she contested the provision in the will that allowed me to purchase the painting. I lost the ensuing lawsuit, and the daughter, despite several very generous offers, refused on principle to let me have the picture. She hated me. I was informed that the Modigliani would be burnt rather than sold to me. I engaged an agent to keep an eye on matters. Two years later, I received a letter from my agent. It stated that the picture had been given as a present to the daughter's lover, a minor Italian film actor. I flew to Rome and bought his contract from the studio. I advised him that he could have the starring role in a film that I would finance if he sold me the picture. He agreed in a flash. Not only did I become the owner of the Modigliani, but launched into a new and extremely profitable business as a film producer.'

'Zubin, don't believe a word of it,' Nadine mocked, from across the room.

Alex winked at me. 'And do you know something? I detest that picture. It reminds me of my wasted life. If I had not become so irresistibly seduced by it, I might have become something worthwhile, a pianist perhaps.' So saying, Alex vaulted a chair, and seating himself at the boudoir grand, struck bravely into Sorabji's 'Le Jardin parfumé'. He played magnificently and I told him so. Then Gris joined us. She was completely naked. Lowering herself

88

onto a wooden seat that looked oddly out of place in the well-furnished room, she crossed her legs and patted the empty space beside her.

'Gris wants to make friends with Zubin,' she said.

I walked across to join her. I felt strangely inadequate as I self-consciously avoided staring at the flaxen isosceles between her slim brown thighs.

'It's not often that I meet a naked girl in a drawing room,' I murmured, extending a hand which she did not accept.

'Gris is not naked,' she pouted. 'Gris merely has no clothes on.'

Curiously enough, I had to concede that it was I who felt naked. I commented wryly about the seat, which felt extremely hard. Alex pivoted on the piano stool and chuckled.

'Gris sleeps on wooden boards. She doesn't even use a pillow.'

I asked her if she was a yogi.

'I just prefer simple things,' she explained. 'Cushions and pillows are too complicated for me.' I must admit that her remark struck a chord in my heart.

'I am trying', Gris said, 'to restrict my choices to essential matters. Self-indulgence is a deflection from that path.'

'Then you are a yogi,' I said.

Gris seemed perplexed. 'Definitions confuse me. They are almost as dangerous as cushions and pillows.'

Nadine joined in. 'That's exactly what Zubin was saying to me about jazz.' She looked at me, wide-eyed and supportive.

'Cut out the crap and keep it simple,' Alex added.

'Alex once played piano behind Bechet in Marseilles,' said Nadine.

Once again, the old bastard impressed me. Nadine seemed almost as proud of the elderly Greek as she was of me. More perhaps. She sensed that I was drowning.

'You look terribly uncomfortable,' she whispered. 'Come

and sit beside me, darling.' I made my way to the couch. Alex sprang down on the other side of her. Leaning across Nadine's lap, he asked me if I minded his kissing her fingertips. I told him that depended on Nadine, but I couldn't mask the hint of menace in my voice. Gris seemed amused.

'Are you jealous of Alex?' she asked.

'No,' I lied, in a flat, unconvincing voice. Nadine offered her fingertips to Alex. He held them and looked playfully at me.

'Not without Zubin's express permission.'

'Let's not be childish,' I snapped. It was clear to everyone that he had rattled me.

Gris turned to me. 'Is anyone jealous of you?' she asked.

'I am,' Nadine replied loyally. But I suspected that nobody really believed her.

Gris burst out laughing. 'You mustn't protect him, Nadine,' she reproved.

By now, Alex knew that things had gone too far. He wagged an admonitory finger at Gris.

'No more games, please,' he pleaded.

Nadine squeezed my hand. 'Can't you see that Gris is only clowning?' she asked, comforting me with a kiss. I looked at her, sullenly.

'I thought Alex was the clown,' I joked. But it came out like a sneer.

Suddenly, I was aware that the verbal exchanges were a sort of mad ensemble playing, and not only was I getting the timing and tone wrong but I was coming in at the wrong places. Even Nadine's protection was misguided, for it only served to underline my vapidity. Alex tiptoed carefully to the piano. We were into clowns again. Gris giggled at his mimetic movements. He sat at the piano stool, spinning around several times with his eyes closed, then, facing the keyboard, played Satie's *Le Piège de Méduse*. Gris leaned forward and placed a hand on my knee. She smiled. Her clear blue eyes had a compliant

90

quality that I had seen before in other women. The look was friendly and intimate. For a comforting moment, I did not feel like a victim. I smiled back.

'Will you learn to like me?' she whispered.

'Of course,' I murmured, trying now to get my crumbling act together.

Nadine rested her cheek on my shoulder as we listened to the music. I glanced discreetly at Gris's body as Alex played. Her flawless skin was the colour of teak, her long curved breasts firm as moulded bronze. We looked at each other again, briefly. Her lips parted slightly in the suspicion of a smile. A covert smile this time, with violet undertones. Before I could avert my eyes, she jerked one leg away from the other, to reveal a fold of deep pink below the yellow fuzz. I felt horny. Instantly. I glanced at Nadine, whose eyes were closed as she listened to Alex. Then I felt threatened again. I wondered if Gris was acting on Alex's instructions. Was her attempt to arouse me devised to create a rift between Nadine and me? Was Alex an unscrupulous bastard? What games were we really playing? I looked across at Gris. She moved back on the bench, gently raising her thighs. It could have passed for a fidget. I glimpsed labial folds and imagined, without certainty, a flash of her cerise lacuna. Gris looked at me, her face open and guileless. My heart fluttered. I turned away, swollen with brutish lust, unable to endure her nakedness a moment longer.

When Alex finished playing, we clapped appreciatively. Gris jumped up and asked Nadine to tell her about our five days at Bormes.

'Tell me about the honeymoon.'

'And me,' pleaded Alex.

'Not you,' Nadine said to him, blushing. But there was pleasure in her eyes as well. Then she left the room with Gris.

After the girls had departed, Alex poured me a cognac.

We exchanged the usual small talk, avoiding with circumspection any reference to Nadine and our plans to return to England. Yet as we smoked and drank, we moved, despite our obliquities, in ever-decreasing circles, to the theme that was uppermost in our minds.

After the third large brandy, I sensed that it was time to be frank with the Greek. But it was Alex, with characteristic adroitness, who took the initiative.

'I have no recourse', said Alex finally, 'but to tell you the truth. It would be unfortunate if you misunderstood the nature of my relationship with Nadine. First things first. I am impotent.' I regarded him quizzically. Alex continued. 'Worse than that. What sexual inclinations I possess in here,' he tapped his head, 'are now almost minimal, and can be conveniently purged with a Bach concerto or ten lengths of the swimming pool. It is true, I love Nadine dearly, but because of my limited aptitude and, indeed, propensity, our bond is essentially Socratic.' I expressed my regret at his condition. Secretly, I prayed that the tricky Greek was not lying. I shuddered to think of my chances had Alex been an entire man.

'While I do not resent Nadine's association with other men – it is only natural that she should find physical fulfilment – I must admit to being unhappy about her decision to leave Rayol.' He paused for a moment, then suggested that I should join his entourage.

'That's impossible,' I said, 'I'm a jazz musician and most of my work happens to be in London.'

'I'm a musician, too,' he said. 'Perhaps we can work something out down here. It's a big house. We have twelve bedrooms. Stay as long as you like.'

I shook my head. 'I don't think that would work.'

Alex eyed me carefully. 'Do you trust me?'

'Not entirely,' I admitted.

He laughed and slapped me on the back. 'I like you. Few men would confess to that.'

'I suppose I'm pissed,' I said.

Then Alex outlined an extraordinary plan. 'If Nadine and you decided to live here, I would be quite prepared to restrict myself to a suite on the upper floor of the house. I will give a written undertaking that I would not speak to her at all. My lawyers will arrange a contract on that basis.'

The idea of Alex being a prisoner in his own house appealed to me. I imagined him peeping down at Nadine through the bedroom shutters.

'The situation would be quite untenable,' I laughed. 'You would merely be demonstrating in a most dramatic manner the contrast between my ridiculous possessiveness and your great magnanimity.'

'You are far too clever for me,' Alex sighed. But neither he, nor I, really believed that.

I found Nadine lying on the bed watching the fireflies through the balcony door. I was tired and slightly drunk.

'I suspect', I said, 'that Gris is trying to make me.'

'You?'

I confessed that I'd been aroused by her exhibitionism.

'I'm sorry for you,' Nadine drawled. I sensed that we were on the verge of our first quarrel.

'At first,' I said, imprudently developing my notions of Gris's sexuality, 'I imagined that Alex had put her up to it, but on reflection . . .' I paused and waited for Nadine's response. There was none. I continued. 'Well, anyhow, I have an instinct about such things.'

Nadine closed her eyes. I unbuttoned my shirt and slipped down my denim trousers.

'Look, I'm not crazy. I think Griselda has the hots for me.'

Nadine opened one eye. 'Oh yeah.' She levered herself up on her elbows. Our eyes met.

'She's a lesbian, you arrogant prick.'

At dinner, Gris wore a long-sleeved black dress, black gloves and a black hat that drooped over her shoulders like an umbrella. I noticed that her eyes were red-rimmed, as though she had been crying. I knew that the comprehensive occultation of her body must have been due to my stupid remarks to Nadine. Gris remained silent throughout most of the meal, while the three of us chatted amiably. Suddenly she turned to me.

'When are you leaving us?' she demanded tearfully.

'Griselda,' Alex reproved. He shook his head at her.

'Well,' I replied, 'Nadine and I had decided to leave the day after tomorrow.'

'But Nadine has other business this week,' said Gris. There was a malicious edge to her voice. I glanced at Nadine. She appeared nervous and did not reply.

'I'm sure Alex will excuse her,' I said, looking at the Greek and fishing for some response. But he sat staring glumly at his plate.

'Couldn't we go to Nice tomorrow?' Nadine asked Alex.

'If that's what you want,' he murmured. Gris showed her large white teeth in a wide conspiratorial smile.

'Can everything be arranged at such short notice?' she asked.

'Of course, of course,' Alex said, adding, 'We'll leave early. I'll make the necessary telephone calls tonight.' The rest of the meal was completed in funereal silence. Each one of us, except Gris, seemed to be burdened with dark and uncomfortable thoughts.

In the bedroom Nadine undressed and slipped between the sheets.

'This Nice trip of yours sounds mysterious,' I commented brightly, kicking off my shoes.

'Business,' she muttered.

'When will you be back?'

'Tomorrow night, perhaps.'

'I'll miss you.'

'That's life,' she yawned. I switched off the light and, lifting the sheets, curled against the silky warmth of her ensellure. I moved my hands around her body. She shifted away from me and turned around.

94

'What's the matter?' I asked.

'I'm pooped.'

I buried my nose between her perfumed breasts and, closing my eyes, fell asleep almost immediately to the drone of the cicadas. Just before dawn, Nadine straddled me. I gripped her buttocks as she found and sheathed my hardness.

'I love you,' she said, taking me with quick manic thrusts. When she went limp we rolled over, she below me, comforting me in plushy wetness as I streamed into her. She nestled on my damp shoulder. I traced a finger around the wonder of her face. Then we fell asleep again.

When I awoke next morning, Alex and Nadine had left for Nice. I dressed, had a cup of coffee, then went out into the garden. I heard the sounds of typing and, peering in through the windows of a yellow gazebo, saw Gris at work. She was wearing spectacles and headphones. Her fingers fluttered rapidly over an electric machine. I noted with guilt that she was dressed in a conventional summer dress. From the pool came a familiar gurgling noise. It was Hafiz. I joined him.

'Hallo,' I called to the tiny black poet.

Hafiz swam lazily to the side of the pool and pulled himself onto the side. He rubbed his red eyes, which protruded like the smooth segments of an egg.

'So, you're the man,' said Hafiz, eyeing me with amusement.

'I don't know what you mean.'

'Nadine's tiger,' Hafiz replied insolently.

'We intend to be married.'

Hafiz exploded with laughter. 'Not Nadine, man,' he cried with genuine disbelief.

'That's the ultimate idea,' I said irritably.

'Chickenshit.'

'You speak excellent English,' I said.

'University of Michigan, darling,' Hafiz explained.

'Have you written any poetry in English?'

'You're not really interested in poetry,' Hafiz observed scornfully. 'That's just patronising garbage. I bet you're thinking: I'd like to kick this black bastard's arse.'

'Don't be silly.'

'There are two kinds of whiteys,' Hafiz observed. 'The black-arse kickers and the black-arse lickers.'

'I'm not white,' I protested.

'What fucking colour are you?' Hafiz demanded.

'A sort of brown, I suppose,' I said. 'I'm a Mede.'

Hafiz slapped his wet thigh and writhed with helpless laughter. 'Are they affiliated to the human race?'

'We are a very ancient people,' I observed with disdain.

'Where were you born?' Hafiz demanded.

'India,' I replied.

'Then', Hafiz advised, 'you're an Indian, man. That Mede hokum ain't going to fool the arse-kickers. And you'd better get a bit more sunburn on that off-white ass of yours so that we all know which side you're on.'

I turned away in disgust. Hafiz was the most repellent creature I had ever met. As I returned to the house, I heard the poet shout, 'Hey, Medey.' I looked back sourly. 'Did you know that little Nadine was pregnant?' he crowed. I felt my knees weaken at the question. I walked slowly back.

'What did you say?'

He was hugely amused by my bewilderment. 'You see,' he said, 'I've got this uncanny ability to tell if a chick has got a mouse up her chimney long before she starts knitting bonnets. I'd say Nadine was about ninety-three days gone, give or take an hour.'

'You're mistaken,' I said, swamped by dark and apocalyptic fears.

'I wouldn't have told whitey a thing like that, but you, being one of us, I'd hate to see you screwed.' He giggled hysterically.

I told myself again and again that it was impossible as I ran towards the house. I was overcome with nausea and

96

an overwhelming desire to urinate. I locked myself in the lavatory, trembling uncontrollably as I purged my bladder. Then I went back into the garden to the yellow gazebo where Gris was working.

'You look dreadful,' she remarked, lifting off her headphones.

'I know', I said slowly, 'that Nadine is pregnant.' I slumped into a canvas chair by the gazebo door. Gris's features did not indicate surprise.

'Who told you?' she enquired smoothly.

'I know,' I repeated, outstaring her big blue eyes.

'You don't deserve her,' Gris reflected.

'I want the whole truth.'

'A shit like you deserves it,' she retorted.

'Well?'

Gris told me that Alex's marriage had produced only one child, a severely mentally and physically damaged girl who had died in an automobile accident. His wife Clare, who had been badly injured in the crash, survived their daughter by only three weeks. Alex's legacy from the tragic incident was spinal and genital damage which resulted in his permanent impotence. He had met Nadine about twelve months before I did and they became friends. He asked her to work for him and live at Le Rayol.

Nadine soon learned that what Alex wanted more than anything in the world was another child. When she discovered that it was possible for Alex to realise his ambition by donating his sperm to a suitable recipient, she offered to bear his child. It was a typically generous and open-hearted gesture. And what made it right for Alex was that he was deeply in love with her. After a series of attempts, Nadine became pregnant. Alex was ecstatic. Then she met and fell in love with me. That was a development nobody expected. But Nadine had second thoughts about our affair and attempted to end the relationship. After my long phone call, she changed her mind again. Alex advised her to spend five days with me at Bormes before she decided her future. And he offered with a generosity to match Nadine's, to have her aborted at a private clinic in Nice, should she decide to return to England with me. On the other hand, if things didn't work out between me and Nadine, she would not proceed with a termination.

'Why didn't she tell me?' I groaned.

'Because Alex insisted that you should not know about the pregnancy. He believed that it might have affected your relationship with Nadine. And having met you, I am inclined to agree with his assessment.'

'I want to speak to Nadine,' I demanded.

'I'll try to get her at the clinic,' Gris said.

We went into the house and she dialled a number. After about ten minutes, she managed to contact Nadine and handed me the phone.

'Nadine?'

'Yes?'

'I know all about it, darling.'

'I'm so confused, Zubin.'

'Me too.'

'Are you angry?'

'No.'

'Don't you want me to go through with it?'

'Of course not.'

I could hear Nadine crying at the other end.

'We have no right,' she said.

'I agree.'

'The child belongs to Alex.'

'And you.'

'It was all my fault.'

'I'll be gone before you return.'

'Will you write?'

'Yes.'

'I love you,' she whispered. There was a long silence.

'Nadine?' But there was no answer.

*

Meehan poured Zubin another drink.

'You returned to England?' he asked.

Zubin nodded.

'Do you want to talk about what happened before they brought you here?'

'Nothing much to it,' Zubin said.

'I remember there was a plaster on your leg,' Meehan recalled.

Zubin managed a thin, unreal smile.

'It was several months after I got back from Le Rayol. Alex phoned me at the Snaffle Club. He told me that Nadine had died giving birth to their stillborn child. The infant was terribly flawed. I listened very calmly to what he had to say. I had been expecting the worst for a long time; I knew that things would not turn out well. I went straight on to play after talking to Alex. I played "Ain't Misbehavin'". Like the first time I saw her. I floated away, shut my eyes and remembered her. Her laughter. Then I went back to the dressing-room and tried to hang myself. The rope snapped and I just broke my ankle.'

Meehan reached out and gripped Zubin's hand. Zubin was crying. Sobs convulsed his thin body. 'I'm all smashed up inside, Meehan,' he said. 'I'm finished.'

'You know,' Meehan confessed gravely, 'I don't think I'm cut out for this fucking job.' He put an arm around Zubin and led him gently back to his cell.

Zubin sat quietly. A beam of light from the outside corridor slanted through the bars of his window and fell in three long rectangles of light on the floor before him. Apart from this, the room was in darkness. He rose after some time and found the skein of rope where he had thrown it. Zubin unravelled the rope and estimated that it was fifteen feet in length. He moved the rope through his small soft hands, feeling its strong entwined smoothness against his fingers and palms. He did this again and again. And, for the first time since he had lost Nadine, he felt tranquil, at peace with himself. He climbed onto the table and threw one end of the rope over the beam. Then he fashioned a noose. It was a very good noose. He jumped down, unlocked his saxophone case and took out his instrument. He scrambled back onto the table, arranging the noose securely around his neck. He closed his eyes, put the tenor saxophone to his lips, and blew.

Meehan lay on his bed across the square, listening to the velvet sounds of Zubin's saxophone drifting through the warm summer darkness. He was glad that the little Mede was playing 'Ain't Misbehavin''. And playing it right out of his skin.

Evenings at Mongini's

· · ·

Although Freni Kaka did not entirely believe Dr Cutty Vakil when he declared that she sang *Bist du bei mir* as well as Elisabeth Schumann, the conceit never failed to suffuse her body with a voluptuous flush.

'Oh Cutty,' she'd protest, fluttering her fingers with a quick wrist movement, 'it's unkind of you to mock me.'

'But my dear madame, your voice is quite divine. Feel my hands. They're trembling with excitement.' He captured her hand adroitly with his palms, then pressed it firmly against his bony chest. 'And my heart palpitates like a supercharged Lancia. I ask nothing more than to expire at your feet.'

Freni made a monkey face at Jamshed, her husband, who appeared to be mildly amused by Cutty's clowning. He stood awkwardly in the corner, rattling the bead curtain, owlishly beatific, like an overweight teddy bear. He watched Cutty brush Freni's hand with his lips before releasing it.

'I'm sorry, Jamshed,' Cutty confessed. 'I am unable to dissemble a moment longer. I adore her.'

Jamshed, who found it difficult to conceal his embarrassment when Cutty flirted with his wife, clattered through the beads onto the veranda, where the oilskin blinds were flapping noisily in the wind. Cutty led Freni out by the hand. Jamshed smiled. He looked a little tense when Cutty pursed his lips and made kissing noises at Freni. She directed a cautionary frown in Cutty's direction before disengaging herself and joining her husband. She moved a reassuring arm around Jamshed's back.

Cutty was forty, tall and uncommonly thin. He was

occasionally mistaken for Mohammed Ali Jinnah. His pale grey eyes were deep-set and looked freakishly mismatched in a dark, corvine face. He had a dry, ominous cough which was intrusive for those who were unused to its morbid clatter. On the rare occasions when he did not have a Gold Flake between his lips, Cutty smiled. And he was a great smiler, despite stained teeth that seemed as insubstantial as sandstone. He dressed elegantly in shrimp-pink sharkskin and had a fondness for ornate rings and cufflinks. Shortly after qualifying he was the focal point of a *cause célèbre* in Baroda, where he had his first practice. Accused of buggering a young nephew of the Gaikwad, he was eventually acquitted but was nevertheless obliged to leave Baroda State as expeditiously as possible. He resumed his practice in Bombay, where he married a widow who was several years his senior. Within a year she had lost her mind and was committed to the Thana Madhouse where shortly afterwards she took her own life.

'Cutty is an absolute idiot,' Freni observed, after he had gone back into the drawing room.

'A joker,' Jamshed agreed affably.

'What's the matter?' she whispered, reaching for his hand.

'We could lose every fledgling this monsoon unless we remember to secure the blinds.'

'Is it just the bulbuls you're concerned about?'

'What else?'

'Business?'

'Not now,' muttered Jamshed, 'not now.'

They heard Freni's cousin, Pheroza, crash rumbustiously across the under-strung Blüthner.

'Amapola,' sang Cutty in a reedy tenor.

'I believe he's tight,' laughed Freni, amused by the mock bravura of his tremor.

She arrived from the veranda on Jamshed's arm.

Pheroza played with extravagant fluency, blurred by an indulgent application of the bass pedal. Her red velvet gown had a daring décolletage. Pheroza was rather vain about her large, not unattractive breasts. Her shining raven hair was secured by a black band and embellished with a silver Kashmiri comb. She was tall and handsomely constructed with sultry lips, an imperious arched nose and heavy-lidded eyes. Freni considered Pheroza majestic and utterly beautiful but men were generally intimidated by her. Although her parents were quietly desperate at the fact that she was unmarried at twenty-six, she had, unbeknown to them, been the mistress of her uncle for nearly ten years. The uncle, her mother's eldest brother, had made his fortune in dairy products. He had more than adequately secured Pheroza's future: he had leased an apartment above her bookshop, where they met every Friday. Although Pheroza was extremely fond of him, she was not above mischievous allusions to her septuagenarian lover's acutely diminished powers. These revelations about Uncle Homi were, of course, for Freni's ears alone.

Freni and Pheroza had no secrets from one another. The prospect of spending the weekend together made Freni glow with happiness. They usually talked until dawn. A sleep-stricken Jamshed invariably made a ritual appearance in his striped night-shorts just before cock-crow to enquire whether they realised that it was four o'clock and to reprove them for disturbing his bulbuls. This never failed to provoke much hilarity and hoots of good-natured derision.

It was a propitious weekend, for the monsoon had just arrived. Freni was always a little giddy with excitement when the rains came. She spoke a little faster than usual and seemed more sharply aware of the sounds, smells and objects around her. During the summer of nineteen forty-two, Bombay experienced particularly heavy rain. Storm drains and sewers, swollen with turbulent water, displaced manhole covers. The bloated corpses of street animals were stranded on the pavements and alleys as each tide subsided. Quickening breezes gusted the musk of the Arabian Sea, the smell of damp quicklime, plaster of crumbling buildings and the sweet, sharp whiffs of putrefaction through the city. It was a familiar and, to Freni, a not unpleasant mingling of odours. She felt it was a vaguely erotic smell. Jamshed was astonished when she made this observation to him.

'It's a dreadful stink,' he protested. 'I really can't stand it. That's why I light jasmine agarbutties when the flood-waters recede.'

Jamshed was very proud of Freni who everybody agreed looked like Hedy Lamarr, but he had reservations about some of her fanciful ideas.

'You read too much,' he once complained. 'All those books excite your imagination and encourage expectations that I cannot satisfy. You are far too heavily educated for the wife of an ordinary asafetida exporter. You have a tricky nature, like your crazy Aunt Silla, who jumped from the dress circle of the Cowasji Jehangir Hall. Always mixing things up, dirty things with clean things. Your music is a symptom and, like all musical people, you are too highly strung.'

Then in the darkness of their bed, he enquired anxiously, 'Do you ever think of other men's organs?'

'Cocks?' Freni asked.

'Don't be dirty, for God's sake.'

There followed a long silence, broken by Jamshed.

'Well?'

'Sometimes,' Freni confessed.

'Whose?' demanded Jamshed.

'Nobody's in particular. Just the odd cock dream. Cocks that come in the night, so to speak.' Freni yawned, then added gloomily, 'I'm marginally repressed, I suppose.'

'Look,' Jamshed said, 'I have a six-roomed office on Sir Pherozeshah Mehta Road. I employ ten people. I work a twelve-hour day. We have a 1939 Buick with new white-wall tyres and a recent respray. I earn three thousand rupees a month and have one or two potentially lucrative deals in the pipeline. The car, this flat and even your housekeeping are charged to tax. We should be happy with our situation. I could be about to take off. But you talk about the smell of the monsoon making you feel juicy. Do you know what that smell is? Dead dogs, cats, rats and rotting vegetation. What are you, some kind of beast?'

'Yes,' Freni replied quietly.

'I love you,' Jamshed croaked, nibbling at her throat and grappling with her slim body. She allowed him to mount her and thrust quickly to his conclusion. Afterwards, roused by her shaking body, he reached for her face and found it wet.

'What the hell are you doing? Crying or laughing?'

'A bit of both, I think.'

He switched on the light to confirm her statement. 'Like I said,' he grunted, 'too highly strung.'

All this, Freni confided to Pheroza.

After dinner, the four of them played mah-jong. Freni was the skilful one. There were always complaints from the others after she had won several games in succession. Jamshed suggested Brag, but he was always overruled. So they played another game of mah-jong.

'How can anyone be so beautiful, talented and lucky as well?' Cutty sighed, reaching for Freni's hand across the table.

Cutty, who did not live far away, stayed until midnight. Then Jamshed, who had been quiet all evening, started a game of patience.

'Aren't you coming to bed?' Freni asked, looking surprised.

'No.'

'Why not?'

'I have a small problem.'

Freni raised her eyebrows at Pheroza.

'I'd better turn in myself,' said Pheroza, rising.

'I'll see you in your bedroom in a few minutes,' Freni promised her cousin. They kissed. When Pheroza had left the room, Freni turned to Jamshed.

'What's wrong?'

'I must go to Nagpur next week to see how matters are progressing at the prison.'

'You should stick to what you understand,' she reproved. 'You're basically an asafetida man.'

'We could make a lot of money on the prison contract,' Jamshed said.

'A lot of money?'

He nodded.

'Why don't you send old Patel?'

'He's having his hydrocele drained. His testicles are too large for his trousers.'

Freni giggled.

'It's very painful,' Jamshed reflected sadly.

'How long will you be away?' Freni asked quietly.

'A week, perhaps two. Why don't you ask Pheroza to come and stay with you? I'd feel happier if I knew you had company.'

Freni kissed him gently on the nose. 'I'll ask her,' she said, rushing away in excitement.

She did not return for some time, but the squeals of laughter Jamshed heard seemed to indicate that Pheroza favoured the arrangement.

Every morning, after Jamshed had left for the office, Freni cleaned the aviary. She changed the water and seed containers. Jamshed would not allow the Goanese maid anywhere near his precious bulbuls. Then Freni would load some Elisabeth Schumann and Galli-Curci records in her teakwood, eight-valve Mercury. She switched on the radiogram just before stepping into a hot bath and sang each aria with the great divas as she bathed.

Towelling herself afterwards, Freni would examine her slim boyish figure in the full-length bathroom mirror. The one aspect of her body that aroused her dissatisfaction was the tendency to hairiness. She resisted shaving the slight moustache and down on her hands and legs, for she had read that many men considered that lip and body down gave an added sensual dimension to a woman. Even Pheroza agreed that she would be diminished by depilation. Her pubic bush, however, had an extravagant growth which she had to contain. Once a month, she would stand on a double page of the *Jam-e-Jamshed* and prune her dark triangle until it was as precise as a grandee's beard, tidying matters up with Jamshed's shaving cream and razor. She was careful to gather the curly hair clippings in the paper and flush them down the lavatory pan. Pheroza had once told her about a beautiful actress called Madinikar whose pubic clippings were used in a magic spell by an evil jogi who had contracted leprosy. The jogi had purchased them from Madinikar's ayah, and his terrible magic made him irresistible to the actress. Every night, she would drive her silver Dusenberg to the outskirts of the leper colony where he lived. Leaping from the car, she would rush breathlessly to his hut, which was constructed of old cardboard cartons and jute sacks, and gripped by a fevered lust, she would perform any sexual perversion the leper's twisted imagination required.

Her fiancé, a famous film director, followed her one night. He was horrified at what he saw. He consulted a holy sage, and was advised that the only way to overcome the black magic was for the man who really loved her to become a eunuch. This would propitiate the dark forces. The brave film director had himself emasculated at an expensive private clinic. And so the beautiful Madinikar was saved.

'It's a beautiful story,' Freni sighed.

Although Freni told herself that black magic had no rational basis, she was always scrupulous about the disposal of her pubic hair. In India, even educated people tend not to ignore the possibility of malign, incomprehensible forces.

Freni and Pheroza loved ballroom dancing. Dr Cutty Vakil, who had won several medals for the foxtrot in his dog days, would accompany them to Mongini's Restaurant. Jamshed would reluctantly join them. Although Pheroza reported to Freni that Cutty slid his knees between her thighs on the turns and even fondled her bottom when the lights were low, Freni found him a perfect gentleman. But both of them preferred to dance with the accomplished Dr Vakil to the wooden Jamshed, for whom dancing was a palpitating ordeal. It took several brandies and sodas to stiffen Jamshed's resolve. He waited until the floor was crowded before he would hobble cautiously around, clutching his partner like a lifebuoy, just a quarter of a beat behind the music. As a youth, Jamshed had been an amateur boxer with the Zoroastrian Physical Culture Health League. He swore he would rather have faced the most bone-crushing blows than be one of the first dancers on the floor at Mongini's.

Sometimes, Freni and Pheroza went on their own. They listened to the music, sipped a gin and Italian or two and always got up to dance the Latin American medley together. When the Bunty Kadoorie Ladies Quartet played the first seductive bars of 'La Paloma', Freni rose, her cheeks slightly flushed and her palms moist with excitement. Pheroza always led, providing the direction and thrust as Freni undulated gracefully. Freni was adept at undulating. They made it a rule never to accept invitations to dance from strangers, although they were often importuned by lonely English servicemen. Both of them were genuinely saddened at having to refuse, as they were ardent anglophiles and conscientiously supported the war

110

effort. Jamshed would not have approved of his wife and his wife's unmarried cousin in the embrace of unknown tommies, however powerfully they were devoted to the British cause.

When Jamshed went to Nagpur, Freni called for Pheroza each evening at Dinshaw Choprivala and Company Limited, International Booksellers of Fort, Bombay, where Pheroza, who was a Choprivala herself, was the manageress. Officially, Pheroza was staying with Freni while Jamshed was away. It was she who suggested that they could use Uncle Homi's flat one night, should an opportunity arise.

'You don't mean . . .?' Freni whispered, awed by the audacity of the idea.

'Why not?'

'I couldn't,' Freni decided after some thought.

'Then we won't,' Pheroza smiled.

Freni had a cup of tea and a salted biscuit with her cousin, leafing through the latest batch of British and American periodicals while Pheroza completed her orders for the shippers, typed out the last of the invoices and cranked up the day's receipts on the addograph. Pheroza could distinguish most of the magazines by their respective smells. The *National Geographic*, she claimed, had an odour of warm starch, while the overseas edition of the *Daily Mirror* smelled of oatmeal biscuits. *Harper's Bazaar* reminded her of puppy's breath and *Punch* had the faint scent of soap and spearmint. The *Illustrated London News* had the merest suggestion of *crème de menthe*, while *Life* was wet sawdust. Pheroza's power of smell was celebrated, and as a rather unusual party trick she would identify magazines blindfold. The merest sniff was enough, and her range extended to the vernacular press. The *Jam-e-Jamshed* was pure mutton fat, while the *Hindu* had the antiseptic aroma of iodine.

As the great clock of the Rajabhai Tower struck six-thirty, Freni and Pheroza walked from the premises of

Dinshaw Choprivala and Company Limited to Mongini's. Earlier that day, Jamshed had phoned Freni to warn her that the left-wing weekly *Blitz* was running a scurrilous story about his prison contract.

'You're not to worry, darling,' he said.

'Are you sure you're not in any trouble?' she asked.

Jamshed laughed. 'Everything has been taken care of.'

But she did not expect to see hundreds of yellow fly-posters advertising the 'Ammunition Box Scandal', with Jamshed's photograph below it, all the way along Hornby Road.

'My God,' she gasped, 'they've made my Jamshed look so fat and dark.'

'Did you know about this?' screeched Pheroza.

'I hadn't realised that things had gone so far,' said Freni.

She bought a copy of *Blitz* from a roadside news vendor. They stood on the pavement and in the failing light rapidly read the front page. The article described how Jamshed Kaka, a small-time asafetida exporter, had procured a contract to repair and repaint damaged ammunition boxes returned from the Burma Front. It was estimated that ten thousand boxes a week were involved. For this contract Jamshed Kaka was paid five rupees per box by the Ordnance Depot. Mr Kaka, the paper stated, did not possess a factory or the resources to fulfil this contract. The damaged boxes were sent to Nagpur Jail, where Indian political prisoners were detained. It was alleged that the boxes were repaired and repainted by these political prisoners, under the direction of Colonel Pavri, the governor of the prison and a second cousin of the profiteering Kaka. The affair had deep political implications, for anti-British, Indian patriots, many of them pacifists, were being forced to assist the British War Effort by reconditioning ammunition boxes. A profit of nine thousand rupees a week was being divided between Jamshed Kaka and Colonel Pavri. Pheroza made a rapid calculation.

'That's over four and a half lakhs a year,' she declared.

'Jamshed is doing very well. You'll have to move to a smarter district. Malabar Hill, perhaps.'

'I only hope he doesn't go to jail,' murmured Freni. She looked wide-eyed with anguish.

'He's making far too much money for that. Jamshed will be able to bribe his way out of hell, at the rate he's travelling.'

'He should sue the bastards,' Freni said. She felt bitter at the unfairness of life.

They continued their journey to Mongini's.

'Litigation is the last thing he needs,' reflected Pheroza.

'Poor Jamshed. How he must have suffered,' said Freni. 'Do you really think he's been profiteering?'

'Of course,' Pheroza smiled. 'And I approve of enterprising entrepreneurs. I didn't believe that Jamshed had it in him.'

'I really can't accept that my husband is a profiteer. My God, I don't feel like a profiteer's wife. I don't possess diamond rings, pearl necklaces, not even a Favré Leuba pendant watch. Do you know, I've only got three pairs of silk camiknickers and still use the old gharial-skin handbag he bought me five years ago. We don't even drink imported gin, damn it.'

Pheroza squeezed Freni's hand as they entered Mongini's.

'Cutty has asked me to marry him,' she confided.

Freni seemed slightly surprised. 'Congratulations.'

'I realise he's a bit of a pederast,' Pheroza declared, 'but I do feel that marriage is what I need. Respectability, darling. Cutty is considerate and a perfect gentleman, so I'm willing to overlook the odd buggery now and then.'

'And Uncle Homi?'

'I daresay he'll be relieved. At seventy, there's very little future in maintaining a young mistress.'

'I like Cutty too,' Freni remarked.

'Of course,' Pheroza said as she lit a black Russian

113

cigarette for Freni and then one for herself, 'if things don't quite work out, I may be obliged to take a lover.'

Freni grinned. 'A younger one this time.'

Pheroza raised her glass and winked.

Freni hummed tunefully with the music, then leaned forward and murmured. 'Don't look now, but those two Europeans at the next table have been staring at us ever since we came in.'

Pheroza dropped her handkerchief on the floor. From the cover of the table she glanced in the direction Freni indicated.

'The short man with shining black hair and spectacles looks like Janki Dass,' she observed.

'Isn't he the cyclist who advertises Indian tea?'

'That's right. I introduced him to you in the bookshop, last year.'

'I remember now. He had enormous hairy thighs.'

'You must be thinking of the advertisement. His thighs were not on view in my shop.'

'Ah.'

'And the thin one with the quiff and Errol Flynn moustache reminds me of Uncle Homi.'

'Uncle Homi is seventy.'

'A younger version. I have several early photographs.'

'I really can't see the resemblance,' Freni replied.

Later, as they danced, she was clearly troubled by the men's persistent stares. Her palms became damp and an inexplicable shiver made the fine hair on her arms rise.

'Somebody is crossing my grave,' she shivered.

'Don't let them concern you, my love.' Pheroza was always protective.

When they got back to the table, Freni moved her head behind a menu card. 'Errol Flynn has a squint.'

'So has Uncle Homi,' Pheroza laughed.

'So he has,' said Freni, astonished by the coincidence. They giggled and shook until the tears rolled down their cheeks.

'We are behaving rather immodestly,' Pheroza warned.

Freni lowered her head and shook helplessly.

'As a matter of fact, darling,' Pheroza said, 'I've suddenly realised who they are. I think I know them.'

'Know them?'

'They're Russians,' Pheroza declared. 'The thick-set one who looks like Janki Dass is Vladimir; the tall, thin one with the moustache is Mischa. I met them at the Indo-Soviet Friendship Society. They showed a dreadful propoganda film called *No Greater Love*. I helped to organise a literature stall at the joint cultural exhibition that preceded the film.'

'What horrid haircuts,' sniffed Freni.

'Mischa is quite a card. I wouldn't be surprised if he asked me to dance.'

'What are they doing in Bombay?' Freni asked.

'They're chauffeurs at the Russian Embassy.'

Freni screwed up her face. 'Chauffeurs?'

'There's no stigma to being a chauffeur in the Soviet Union.'

'It indicates mediocrity anywhere.'

'Men are men,' Pheroza drawled coarsely.

'Those dreadful light-blue suits. How baggy they are. Oh shit, I think they're coming . . .'

'Be sweet to them. Think of the terrible news from Stalingrad.'

'*Prosit*,' said Vladimir, touching a glass to his lips before directing a generous mouth filled with glistening white teeth at them. The Russians used a dozen or so German and English words to communicate with foreigners. Freni felt faint and slightly nauseous. Pheroza had already taken Mischa's proffered arm.

'I don't think we can refuse,' she hissed. As Bunty Kadoorie on the accordian wheezed her way into 'Green Eyes', Freni and Pheroza discovered that despite their lack of sartorial elegance, Vladimir and Mischa were stylish, if somewhat old-fashioned, ballroom dancers. After the medley, they accompanied the girls back to the table and ordered four large vodkas on the rocks and a dozen chocolate cakes. Later in the evening, in the ladies room, Freni complained that Vladimir was dancing too close.

'Mischa too,' laughed Pheroza.

'I feel', said Freni in a slightly slurred voice, 'that we should escape before we are irretrievably compromised.'

'What? With a comfortable Embassy limousine to ride home in?'

'My God,' said Freni dolefully. 'This is going to end badly for us. You mark my words.'

On the way home, Vladimir parked the car on a dark area of wasteland near the sea. Pheroza and Mischa occupied the rear seat while Freni sat beside Vladimir in front. Vladimir slipped his arm around her shoulder, kissing her gently on her right earlobe and cheek. He leaned closer to her and, putting his mouth to hers, moved his hand onto her breast. Freni jerked nervously away.

'Pheroza,' she called huskily, turning her head.

There were low moans and sounds of noisy osculation from the rear seat.

'It's time we went home,' said Freni, a note of despair in her voice.

Vladimir made another attempt to kiss her, which she allowed reluctantly with clenched and unresponsive lips. He placed a palm on the upper part of her thigh. She felt its heat invade her flesh. Freni lifted his hand away tremblingly. Her defensive response became an ardent hand-clasp, the back of his hand against her pulsing stomach. Then, inexplicably, she accepted the persistence of his lips and took his probing tongue as they kissed. Vladimir undid the buttons of her blouse, slipping his hands across her warm, bare skin to her back, where he unfastened her brassière. Oh shit, Freni thought. Oh shit. He cupped her unsheathed breast, gently caressing it before lowering his head in the darkness to take her nipple in his hot mouth.

*

116

Dr Cutty Vakil phoned her the following morning before nine.

'My dearest Freni, where were you last night? I called at ten and you were not at home. With Jamshed away, I didn't know what to think.'

'Pheroza and I met some friends of hers from the Russian Embassy,' she explained sleepily.

'Oh?'

'At Mongini's.'

'I adore the Russians,' Cutty enthused. 'Chekhov, Tolstoy . . . not to speak of Tchaikovsky and Rimsky-Korsakov . . . and those magnificent dancers, Nijinsky, Pavlova . . . ah, Pavlova. Did you know that she danced at the Taj Mahal Hotel, here in Bombay?'

'It's a pleasant thought,' said Freni flatly.

'I'm ringing you to see whether Pheroza and you would join me for dinner tonight.'

'Not tonight, Cutty. Pheroza and I are going to the pictures.'

'Where? I'll accompany you.'

'It's a bit difficult, Cutty. We've been invited by her Uncle Homi.'

'That goat? Pictures? He must be eighty if he's a day, and almost blind.'

'He's seventy.'

'Did you know he has a soft spot for my Pheroza?'

'*Your* Pheroza?'

Cutty laughed nervously.

'He's very fond of Pheroza,' said Freni.

'Put it that way if you want. I've warned her not to trust the old bounder. Did you see the story about Jamshed in *Blitz*?'

'Wasn't it awful?'

'What excitement . . . my word, what excitement.'

'I'll have to hang up, Cutty. There's somebody at the front door.'

'Perhaps tomorrow?'

117

'Perhaps.'

It was the postman at the door. He had called with a parcel she had to sign for: a box of halva from Jamshed in Nagpur. She decided to take it to the intimate party Pheroza was giving that night at Uncle Homi's flat. Vladimir and Mischa were bringing vodka, smoked salmon and beluga, while Pheroza was providing samosas and iced taragolas. And Freni had enough Latin American records to last all night. A similar party had followed the petting in the embassy limousine. It was such a success that they had decided to hold one every evening while Jamshed was away. Their appetite for close dancing was now quite excessive. They danced with Vladimir and Mischa in the dark, wearing nothing but their underwear. And every now and again, until daylight, they took it in turns to put Uncle Homi's bedroom to good use.

Cutty had begun to ring Pheroza early in the evening when she got home from work.

'I've decided to take you to Mongini's tonight.'

'Oh Cutty, I've had a migraine all afternoon.'

'What about dinner? The three of us?'

'Why can't we celebrate with our usual foursome when Jamshed returns?'

'I feel neglected,' complained Cutty. 'I haven't seen either of you for ten days.'

It all ended suddenly. Vladimir and Mischa were to be posted back home. They brought presents for the girls. A large Russian doll for Freni and a balalaika for Pheroza.

'Perhaps we'll all meet again after the war,' Freni said sadly.

They didn't dance much the last night. Pheroza and Mischa had Uncle Homi's room, while Freni and Vladimir made themselves comfortable on the large sofa. Freni cried and Vladimir comforted her. In the few days they had been together, she had grown addicted to his presence. She would miss him. Yet her regret was also tinged with a feeling of relief. She had begun to wonder how much

118

longer she would be able to endure the intense and unreal relationship.

'Like animals on heat,' Pheroza remarked, summarising their adventure with the Russians.

'Wasn't there more to it than that?' Freni asked, bewildered at Pheroza's observation.

But Pheroza just squeezed Freni's hand affectionately and laughed.

The following week, Freni received a telegram that Jamshed was returning. She met him at Victoria Terminus. He bounded out of his first-class compartment and almost lifted her off the ground with an uncharacteristic demonstration of manic affection.

'My God, Jamshed. Have you gone mad?'

'I've got a basket of mangoes for you.'

The coolie laid the basket on the trolley beside his luggage.

'I hope you've been a good girl.'

'Naturally,' she smiled, inhaling the smell of sweet turpentine and warm straw rising from the basket of Alphonse mangoes. It was a smell of childhood and happiness. She was suddenly very pleased to see Jamshed.

'What are you grinning at?' he asked, swinging her hand between them as they walked down the platform.

'I'm pleased to see you,' she said, looking sideways at him.

'And I, you,' he said, hooking her arm in his, as they went out to find a taxi.

It was mah-jong again the next evening. Pheroza and Cutty arrived together. Freni noticed the solitaire diamond on Pheroza's finger.

'My God, it's huge,' she cried, pointing it out to Jamshed.

Cutty quickly accepted responsibility with an imbecilic grin. His face almost melted with pleasure.

'It's just point nine five of a carat, to be precise,' he informed them.

'Are congratulations in order?' asked a confused Jamshed. 'What has been happening during my absence?'

'We've decided on a quick job. Pheroza and I are getting married before the end of the month,' Cutty explained. Pheroza flushed. She seated herself at the piano, fiddling with the height of the stool. Freni bent down and kissed her on the lips as she lifted the lid of the Blüthner. She boomed her way floridly through a Sousa march.

'It's "Under the Double Eagle",' said Freni.

'She plays it quite superbly,' Cutty enthused. 'I'm buying Pheroza a white Bechstein for our new house.'

Freni joined Pheroza at the piano. 'I hope you'll be happy,' she whispered, stroking Pheroza's shoulder tenderly.

'I'm a tough bitch,' Pheroza confided, 'with a repertoire of survival techniques that would amaze most men.'

'Oh, I'm so glad you're tricky,' breathed Freni. 'A woman has to be really tricky to survive in Bombay.'

'Anywhere.'

'Do you miss him?'

'Mischa? Not at all.' Her fingers slid mischievously into 'Kalinka'.

'And you?' she enquired, vamping as she turned her face to regard Freni.

'He had a nice mouth,' Freni mused.

'There are plenty of nice mouths in Bombay.'

'Would you do it again?' asked Freni.

'I never exclude any possibility in life. And you?'

'Never,' Freni said with resolution. 'Never.'

Pheroza stopped playing as Cutty led Jamshed forward, waving a hand for attention.

'I have to inform you, Pheroza my darling, that my dearest and best friend, Jamshed Kaka, is now officially a millionaire. We must toast this wonderful prosperity.'

'Only in rupees, of course,' Jamshed explained diffidently.

'I was quite astonished when he told me the news last night,' Freni said.

'We read about it in *Blitz*,' Pheroza said.

'Damn *Blitz*. Those communists have caused enough trouble.'

'My accountant confirmed last week that poor hard-working Jamshed Kaka was worth several million rupees,' Jamshed joked.

'Several million,' whistled Cutty. 'And do you know what, Pheroza, my dove? Jamshed is buying Freni a racehorse.'

'We haven't taken a definite decision yet,' said Freni. She looked embarrassed.

'I suppose it's the notorious ammunition box contract that's responsible for your sudden wealth,' remarked Pheroza, wide-eyed.

'That helped, of course. But I've recently landed something very big with the US government.'

'More ammunition boxes?'

'No, coffins,' laughed Jamshed. 'I have a contract to provide polished teak coffins with brass handles and inscription plates for all American servicemen killed in Southeast Asia.'

'The more bloody Americans the Japanese kill, the richer our Jamshed becomes,' Cutty cried with wild excitement.

'It sounds quite bloodthirsty, put like that,' mumbled Jamshed.

'How many corpses are you hoping to accommodate?' Pheroza asked.

'He's not hoping for anything, Pheroza,' Freni snapped with untypical asperity. There was an awkward silence.

'Fifteen thousand is the number of dead they've forecast,' said Jamshed, glancing glumly up at the ceiling. Nobody spoke for a while. It was as though they wanted to dignify the sacrifices of those young Americans who would soon be making Jamshed a packet. It was Cutty who broke the spell.

'Mah-jong time, children,' he called, 'mah-jong time.'

Pheroza and Cutty Vakil honeymooned for six weeks at his family bungalow at Marbleshwar. Jamshed put in a bid for a villa on Malabar Hill overlooking the Arabian Sea. When Pheroza was away, Freni read *Resurrection*, *The Death of Ivan Ilytch* and *The Cossacks*. Jamshed grew a moustache and went on a diet. He ordered a beige Cadillac from the Bombay Garage. Freni was halfway through *Crime and Punishment* when the Vakils returned.

'It's so depressing,' Freni complained, when Pheroza asked her how she was enjoying the Dostoevsky.

Cutty had reserved a table that night at George's Restaurant, an Irani shop tucked away in a narrow side street near Jamshed's office. They were noisily delighted to be together again, shouting, touching, kissing, and at times crying with excitement. They made a boisterous entry into the restaurant, rattling the brass cage of the somnolent, grey Zanzibar parrot in the hallway. Cutty said the parrot had once belonged to General Nicholson, who had been killed in Delhi during the Mutiny. Freni looked thoughtful. She made a mental calculation.

'That was eighty-five years ago,' she said with awe.

'It's a very old bird,' Cutty assured her.

They took their usual private room upstairs, inhaling the warm spicy smells from the kitchen as they climbed the narrow staircase. Once they were settled in the room, Jamshed led a solemn charade, striking the glass saltcellar against the table for silence. He took off his Polaroid sunglasses (he had recently taken to wearing them at night), and laid them on the starched white tablecloth.

'Acting in my capacity as annunciator – ' he began.

The other three interrupted him with clapping and boos. Jamshed held up his hand for silence. 'It is suspected,' he said, 'that Freni is with child.'

122

'What kind of lame-dog annunciation is that?' Cutty derided, 'and suspicion is not a scientific state of mind.' He turned to Freni. 'How many periods have you missed, Mrs Kaka?' Of course, Cutty, like everybody else, already knew the answer.

'Two,' she giggled, unable to maintain a straight face.

'Which is the same number', observed Cutty, giving his wife an affectionate squeeze, 'as your cousin Pheroza.'

The girls reached across the table and embraced emotionally, tears flooding their dark lustrous eyes. This was despite the fact that they had already discussed the matter between themselves on three occasions earlier in the day, weeping copiously each time. The Chaplinesque waiter with a crooked mouth allowed himself a smile before running out to return with a marigold for each of the ladies. He had known Freni and Pheroza since they were little girls.

Jamshed punched Cutty playfully on the shoulder as Cutty with contrived gravity looked over the menu card at the waiter. He recited their usual order.

'Two mutton biryanis, two moorghi chops with moghlai rotis, four iced faloodas and firnee to follow.'

After the waiter had hurried away with the order, the four friends beamed. They contemplated the rosy future that lay before them, wallowing in the happy thought that they were together again. Life had never been quite so wonderful. Then they laughed for sheer joy. And they laughed madly, with an outrageous lack of moderation and restraint.

The Pathan's Girl
• • •

When Nigel Drinkwater was first appointed managing director of Duveen's Chemicals, located at Chembur, just outside Bombay, his wife Lorna couldn't wait to sail out to India. Her life in Radlett, which seemed to have entered a phase of grey quiescence after the boys had gone to boarding school, was suddenly filled with strange images and expectations.

She prepared for her new life with characteristic thoroughness. The six months before they embarked on the *Hindustan* were employed reading everything she could about India. When Nigel came home one day, with a packet of large photographs of the house in which they were to live, Lorna laid them out on the carpet, bending her dark, shingled head over them for hours. Duveen's personnel department had commissioned a local photographer to record the interiors of the six bedrooms, three bathrooms, lounge, dining room, staircase, study, kitchen, pantry, verandas, garages, stables and servants' quarters. There were pictures of the garden, fish pond, tennis court, terrace and swimming pool. In all, there were eighty-five photographs, with details of their orientation inscribed on the backs. There was also a file with additional information about the servants, local customs, fauna, flora, food, climate, social life, and useful advice for senior covenanted staff and their families.

'Did you know we are entitled to eleven servants?' Lorna asked, with a hoot of incredulity. Nigel smiled. He sipped his gin and tonic and regarded Lorna happily. He was pleased about the Indian appointment. It was almost South Africa at one point, but the job had not been as prestigious.

Then Rosenthal had got it. He remembered how drear everything seemed at the time. After Lorna had hinted to her mother that they might be off to Cape Town, he began to want it for her. He felt acutely resentful about her bewilderment when he had to break the bad news.

'They've given it to the Jew,' he said.

'David?'

He nodded, inhaling deeply through his nose. She sensed he was hurt on her account and drew nearer to him, running her fingers through his fine blond hair. He would never have referred to David Rosenthal as the 'the Jew' had he not been profoundly upset. David was an old friend of theirs, and they both enjoyed a good, if not intimate relationship with him and with his wife Peggy. There was, of course, Nigel's eccentric attitude towards the Jews. She didn't care much for those silly Ikey-Mo jokes that he and Barry Ashcroft sniggered at when they were together, particularly after they'd had a few drinks. Anyhow, David and Peggy weren't the big-nosed, hand-rubbing characters that Nigel and Barry guffawed about. They really were super people. Barry seemed to spot Jews everywhere. Lorna couldn't tell the difference, most of the time. And, as far as she was concerned, it didn't matter a toss. Nigel was always on about England needing a short sharp dose of strong government. Barry thought that Mosley had the right ideas but ranted too much. Nigel felt that what England needed was a gentleman with steel. It was a pity Eden was such a liberal softy, they said. Halifax perhaps, Barry suggested.

How Lorna hated politics.

In 1936, the year the Drinkwaters sailed for India, Lorna was forty. She felt betrayed by life. Where had all her best years gone? Nigel had done well at Duveen's; the boys were at Charterhouse; they ran a decent-looking Bentley and employed an Irish maid. She also had a cleaning lady, who did mornings. They belonged to the local tennis club, spent two evenings a week playing bridge and holidayed at

128

Nigel's sister's bungalow at Budleigh Salterton. Then, suddenly, she was forty.

Lorna was tall, slim and athletic. She had dark brown hair, greying slightly at the sides, blue eyes, a fine long nose and a large mouth. In her younger days she had laughed a lot. Sometimes when she lay in bed at night she tried to remember that laughter, and wondered what had made her so happy. But she could never recapture the feeling of those days. Perhaps she laughed at nothing.

She had met Nigel at a dance in Cheltenham, where she had been a nurse. She had thought him unbelievably handsome. He was blond and as proud as a Teutonic god. He had platinum lashes, pale blue eyes and big strong hands. She was fascinated by his hands. He had just come down from Cambridge, at twenty, a year younger than was usual. He kissed her after the second waltz and on the way home she allowed him to touch her breasts. That was quite daring for 1918. Then, on their second date, he unbuttoned her blouse and took one pink mamilla between his lips. They were picnicking in a spinney not far from her house.

'You have elegant breasts,' Nigel said, 'beautifully turned up at the ends. They look snooty and extremely well bred.'

She considered that deliciously droll. It was his combination of intelligence and sensuality that first excited her. It was almost unbearable waiting for the honeyoon. And that was the first disappointment of her life.

After the boys were born, Lorna's life began to ebb away. Nigel drank rather a lot, but that was about average for the Duveen's executive set. He had put on a lot of flesh and, although he was still a handsome man, his face was beefy and rufescent. His neck had coarsened and grown two collar-sizes thicker. Sometimes, as they played bridge, she could see him as he once had been, but his movements had slowed. He preferred playing life, like his tennis, from the base line. But with weight Nigel acquired authority. He had, she felt, been evolving over the last ten years into a managing director.

Barry Ashcroft and his wife Wendy had been living in Bombay since 1933. Their second tour of duty coincided with the Drinkwaters' first. Long before the *Hindustan* sailed from Tilbury, Lorna had planned tennis and bridge evenings with the Ashcrofts. She realised, of course, that Bombay would not be Radlett in the tropics, but Wendy assured her that the British made a jolly good show of replicating life at home, as far as possible. Then she had a last-minute panic about the eleven servants. Would she be able to remember their names?

'That won't be necessary, darling,' Wendy laughed.

And shortly before they embarked, a strange thought occurred to her in the middle of the night. She shook Nigel awake.

'What about Yorkshire pudding?' she asked.

'What about it?' he grunted.

'Do you think the cook will be up to making one?'

'You may have to teach him a few of your tricks,' Nigel yawned, 'but the Indians are very quick at picking up elementary things.'

In the end, it was not like that at all. Her servants ran everything. She showered three times a day, rode for an hour in the morning, swam, read, took her first small gin at four in the afternoon and changed for tennis at five. She was astonished at the sticky unpleasantness of the heat, sweat drenching her body the moment she walked on to the burning concrete court. By the time they were ready for the first set, she was soaked, as though she had fallen in the swimming pool. After each set, the bearer brought out iced lime juice and fresh towels. At half-past six they trooped in for showers and drinks on the terrace.

'Do you know,' Lorna remarked to Nigel after they had been at Chembur a month, 'that we're getting through two bottles of gin a day?'

Nigel did not appear to consider that exceptional.

'We do a hell of a lot of entertaining,' he said, 'and Sam McAbe shifted quite a bit this evening.'

Before they had been at Chembur a year, it was three bottles a day. It was time, Lorna thought, for her to stick to lime juice.

It was Wendy who first noticed him. He was a tall young man who arrived on his bicycle along the back road, adjacent to the trellis that bounded the tennis court. He appeared just as they were knocking the balls about before the first set. He dismounted, then, leaning his machine against the trellis, stood almost motionless watching them playing. He was dressed in buff nankeen trousers and a black shirt.

'We have an audience,' Wendy said, waving a racquet in the young man's direction.

'A Pathan,' laughed Barry. 'We all know why he is here.'

'Why?'

'White women's limbs drive those fellows wild. Their own females have to go about in tents, covered from their heads to their toes.'

'I think he's rather cute,' giggled Wendy, preparing to serve.

Lorna was intrigued by the stillness of the man. He scarcely moved for one and a half hours. Then, when they went in for their showers, he climbed on his bicycle and pedalled slowly down the road.

Two evenings later, he was there again.

'It's Wendy's boyfriend,' shouted Sam McAbe.

They all stared back at the man, who must have been aware that they were discussing him. He was as motionless as before.

'I think he's got a bloody nerve,' said Barry.

'It's a public road,' remarked Lorna.

'It would do no harm to report him to the police,' suggested Nigel. 'One never knows what these bounders are up to.'

'Calculated insolence, that's what it is,' fumed Barry.

131

'What the sod needs is a whack or two across the arse with a stick.'

'I suspect', Nigel said to Wendy over drinks on the terrace, 'that your Pathan friend is probably a workman from Duveen's. I shall place the back road out of bounds tomorrow. That should put an end to his troublesome presence.'

'Can you really place a public road out of bounds?' Lorna asked.

'We can do anything we want, darling,' Nigel said, swirling the contents of his glass around. He looked at her and smiled. It was almost a friendly smile. 'This isn't Radlett, you know.'

Duveen's provided Nigel with a company Humber and a chauffeur. One afternoon, Lorna was surprised to see him arrive home in a green Wolseley Hornet. He got out and called to her. She came down from the terrace.

'It's yours,' he said, throwing her the ignition key.

She went up to him and kissed him on the lips.

'Steady on,' he murmured, *pas devant les domestiques*, old thing.'

There was nothing Nigel could have bought Lorna that would have given her greater pleasure. She now spent most of her time in the Wolseley, visiting her friends in Bombay and exploring the roads in the countryside around Chembur. She stopped the car in remote clearings, fed wild monkeys, saw spotted deer, jackals and, on one occasion at dusk, a black panther.

After nine o'clock on most evenings, Nigel was rarely sober. He did not fall about, get sick, or do anything obviously silly, but he breathed unevenly, spoke with a slight slur, and fell asleep suddenly, though he usually had the courtesy to wait until his guests had departed. His snoring made it impossible for Lorna to sleep in the same room.

'You don't mind my using another bedroom, do you?' she asked anxiously, squeezing his hand.

Nigel eyed her with puffy-eyed equanimity.

'Help yourself, old thing,' he said, jabbing one of his bread soldiers savagely into a soft-boiled egg. He prayed that she wouldn't carry on about the drink and was vastly relieved that the matter had been so pacifically resolved.

As she sipped her tea, Lorna saw before her a fat old man bent ravenously over his breakfast. It was a trick of the light shining behind his cropped blond hair, transforming it into hoary stubble. He looked up suddenly and noticed the look of alarm in her eyes.

'What's the matter,' he asked, 'seen a ghost?'

Lorna shook her head. Then, thrusting her chin forward, she simulated a funny smile shape with her mouth.

'Sam McAbe is taking me to the Jogeshwari Caves today.'

Nigel nodded. 'Bring him back for tennis tonight. Barry can't make it.'

'I'll ask him,' she promised.

It was three o'clock when Sam and Lorna got back from Jogeshwari. She ordered tea and they went out onto the terrace.

'I nearly managed it in the caves,' he said.

'What?'

'Kissing you.'

'Oh, Sam.' Her voice conveyed disappointment. She was very fond of the short square Glaswegian with thinning ginger hair. A structural engineer, the same age as herself, he had decided to take his six months' home leave in India. His keen but not intrusively well-informed interest in Indian culture took Lorna to places she would not have normally visited, like ashrams and yoga centres. He had even, much to Nigel's amused derision, given her a translation of the *Bhagavad-Gita* for her birthday. He had solid doggy virtues, like cheerfulness and dependability. Lust, however, was not something native to his guileless nature. Now Sam's admission of his feelings for her had produced a tension in their relationship that Lorna did not welcome. He was mooning. And mooning made her uncomfortable.

133

The bearer brought in the tea, then withdrew. Sam looked disconsolate. He had just made a muttered declaration of amatory intent.

'I mean it, you know, Lorna.'

'Perhaps we're spending too much time together,' she suggested brightly.

They sipped their tea. Sam was not a ladies' man. He had never been easy with women and, rather late in his life, had concluded that his Calvinist temperament might have been the principal impediment in his dealings with the opposite sex. The moment Lorna rose to go to her shower, he came awkwardly to her. But hot pursuit was not in his grain. He aimed his lips in the direction of hers. Lorna turned, as quickly as a startled bird, receiving Sam's mouth just below her right ear.

Just before they ended their next game of tennis, the young Pathan was there again. On this occasion he did not dismount. He sat on his bicycle at the far end of the road, looking at them through the fronds of a palm that grew beside the pavilion. Lorna could just distinguish his face framed between the green leaves, still motionless and watchful.

'I don't like him,' Wendy decided, missing a ball.

'Oh, for God's sake, ignore the bastard,' shouted Barry, for she had lost them a crucial point.

'He probably likes tennis,' said Lorna. Her game had improved a great deal in Chembur. Probably as much as Nigel's had deteriorated. Often, Nigel sat out after a set and Sam took his place.

The reappearance of the Pathan had made everyone edgy. Nigel walked to the trellis, nearest to the young man, and shouted. The Pathan did not move. Nigel waved him angrily away. When the others saw that the man appeared to be deliberately defiant, the game stopped. The players joined Nigel at the trellis. Lorna sensed that the situation had got suddenly out of control. She placed a restraining

134

hand on Nigel, who was trembling with rage. Barry shouted abusive remarks.

'He's doing no harm,' Lorna said, looking towards the young man and shrugging her shoulders to convey to him that she, at least, had no wish to be unpleasant. The young man looked straight at Lorna and smiled. He had a lean hawkish face with kohl around his eyes. Then very slowly, and with dignified arrogance, he cycled away, wishing them a 'salaam alaykum', as he went.

'The next time that cocky wog appears, I'm going to hit him,' vowed Nigel.

'You'd better be careful,' Sam said. 'These Pathan blighters are quite handy with the knife.'

Two nights later, after dinner, Lorna drove out to the village Irani shop, about three miles down the road. The proprietor used to stock Turkish cigarettes for her. She bought two hundred Abdullahs and was just coming out of the place when she saw him. The Pathan. He stood by her car, watching her. She stopped and smiled at him, nodding politely. He nodded back, smiling and settling his hair with one hand. He waited until she started the engine before he had the courage to speak. As she drew away, she thought she heard him call, 'Good evening.' She watched him in the rear-view mirror, silhouetted in the shop lights. He half raised a hand to wave her farewell.

At a house party for Sam's birthday, the Scotsman danced with Lorna long after the last of the guests had gone. Nigel had been one of the early casualties of the night, being helped into bed just before midnight.

'It's two o'clock,' Lorna said, as they shuffled around the terrace.

Sam disengaged himself from her for a moment and switched off the light. He grasped her with more confidence in the darkness, enveloping her in his strong arms and drawing her close to him. Lorna kicked off her shoes and leaned against his shoulder. She was very tipsy but conscious that she was being irresponsible about Sam's emboldened hands. She allowed him to slide a palm over her breasts. He kissed her. As their mouths met, his pretence at dancing ended. He caressed the contours of her bottom, drawing her to him. They kissed again and he moved a hand up her dress.

'Can we go to your room?' he asked.

Lorna did not answer but led him through the darkened lounge to her door. They did not switch on the light when they got inside. She wriggled out of her dress and allowed him to draw her knickers down her legs. And a moment before she laid herself on the bed, she whispered, 'You'll have to wear something.'

'Oh aye,' he said, fumbling about in his wallet.

She waited, listening to the rustling of the packet as he prepared himself. When he fell on her, little happened. She felt him struggle between her thighs. Lorna moved a guiding hand down to his detumescent flesh, folded inside the protective sheath.

'What's the matter?' she asked.

'I'm sorry,' Sam replied. 'I must have had more drink than I thought.'

The young Pathan never returned to watch the tennis. Nigel congratulated himself that he had frightened him off, while Barry claimed that his word in the ear of the local superintendent of police had probably done the trick. Lorna, however, saw him regularly. At first, their brief encounters were outside the village shop where she bought her Turkish cigarettes. They wished each other good evening and smiled. For some weeks, that was all that occurred. What was possibly more significant was that Lorna told nobody about her exchange of greetings with the young Pathan. She understood that both of them were playing a game. She felt that he had guessed that at least part of the reason for her increasingly frequent visits to the shop at night, was to see him. But he seemed content to wait, gradually to infiltrate her dreams and to encompass her needs. She felt sure that he apprehended, as only players of their sort of game could, that the movements of

the hunter and the hunted have to be almost imperceptible; that the intense pleasure of the game resides in
forgetting who is the hunter and who the hunted. And
that their covert complicity was a madness that could lead
to a resolution that neither of them, at the last throw,
might be able to evade.

One night, she saw him standing in a deserted stretch of
country, a mile from the village. She picked him out in the
Wolseley's headlights and slowed, acknowledging his
raised hand with a wave of hers. She did not stop, but
suspected that he had now positioned himself some distance from the lighted shops in order that their signals
would not be observed. On two subsequent nights, Lorna
drove past him, exchanging what appeared to be innocent
gestures but which were, for her, charged with an excitement she was finding it difficult to contain.

The night Lorna finally stopped, she left the engine
running. He approached the car and looked through the
near-side window. He smelled strongly of an Indian perfume and when he spoke, she noticed that his teeth were
stained with betel nut juice. Lorna knew that the difficulty
of being able to communicate verbally with one another
would never be overcome. But she recognised that the
very poverty of their common vocabulary might precipitate
a more physical congruence.

'My name', he said, 'is Zia.'

She saw that he was quite young. Barely thirty, she
estimated. They touched hands in a self-conscious hand-
shake, perfunctory and not ardent or presumptious on his
part. She was grateful for his shy diffidence, which she had
not expected.

'And my name', she said, 'is Lorna.'

He appeared not to know what to say. They looked at
each other, smiled shy smiles of almost virginal modesty,
then averted their eyes.

'I have to go now,' Lorna said. He did not attempt to

detain her. As the car moved away, he called out to her in stilted English.

'You are beautiful,' he said.

Lorna found herself trembling as she steered the Wolseley towards the house. Zia, she said to herself. Zia, she repeated, half singing the word. And after her shower, as she lay in bed, she uttered his name, again and again, like a young girl who had never been taken.

The Drinkwaters were delighted by a report they had received from Charterhouse. John, it was suggested, was scholarship material; he was being aimed at Balliol to read Classics. Nigel was exalted by the news. He privately hoped that John would enter the Foreign Office, a career that he had once wished for himself until his precocity and competence in science had diverted him along commercial tributaries. Mark, their younger boy, was also doing well. They were gratified that their sacrifices in keeping the boys at a decent school were now being rewarded. Nigel read then reread the report aloud to Lorna. She had not seen him so excited for some time. And, as they talked about their sons, Lorna felt homesick. It was the first time. She was overwhelmed by a desire to escape from Bombay and return to Radlett. The wonderful news about John and Mark came as an affirmation of the kind of life she had always persuaded herself she wanted; the sort of respectability and achievement she imagined the family should pursue. Suddenly she was afraid of what was happening to her in Bombay. It was as though the heat had opened her like a flower, revealing within her a canker that had lain concealed for many years. She knew that what she was about would inevitably damage not only the dedication of her marriage but her dignity as an Englishwoman. And there were days when she cared. But she also feared, knowing herself, that there would be days when she did not.

'I'd love to see the boys before Christmas,' she said to Nigel. She had lately directed herself towards a reconciliation with him. He did not seem averse to her returning to England before the end of his tour of duty, but showed little enthusiasm to address the disharmony of their relationship. He was drinking more than ever.

'I don't think this place suits you,' he said quite gratuitously one night.

There was an implication in his words that she did not immediately comprehend.

'You don't feel that I am capable of becoming a good memsahib?' she asked. Her tone was light, self-deprecatory and good-humoured. Nigel dropped his spoon irritably in a half-inch of unwanted minestrone and regarded her with tired despair. He screwed up his serviette.

'You are not a serious woman, Lorna. You will be far better off in Radlett.'

'What do you mean?' she asked, fearful of what he had discovered.

Nigel shook his head then rose, abandoning the table, as the bearer brought in the crumbed pomfret.

Sam McAbe dropped in unexpectedly the next morning. Lorna had just dismounted from her grey Arab mare. She handed her over to the young sice as Sam came into the stables. He kissed her on the cheek. She was genuinely pleased to see him.

'Am I forgiven?' he asked glumly.

'Of course,' she laughed.

He had come to invite her out for a trip to Elephanta.

'More caves?' she mocked.

'The Shiva is superb. And I've got my own transport.'

'A boat?'

'I've bought a dinghy. Been tacking around the harbour all day.'

'Is it safe?'

'I'm an experienced sailor,' he told her. 'I did quite a bit of sailing in the Clyde.'

They made arrangements to sail across to Elephanta in Sam's boat the following Sunday.

'Nigel might be able to come,' she suggested.

Sam made a sour face. 'I wanted to seduce you,' he said, trying the joke on for size.

'What, again?' Lorna asked with grimace.

Sam laughed sheepishly. For some unaccountable reason, Lorna felt happy and not threatened. She took his arm and walked with him back to the house.

Lorna had not driven down to the shop for a month or more. She decided that it was prudent to keep away from Zia, recognising in a moment of lucidity the essentially brutish nature of her interest in the young Pathan. It was Wendy who alluded to Zia when she arrived with Barry for an evening of bridge. They decided to play on the well-lit terrace, from where they could be seen from the back road.

'Do you remember your Pathan friend?' Wendy giggled.

'My Pathan friend?' Lorna asked.

Nigel dealt the first hand.

'He's out there. On the back road. Barry caught him in the headlights. Sitting on his bicycle and looking up at the house.'

'I wonder what the bugger's game is?' mused Nigel, venturing a 'one no trump'.

Lorna shivered and looked out into the darkness. She imagined for a brief moment that she saw a bicycle light flickering behind the shrubbery. She got up after the first hand. She looked down and found Nigel observing her.

'I'd rather play inside,' she announced. 'I don't feel like sitting out here.'

There was no dissent from the other three. They filed into the lounge. Lorna drew the curtains and Wendy dealt the second hand of the rubber.

Although Lorna had not seen Zia for some time, she

140

understood that he had been observed cycling around the property at night. Then, one evening, Nigel told her that a young Pathan had been arrested on the back road. He had been carted off to the local chowki. Nigel thought a charge of loitering with intent would be a formality.

'Is it the same man?' Lorna asked.

Nigel nodded, smiling at her. 'I was determined to teach the bastard a lesson.'

'You?'

He shuffled through some paperwork he had brought home from the office. 'Had a quiet word in the ear of the super. Barry's friend, you know.'

'What will they do with him?' Lorna enquired. Her heart pounded. She felt sick.

'Not much. Beat the shit out of him. Give him a good scare, I suppose. Then let the bugger go.'

'That's horrible,' she said.

Nigel regarded her with amusement. 'In the good old days, they used to fire Pathans who got above themselves from cannons.'

Lorna though about Zia for several days. Then, one night, she decided to drive out to the shop for cigarettes and see if he was still around. She wouldn't stop, of course, but she wanted to know whether he was all right. She felt responsible for his punishment and couldn't bear the thought of the pain he might have suffered because she had irresponsibly encouraged his interest. Was he still there, waiting for her? How long did he wait? She remembered the night she came back, repeating his name. He was such a gentle man. How dare the police beat him. She felt ashamed to face Zia again, but she knew that she could not live with herself until she had.

'Where are you going?' Nigel asked. It was unusual for him to be interested in her movements. He was reading Dornford Yates's *Jonah and Co*. Nigel loved Dornford Yates.

'I'm off to get some cigarettes,' Lorna said.

'I've got fifty Gold Flake in the bedroom.'

'I feel like a Turkish.'

'Be careful,' he called pleasantly, turning to his book again.

She drove out. She was still unsure, as she breezed along the dark country road, whether she really wanted to see him. As she approached the stretch where he usually waited, and saw that he was not there, she felt vaguely depressed. She wondered what the police had done to him.

But when Lorna came out of the shop, she saw Zia standing by her car.

'Good evening,' he said, smiling as though nothing had happened.

'Hallo,' she said, overjoyed. She found herself crying with relief. 'Police?' she asked, wiping her face with her handkerchief.

Zia laughed. He lifted his palms towards her to indicate that all was well.

She got in the Wolseley and started the engine. 'Can I take you somewhere?' she asked.

He smiled vaguely. She sensed that he didn't understand. She patted the passenger seat beside her. Zia moved around the car. He opened the door and climbed in. She noticed that he was wearing baggy white trousers and gold-trimmed sandals. They looked at one another. There was no need for words. The question was asked and answered.

Lorna drove back into the country. She stopped after they were out of sight of the shops and switched off the engine. Zia did not reproach her for her long absence. He had waited patiently. Something he had seen in her eyes, perhaps, had told him that she would return. She was surprised by how peaceful she felt, sitting beside the young Pathan. She glanced at her watch. It was ten o'clock. Half-past four in England. She had a momentary vision of another reality. The High Street at Radlett. She turned to Zia, inhaling his scent of cheap perfume and sweat. He did not touch her.

'Will you come to my room?' he asked politely.

He was solemn and curiously respectful. Lorna looked at the quiet young man, half-seen in the darkness of her car. She nodded.

Zia pointed up the road. She started the car and drove in the direction he indicated. She thought briefly of Nigel reading his Dornford Yates and drinking gin and tonic. Zia indicated a narrow gully through the trees on the left. She turned the Wolseley, bumping along a lane towards a cluster of huts around a two-storied plaster building that appeared to be a grain store. She stopped the car. He motioned her to follow him. It was difficult for her to see as they picked their way past the huts. Some of them were illuminated by oil lights. A dog barked and she heard a baby crying. Lorna was aware of the faint fecal odour of inadequate drains, urine, and the warm aroma of recently cooked curry.

Zia led her behind the grain store, through a doorway, up some stone steps to the first floor. He unlocked a door and invited her into a dark room. She recognised the smell of his perfume, with a mingling of coconut oil, kerosene and raw onions. He lit a lantern and balanced it on a stone shelf beside the drain. The room contained a large wooden bed, a bamboo chair and a tiled washing area below a brass tap. Zia locked the door. He held out his hand and grasped hers. He came close against her, but did not use her mouth. He kissed her on the neck and cupped her breasts in his palms. She felt the hardness of his risen flesh against her. Zia drew her hands down, placing them inside his trousers. She held his swollen cock with her cool fingers, pleasuring the thick stem with gentle movements. He lifted her skirt and slid a hand up between her thighs to feel her wet accessibility. Then, without a word, he moved away and undressed. Lorna removed her own clothing. She lay on the bed, parting her thighs to allow the young Pathan to slip quickly into her.

*

143

Lorna and Zia made love at every possible opportunity. During the period of the affair, which lasted six months, she expected signs that she knew must come. They took no precautions and she waited for the time when she would miss a period. Eventually, she did. First one, and then another. She had wanted, more than anything else, to feel life quicken within her. She needed to experience once again the thrust of a child in her womb. And as Zia's sperm streamed into her, Lorna felt liberated by the joy of their union. She was certain that Zia and she would make a wonderful child.

Lorna was now conscious of her increasing alienation from her husband and friends. She was taking greater risks in visiting her lover. She knew that it was a narrow relationship, impossible to sustain indefinitely. But she had learned from Zia something about her own sensuality and the nature she had tried to suppress for many years. She had already decided to return to England before the existence of her child became evident. She would write to Nigel about the affair once she was back home. Divorce, of course. Other lovers, perhaps. Lorna was optimistic about her future.

One afternoon, just before she was due to leave Bombay, she was sorting through some luggage they kept in a storeroom. There, on a dusty shelf, she saw a cardboard box that she recognised. It was where Nigel kept the contraceptives. She wondered why it was there and not in the bedroom. She lifted the lid and was startled to discover white ants swarming around in a nest of floury paper and shredded rubber. She closed it and carried it out to Nigel on the terrace. Lorna opened the box and held it before him.

'I had no idea they ate rubber,' she laughed.

He regarded her gravely, quite unamused. 'It doesn't matter, does it?' he said.

She placed the box on the table beside him. He was staring at her with a malevolence that could only mean one thing. He knew. She sat down in front of him, calm and without fear. He had probably underrated her strength. As he spoke the words that she had been expecting for weeks, she clenched her mind and prepared to endure the predictable reproaches. Listening to his voice, she perceived in Nigel a weakness that had not been apparent to her before.

'Your motor-car has been observed', he said loftily, 'in a place and at a time, where and when, one would not expect to see it.'

She was tempted to say, yes, it must have been when Zia and I were making love, but she restrained herself.

'You have been seen several times in the company of a young Pathan. I have reason to believe that you have been visiting this man in his room.'

Lorna lit a cigarette. Despite everything, she found herself trembling.

'An Englishwoman, my wife, with a filthy wog,' he hissed. 'What in God's name made you do it with a wog?'

She narrowed her eyes in contempt. 'Because I couldn't find a Jew, I suppose,' she sneered.

'Whore.'

'I'm sorry I've made you unhappy,' she said simply.

'Didn't you consider your sons? Our responsibilities in this place? My position in Duveen's? Your duty to your friends, class, even your country? Did you not consider any of these things when you allowed this black bastard to perform these unspeakable acts with you?'

'No,' Lorna replied flatly.

'What kind of woman are you?' he asked. He stared at her with revulsion.

Lorna sat back in her chair. She took a deep breath.

'I'm sailing out on the *Britannia* next week,' she said, 'and that will be that. We may as well go through the motions for the last few days.'

He got up. His eyes were filled with tears. 'You've ruined my life,' he sobbed, turning his face away.

She watched him weep without restraint. Lorna no longer loved the man. And she knew nothing she could do would console him in his unbearable shame.

Lorna never saw Zia again. She had a pleasant and flirtatious voyage home. A Captain Damian Farrago of the Lancashire Fusiliers pursued her relentlessly. He informed her that he was a Knight of St John, with a palazzo on Gozo and a house in Belgravia. He was a short hairy man with glittering eyes and a luxuriant moustache. They danced, ate, and walked the decks together. A day out of Aden, he laid his cards on the table.

'I say, Lorna, I'm terribly keen on you.'

She smiled and showed him her left hand.

'Nobody need know,' he promised, putting an arm around her waist in the darkness of an upper deck.

'I suspect that you're a cad, Captain Farrago,' she reproved.

And during a day out at Port Said, he kissed her fingers over coffee at Simon Artz's.

'This is the real thing for me, Lorna,' he said, his eyes lustrous with desire.

'Don't be an absolute goat, Damian,' she sighed.

After the fancy dress ball, a day before they reached Gibraltar, she allowed him to take her mouth several times. From that point, Captain Farrago hardly left her side. And on the last night, he danced as close to her as it was socially acceptable for a commissioned officer to do in public.

'I'm besotted by you,' he complained, 'and I don't know how I'm going to live without you.'

'You'll live,' Lorna grinned.

'This could be our last chance,' he implored her.

'Listen, darling,' Lorna confided, after he'd walked her to the cabin door, 'you've been awfully sweet, but I'm three months pregnant.'

The Knight of St John looked gloomy for a moment. Then his face lit up.

'It doesn't matter then,' he suggested, grappling hopefully with her. 'Can I come in?' he pleaded.

They kissed several times.

'It's rather a narrow bunk,' Lorna warned, bolting the door behind them.

Lorna's baby was born in Cheltenham. Despite her forty-three years, it was an easy delivery. An eight-pound baby girl. Her mother turned up with fruit, chocolates and flowers, and, to her surprise, Captain Damian Farrago walked in with two dozen red roses. He was shorter and fatter than she remembered him. He prodded the pink bundle in the cot with a cautious forefinger.

'I feel like the father,' he enthused, bending over the bed and kissing Lorna.

'You're not,' she laughed.

Her mother thought the baby took after their side of the family: dark hair and eyes. Both boys were blond, like Nigel.

'My word,' said Captain Damian Farrago, 'isn't she an absolute corker? What are you going to call her?'

'Zia.'

Lorna's mother raised her eyebrows. She did not appear entirely to approve of the choice.

'Zia? Foreign, isn't it?'

'Yes,' cried Captain Damian Farrago, who was an extremely well informed person. 'It's Russian.'

Moving Targets
• • •

Three young people are walking along a promontory above a tumbled breakwater of rocks that faces the Arabian Sea on one side and a sheltered bay on the other. They move slowly in the burning heat of the afternoon sun. The water is calm: indigo on the seaward side, with the merest flecks of white visible near land; more grey-green in the bay, a barely perceptible swell fringed with milky lace fretting through the rocks. The two males carry ·22 rifles at arm's length, and one has a hessian bag thrown over his shoulder. The female has a Holland and Holland twelve-bore, broken and tucked against her side. A canvas cartridge case is slung around her neck. They are all about sixteen. The year is 1944.

The tallest male, Clovis, is lithe, ivory-complexioned, with thick lips, wide nostrils and brown eyes. He could pass for an Italian but is in fact of mixed race. The second male, Zimorowicz, know as Zimmy, is a Polish Jew. He is short and powerful, ponderous in his movements. He has red hair, the narrow violet eyes of a cat, and a broken nose that gives him the distinction of brooding menace. The female, Honey, an Australian, has flowing golden hair, cornflower-blue eyes and the radiance of Botticelli's *Primavera*.

The three belong to families that are comfortably off or at least able to pay the rent of an apartment in Aquamarine, an azure-blue block of flats situated about two hundred yards from the start of the headland they are traversing. Aquamarine is a fancy sort of building. It has avocado plants and weeping figs in imitation Hispano-Moresque pots on every landing. The lifts are panelled in teak, with turquoise and sorrel marquetry borders, burnished brass grilles, cheval mirrors, and even seats in red plush. On the ground floor there is a French patisserie, an air-conditioned barber's shop and a yoga centre. At the rear of the building, protected by high walls covered by bougainvillea, is a well-secured courtyard and a freshwater swimming pool for the Aquamarine residents.

Apart from these three young people, the headland is deserted; nor are there any humans present on either side of the causeway. There is, however, an infestation of large rats, which exist in a tunnel linked to sewage outlets at the far end of the causeway. These ginger-haired scavengers subsist on crabs, cockroaches, dead fish and excrement. They also feed upon each other, devouring their own dead and undefended young, tearing the weaker members of the species to shreds with razor-sharp incisors. Many of them are blind, bloated with disease, and afflicted with ulcers and mange. Yet they move with great rapidity, scrambling up and down the breakwater and swimming short distances between the rocks. The three young people have come to kill the rats.

Clovis, who is more than moderately literate, has read Tolstoy, Shelley, Gogol and Flaubert. Indeed Flaubert has been for some time a constant and fevered passion. And Clovis's familiarity with Gray's *Anatomy*, particularly the section on the female organs of reproduction, inspired an improper haiku celebrating Flaubert's heroine:

> *Madam Bovary's*
> *fourchette, is the golden fob*
> *that hangs from my heart.*

Clovis's friend, the Bengali poet Ajoy Gupta, had these lines reproduced on a Gestetner and circulated around the

English Department of Elphinstone College.

'You are now a published poet, Clovis,' he declared.

When Clovis was nine, he attended a Jesuit school. It was run by Spanish and Italian priests who smelled of sweat, stale brandy and cigars. Clovis was told by an older boy that when serious offences were committed, pupils were whacked on their bare arses.

'Until they bleed,' the older boy affirmed.

'And sometimes', another boy said, 'they don't use a cane.'

Everybody laughed but Clovis did not get the joke.

Gonsalves, a hawk-faced boy of twelve, who was invariably the source of these arcane utterances, established himself as Clovis's protector.

'On Saturday afternoons,' he told Clovis, 'we always visit the carpentry room.' Everybody laughed again. Clovis laughed with them, although he did not understand the implication of Gonsalves's remark.

So when Saturday came, Clovis accompanied Gonsalves and two other boys to the carpentry room. He watched with interest as the two other boys removed their shorts. The younger boy climbed up onto the table and lay face downward, while the older boy mounted and pressed into him from above. The older boy jerked between the cheeks of the younger boy's arse for several minutes. Then they changed places. After the two boys had put on their shorts, Gonsalves turned to Clovis.

'Now it's our turn,' he said.

Clovis was slightly nervous but he did not show it. He undressed and climbed onto the table, lying on his stomach, his face pressed against the rough surface. He shut his eyes and inhaled the perfume of wet cedar shavings. He felt Gonsalves above him, his hardness thrusting between his thighs. It seemed to go on for ages but when the wetness came he sensed that it was his turn to

153

be on top. Clovis imitated what he had seen, rubbing himself against Gonsalves for a minute or so, then stopped when the dry friction made him sore. He got off. Nobody spoke much on their way back to the playground.

They visited the carpentry room every Saturday afternoon until Father St Jerome Ambrosiano-Moretti caught them *in flagrante delicto*. The older boys were expelled. Clovis's mother thought it might be prudent to send him to another school. For some obscure reason she felt that a Protestant establishment might be safer. And that was how he came to Cathedral, where he met Zimmy. The incident at the Catholic school was something Clovis never talked about. Occasionally, however, he would see Gonsalves's saturnine face in his dreams and be strangely stirred by the smell of wet wood shavings.

Zimmy, who despised books, was vaguely disturbed by Clovis's attachment to them.

'Listen, too much small print gives me the creeping shits.'

Even Clovis's collection of *fin de siècle* dirty postcards were too distanced from the glossy reality Zimmy's imagination demanded.

'Brother, all those funny old ladies with massive tits and hairy fannies. If Paris is like that they can stick it up their bum-holes. My blubbery stepmother is juicier than those dames.'

'Your stepmother?'

'She has breasts like pink melons and see-through ginger fuzz.'

'You've seen her?'

'Sure.'

'She doesn't mind?'

'I peek at her through the bathroom air vent. The mad bitch showers seven times a day, so it's easy.'

'My God.'

'You want to see her?'

'You bet.'

'It'll cost you five rupees.'

'It's a deal.'

Clovis lived with his maternal aunt. His father, an Armenian manganese exporter, lived in Kandy with his Singhalese mistress, a Kathakali dancer, while his mother, who was given to mysticism, spent most of her time with her Buddhist friends at an ashram near Kalimpong. Clovis's aunt was a *café au lait*, mottled Mauritian with bulbous eyes, buck teeth and tightly permed, hennaed hair. Her thin forearms were covered in gold bangles. She detested Zimmy. Not only had she discovered him sniggering disrespectfully behind her back on several occasions, but she suspected him of deflowering Albertine, the Zimorowiczs' squirrel-eyed Goanese maid whose elder sister, Sarah, she employed as a seamstress.

'Your little Albertine has developed an experienced wiggle when she walks, Sarah. I'm convinced that dreadful Jewish boy has ruined her. We must arrange for Dr Fernandes to examine the poor child. If the girl is no longer *intacta* it could be a matter for the police. How old is she?'

'I don't know, madam.'

'Does she have pubic hair?'

'I don't know, madam.'

'You have a moral responsibility for Albertine, Sarah. Do you understand that?'

'Madam?'

'Is Father Ignatius Albertine's priest?'

'Yes, madam.'

'I'll have a quiet word in his ear. Ignatius is a man of the world.'

Zimmy's stepmother disliked Clovis, whom she considered conceited and slightly effeminate. She was a heavy, snub-nosed blonde from Poughkeepsie, and had married her Polish husband in New York during his brief transit through the States with his son, six months after the first Mrs Zimorowicz had been murdered in Breslau during an

155

anti-semitic demonstration. Zimorowicz *père*, an industrial chemist, had, shortly after his second marriage, set himself up in Bombay as a manufacturer of laboratory furnaces and portable electric kilns for gold and silversmiths. The second Mrs Zimorowicz, who consumed several bottles of gin each week and served lethal John Collinses in tall green receptacles that looked more like flower vases than liquor glasses, complained incessantly about the quality of life in Bombay. Zimorowicz *père*, having discovered, a month or two after an unforgivably hasty marriage, that his gentile partner was a coarse and drunken bore, gradually became inattentive to the minutiae of her puerilities. And when she lapsed into a sulky silence for more than two minutes, he programmed himself to look up and murmur with polite concern, 'I didn't quite catch what you said, my dear.' Even in an inebriated condition, Mrs Zimorowicz recognised this to be a strategy of comprehensive indifference. She would become acrimonious.

'Dear God, it's easier for you to shit gold ingots than to open your schmucky gob.'

Mrs Zimorowicz used the occasional Yiddish swearword when she was angry. She had acquired these nasty expressions from a couple of boyfriends she went with in New York, before her marriage. One was a wealthy hosiery wholesaler who valued her for her sensitivity and profound insights into the human condition but was unable to marry her because of a paraplegic and extremely orthodox mama. The other was a comedian, married, with seven children, who spoke rapturously about her sphincter control. He used to slide into bed with her on his way home from the club where he was working. It was usually three o'clock in the morning when he arrived. He made love with energetic urgency, then, twenty minutes and an ejaculation later, signed off with a couple of hilarious one-liners. On the basis of these not unpleasant experiences, she decided that she would like to marry the first reasonable Jew who was available. So when Zimorowicz and son arrived in her life, she went for a touchdown.

156

'You Jewish boys have such a lot of zip,' she confided in her cute, little-girl voice on their first date. The lugubrious Zimorowicz, who was probably the unzippiest human being she could have trawled in a dozen passes across the city, was inexplicably flattered by this patently unperceptive observation.

'I suppose that's true,' he reflected, mushing her hand in warm response.

The following week, over several vodka martinis in a quiet bar on the East Side, when she expatiated once again on Jewish vitality, he rashly decided to lay her without delay. He resolved to marry her in a spasm of exaltation as she fluttered beneath his substantial body, demonstrating her intense satisfaction with piteous and primeval squeaks. Thus, their bonding, like many such conjugations, had a simple and sentimental genesis.

2.

When Clovis, Zimmy and Honey reach the end of the causeway, they do not hear the familiar squealing and scraping of the rats retreating to their tunnel. The first operation is 'flushing out'. This is relatively hazardous, for one has to be close enough to fire the twelve-bore into the narrow entrance of the tunnel. This frightens the rats into the open. Apart from the danger of ricochet from the shot, there is a slight risk of being bitten as the rats emerge in terror, running at anyone who is in the way. Clovis, who is the most adroit of the three, usually flushes out, while Zimmy and Honey stand with rifles on the two concrete breakwaters nearest the entrance to the tunnel to pick off the rats as they emerge into the bright sunlight. On this occasion, Honey feels that she should flush out, as the Holland and Holland belongs to her father. Having loaded the gun, she reconnoitres the area around the tunnel, pacing out her projected scramble to the safety of the causeway before the rats run out.

'I can't hear anything,' says Clovis. 'The rats seem to have disappeared.'

'Where the hell to?' muses Honey, pitching a stone into the hole.

Zimmy goes a few yards down the rocks. He finds a sheet of dry tarpaper, rolls it into a wand, lights one end and thrusts the burning paper into the tunnel. It illuminates the rats' lair for several feet. There is no sign of life.

'I'm going to flush out,' Honey decides.

Zimmy and Clovis move back onto the breakwater with loaded rifles while Honey, standing to one side of the entrance, pokes the twelve-bore into the tunnel. She discharges both barrels. The noise reverberates over the causeway and the shot chips fragments of rock from inside the hole. The entrance is obscured by dense white smoke. They inhale the not unpleasant pungency of cordite as they crouch, watchful, observing the opening. There is silence.

'The bloody rats have buggered off,' Honey concludes disconsolately.

Clovis used to visit Ajoy Gupta in the flat below, several times a week. They played chess with chivalry and romance. Queens were never taken without warning, which rather negated authentic sacrifices. Weak moves were allowed again. Pretty endings were particularly prized. Coarse and obvious conclusions were avoided, so they would retrace the game to a point from where more attractive and subtle denouements could be contrived. Occasionally, when a game was played without reprise, it was with such slow and solemn deliberation that it could take several nights. On the whole, they did not approve of clocks.

Ajoy introduced Clovis to Havelock Ellis and the Kama-sutra. He read him Swinburne, whose works he was trying

158

to translate into Bengali, taught him to appreciate ragas, and chewed masala-pan with him as they speculated how Alekhine would resolve a particular chess problem, for they were both Alekhine worshippers. They also talked about the inevitable and imminent end of British rule. Ajoy's elder brother, who was a supporter of Subhas Chandra Bose, had been held by the British at the Red Fort in New Delhi. There was evidence to indicate that he had been tortured.

Clovis had for some time felt an enthusiasm for Indian nationalist aspirations, an affinity he could only discuss with Ajoy and Ajoy's friends as it was a viewpoint his teachers, his family and most of his schoolfriends rejected. He detested the arrogance, brutality, philistinism and narrow racialism of the Raj. On the other hand, he respected British valour; it had a storybook, fife-drum-and-flag quality that stirred his young mind. He understood British idealism but was already beginning to smell the hypocrisy that lay like a dead beast at its heart. Clovis never felt close to the British. He did not like them. But he did enjoy pulling Ajoy's leg.

'Don't you think, Ajoy,' he'd say, 'that there is something almost miraculous about the manifestation of Empire? It is a phenomenon beyond man's dreams. Do you somehow suspect that God might be an Englishman, after all?'

'Balls, my dear Clovis, balls.'

Clovis could not resist praising the magisterial prose of Macaulay and the voluptuous imperialist cadences of Kipling. But these were opinions that Ajoy would not graciously accept. 'You have an infantile infatuation for romantic illusions and lost causes.'

And if Clovis suspected that Ajoy was being less than objective, he still laughed at his friend's endearing pomposity when he smelled blood. Ajoy had complained that Major Bullivant, an Englishman who lived in the building, had wished him good morning for the first time in six years.

'It is impertinent', announced Ajoy grandly, 'of the British seriously to expect that the terminal condition of the Raj would at this late hour be repaired by Bullivant's marginally improved behaviour towards an Indian poet.'

One evening, Clovis found Ajoy inebriated. His breath smelled of fermented fruit, which Clovis recognised as toddy. Ajoy would never drink whisky or gin, which he considered to be symbols of imperialism.

'My brother has been released, Clovis. I had a phone call this afternoon.' Ajoy wept with relief and clasped Clovis in a fierce embrace.

'I honestly believed that the bastards would execute him,' he said.

'I'm glad for you,' whispered Clovis, his eyes welling with tears.

As Ajoy held Clovis to him, Clovis felt the stiffening of Ajoy's flesh against him. He pressed his face against Clovis's, then kissed him tenderly on the mouth. 'Stay close to me,' he pleaded.

Zimmy made a surprising disclosure to Clovis.

'I discovered my father on top of Albertine last night.'

'What do you mean, on top?'

'You know,' Zimmy sniggered.

'But he's an old man.'

'He's over forty, I suppose.'

'Did he see you?'

'Oh yes. When I went to the pantry refrigerator for a guava at about midnight, I heard a panting sound coming from Albertine's room. It sounded just like a thirsty dog. Placing my ear against the door, I heard a lot of heavy breathing and creaking springs. So naturally I opened the door. There was sufficient light from the pantry for me to see everything.'

'My God.'

'They were both naked. My father was jigging about between her spindly legs.'

160

'What did he say?'

'Shut the fucking door, was what he said, except he screamed it like a demented guy.'

'What did you do?'

'I did what he said.'

'How awful.'

'I did okay. He's buying me a Leica today.'

'That's to keep your mouth shut.'

'Fat chance,' Zimmy sniffed. 'I'm going to tell everybody.'

'Even your stepmother?' Clovis asked.

'Sure. Why not? She'll probably shoot the old fucker, then hopefully get executed for murder and I'll inherit everything. Maybe I'll buy myself a racehorse or two, a couple of dozen really crazy Aloha shirts, a few crates of Tennants beer and a red Lincoln Continental with white-walled tyres. I may even marry Honey Crowe. Hey, that would be shit-rich.'

'She'll never marry you,' Clovis reflected.

'She's mad about me,' Zimmy boasted. He slid a green packet out of his iguana wallet. 'I've even invested in some frenchies.'

Clovis managed a grim smile. Zimmy beamed at him. He suspected Clovis looked unhappy.

'I'll tell you what,' he said. 'As a consolation prize, I'll let you sneak a peek at my stepmother taking a shower, for nothing. If we hurry, we'll just be in time.'

'Not again,' grunted Clovis.

Honey's father was a famous racehorse trainer. He disapproved of Clovis and never spoke to him when he visited Honey. So Clovis went round when he was certain that her father was not at home. Honey admitted that she enjoyed kissing Clovis, who had soft lips and probed her open mouth with his tongue. She allowed him to put his hand inside her blouse and caress her satin-soft breasts. And they kissed until their jaws ached. Clovis progressed

161

to moving his fingers inside her knickers. Feeling Honey was for Clovis the most incredible experience of his life. But the first time it happened, she pulled his hand away after several minutes, reprimanding him for his ardent groping.

'You'll make me sore.'

'I'm sorry.'

'Don't use more than two fingers, okay?'

After he left her, Clovis savoured Honey's faint fishy odour on his finger-tips. He placed them against his nostrils from time to time, remembering his secret. Frequently he didn't wash his hands until the end of the day. These were matters he never confided to anyone.

The Crowes had an arsenal of guns. They were kept in a glass cabinet in the hall. Honey was proud of her father's reputation as a hunter. She showed Clovis his collection. Among them were two Winchester automatics, a five hundred State Express, a Fisher sixteen-bore, a Holland and Holland twelve-bore, a Tokorev sniper's rifle, a Lee Enfield and an assortment of lighter weapons.

'He must do a lot of shooting,' Clovis said.

'Daddy's killed seven tigers in the last two years. Hell, even I've shot three nilghai and a pig.'

'I have an uncle who likes killing animals as well,' admitted Clovis ruefully.

'My daddy's done better than that. He's killed a man.' She looked at Clovis with the smug certainty that her remark would astonish him. It did.

'Christ.'

'Well, an abo, to be precise. He was trespassing on our land back home in Australia.'

'What happened?'

'Oh, Daddy got off. Abos don't count for much out there, particularly trespassing abos. Daddy told the judge he thought the bugger was a kangeroo.'

'That's terrible.'

'And he's quite capable of doing it again,' Honey laughed. 'He says that if he knew a wog had had his way with me, he'd plug the bastard in the balls.'

162

'Then let's hope you don't fall in love with a wog.'

'Now you're being really stupid,' Honey growled.

Clovis was uneasy about Mr Crowe, the abo killer. He knew that the Australian suspected that he lusted after Honey. He felt vaguely threatened by the tall, freckled, ginger-haired trainer, who always stared through him with ice-cold blue eyes, as though he did not exist. Clovis sometimes wished that he could be on social terms with the man, if only to prove how well balanced and responsible he was; then he remembered with numbness one of Honey's remarks about her father.

'Daddy thinks that libraries spread diseases. If he had his way, he'd burn most books around anyway. He thinks that real fellers don't waste too much time farting around with books, only nancy-boys and bloody trouble-makers.'

Clovis was heartened that Honey didn't support her father's extreme views.

'He's crazy,' she laughed.

But he realised that he could never develop even a tenuous relationship with the sort of man who seriously held Mr Crowe's opinions. He knew that any progress with Honey had to be covert and risky, in the most deadly way.

Zimmy's stepmother enjoyed bitching about Clovis, directing her malefic suspicions at her stepson.

'Do you really believe that your clever Clovis really plays chess with that perfumed Mr Gupta until past midnight? Shit. That relationship really stinks of you know what. Now don't get me wrong. I approve of Indians. The real Indians, you know, the guys in the Mahabharata and the Ramayana.'

'He's Armenian,' Zimmy protested.

'And the rest. That aunt of his isn't Armenian.'

'So what? She's a human being.'

'There's human beings and human beings, son.'

'Clovis can't help his aunt,' Zimmy said defensively.

'And I feel really quite queasy about Clovis's friend. He's more than a little . . .' She paddled a fat hand before her to indicate ambiguity.

'They're poets.'

'Don't tell me about poets. They mooch around gents' toilets and interfere with little boys' assholes.'

'Clovis is okay.'

'But he's a mongrel. You understand what I'm saying, boy? One has only to see the rock sculptures of Ajanta and Ellora to realise that the Indians are a very special people. They have dignity and wisdom, unlike your Clovis, who's neither fish, fowl, nor Lord knows what. And as for that dreadful aunt of his, she even invited me up for a drink when we first arrived and claimed that she was a Parisienne. She pattered away in the most dreadful pidgin French to support her outrageous claim that she was born in Montmartre. You know what? The old bitch is from Port Louis. She served chartreuse on the rocks at ten in the morning, with hard-boiled eggs and beluga on toast, then sat down at her white boudoir grand and played what she imagined was Debussy. It was a joke. Shambling, fumbling. She could hardly manage two consecutive notes. I was half-minded to walk out while she was rattling around the keyboard, but I'm rather partial to chartreuse so I stayed. That woman has the stink of the whorehouse about her. I wouldn't be surprised if she was a retired madam.'

'I don't like her either,' Zimmy brooded, 'but Clovis is my friend.'

'That sickly perfume she wears. That's whorehouse perfume, all right.'

'It's very strong,' Zimmy agreed.

She turned to her husband with a knowing snort.

'Did you hear your own son? It's the smell I've always complained about on our landing. When are you going to tackle the agent?'

There was no immediate response, but after a while,

Zimorowicz *père* raised his head quizzically from the magazine he was reading, and said, 'I didn't quite catch what you said, my dove.'

Mrs Zimorowicz rose unsteadily to her feet and regarded her husband with weary contempt.

'I'm going to take a shower.'

As she tallulahed slowly across the room, Zimmy went into the hall to phone Clovis, warning him that the show was about to begin again.

Ajoy reproved Clovis for his interest in hunting rats.

'Not many years ago, before the Reclamation was completed,' explained Ajoy, 'thousands of bandicoots lived here. They infested the older properties and spread disease among the inhabitants. Then we installed better drains, pumped the sewage further away, improved the area, built posh apartment blocks on tons of impenetrable concrete and drove the filthy creatures away from our salubrious environment. And there, at the end of the causeway, hidden in dark subterranean mazes, where no respectable person need see them or be inconvenienced by their horror, they perform unpleasant but necessary tasks, consuming the sewage for the nice sanitised residents of places like Aquamarine.'

'You're not developing a Marxist analogy, are you?' asked Clovis.

'Not at all. I see them, unlike the poor British, as irresistibly successful imperialists, the ultimate survivors. I predict that in ten thousand years' time, the rats will inherit the earth, burying the monuments of mankind beneath mountain ranges of rodent defecation.'

'In the meanwhile,' laughed Clovis.

*

3.

The three young people spread out their towels and sit on the flat concrete breakwater on the shaded leeward side of the causeway. They chew their sandwiches and sip spit-warm orange squash. It is oppressively hot.

'What do you think has happened to the rats?' Honey asks.

'Perhaps they've moved closer to the mainland,' reflects Clovis.

'Why?'

'Because we've been killing them out here.'

'But rats are stupid,' grunts Zimmy. 'They don't know the difference between here and there.'

'I feel like shooting at something,' grumbles Honey.

She looks petulant. Clovis points to an oil-drum bobbing about in the bay. 'There you are. Hit that,' he says.

'I need moving targets,' Honey complains.

'My stepmother,' Zimmy suggests.

Honey laughs. Rather too much, Clovis thinks. He notices Zimmy's tight shorts bulging in the front. He closes his eyes and lies back on the rock, feeling the wet side with his fingers. He remembers, without wanting to, the shape and colour of Zimmy's cock. Thick and ivory white with a purple-pink mushroom at the end. He opens one eye and looks at Honey. She meets his gaze, then turns away. He is not sure, but senses a brief glance of complicity between Zimmy and her. He closes his eyes and thinks back to several evenings ago.

Clovis was sitting with Honey on a plank wedged between the water tanks on the terrace of Aquamarine. It was early dark and they looked out at the necklace of light along the Reclamation. The twilight which had just passed seemed to

166

have stayed with them. He felt it was somehow an emana-
tion of their relationship. That last meeting with Honey
had the strange unreality he had once experienced at the
onset of a serious fever.

'You wouldn't want us to go any further, would you?'
he asked diffidently, keeping a hand between her parted
but restless thighs.

'You mean humping?' she enquired.

'I'm ready if you are.'

He tried to ease her head against his shoulder, troubled
that she was less quiescent than normal.

'Don't be an arse, Clovis.'

'I mean it.'

'Well, we couldn't hump over here,' she said, jumping
down from the plank, 'not in a public area, like beasts of
the field.'

'A hotel perhaps,' Clovis said. He sounded unconvincing
and doubtful.

'We'd never get away with it,' Honey sighed. 'Now, my
place is a possibility. Maybe when Daddy's at the races. I'd
have to bribe the servants, of course, and you'd have to
use a frenchie.'

'Naturally,' agreed Clovis, dazed at the prospect. He drew
her to him, but she pushed him firmly away.

'Let's not get tacky again. Daddy's probably out looking
for me.'

'Please.'

'We'll drink orange squash with a shot of vodka and
listen to music,' Honey suggested.

'In your bed?'

'In Daddy's bed. It's quite immense. And we must have
silk sheets.'

'I could', Clovis said, 'bring along my complete set of
Bach partitas.'

Honey looked pained. 'I'd prefer Glenn Miller,' she
yawned. She jigged several paces away from Clovis towards
the terrace parapet and peered down at the street. It was

167

in those positions of relative inculpability that Mr Crowe found them.

4.

'I'm going to sunbathe,' Honey announces, picking up her towel and climbing over the rocks to the other side of the causeway. Zimmy stands up. He turns to Clovis.

'Clovis?'

'I'm okay here,' Clovis murmurs.

'Look after the guns,' Zimmy calls, following Honey.

Clovis turns his eyes towards the sheltered bay. He knows that he has no choice but to let events take their course. He stares out at the line of fishing boats drawing their nets in to the crescent of yellow sand across the water. He sits up and picks some small stones from between his toes. He takes off his sandals and strikes them against the rocks. From the other side of the causeway he hears Honey laugh. Zimmy is saying something. Honey laughs again. Then there is silence. Tiny spider crabs meander over his sandals and a quick breeze gusts against his back. He looks at his watch. They have been gone for more than an hour. He knows now, for certain. It does not matter any more. He stands up and gives a warning shout.

'Zimmy!'

There is no answer. He waits a few minutes, then, carrying the guns, makes his way up the rocks onto the causeway and looks down. Honey is sitting up, gazing out to sea, while Zimmy stands, arms folded, against the causeway wall. Clovis finds the apartness contrived and offensive.

'I'm thinking of going back,' he says, placing the guns carefully above their heads on the wall. Honey looks back at Clovis but does not smile. Zimmy grins foolishly.

'We've been sunbathing,' he says.

As he turns away, Clovis hears the squealing from below his feet. Suddenly the air is filled with high-pitched screeching and the swelling chirr of rats. Honey leaps up and grabs her gun. Zimmy takes his.

'They're back,' Zimmy shouts exultantly, vaulting onto the causeway and jumping down to a rock above the tunnel. It is now four o'clock. Honey scrambles along towards the end of the causeway, panting with excitement.

'Don't use the twelve-bore unless you're facing the water,' warns Clovis, clambering after her. From the corner of his eye, he sees an empty green packet flitting through the rocks like a butterfly. It blows into the shallows, stranded against the wet shingle.

From a conduit above Honey's head rats appear, slithering down the slime of the wall. Zimmy fires. Clovis picks off a pregnant female running blindly into the sea. Honey whacks the plushy, orange body of another with the butt of her gun. There are rats everywhere. Zimmy is bitten on the thigh. He tears the creature from his flesh and throws it savagely against the wall. Honey screams, ducking as rats jump over her head. They seem to be driven by an inexplicable frenzy, filling every crevice with their squeaking squirming bodies. Honey discharges both barrels into a pyramid of rats climbing a breakwater. Clovis aims at one running along the wall, then sights Honey's golden hair rise before him as he fires. She falls instantly, crashing past the rocks into the water. Zimmy springs down ten feet from the causeway, kicking rats away to reach her. He looks up in anguish. Clovis advances, leaping from rock to rock. Honey's face is badly gashed along one cheek. There is a blue bullet hole on her brow above her right eye. Zimmy gathers her in his arms.

'Christ,' he mutters, 'she's hurt bad.' He climbs back and places her gently on the causeway. Clovis kneels over her, looking intently at her still white face. Twittering rats swarm over and past them. But they are no longer concerned by rats.

'It was an accident,' Clovis says.

Zimmy scoops Honey up in his arms and runs towards the mainland. Clovis jogs beside him, carrying the guns.

'It was an accident,' Clovis repeats, several times.

Clovis stares at Honey's pale face. He knows that she is dead. Zimmy looks before him hopelessly, tears streaming down his face. But Clovis cannot cry. From Aquamarine and the buildings around, people emerge, as though they sense that something terrible has occurred. And as the two boys approach them with the dead girl, those who came to see begin to run fearfully towards them.

Keep Smiling
. . .

When Sultan Buckrabhoy saw his seven-year-old gelding Dream Time beaten two short heads at Mahaluxmi, he smiled; not because he liked to lose but because, whatever misfortune came his way, Sultan always tried to smile. A smile was his trademark and the saying, 'keep smiling', was never far from his lips. And although his racing stable of seventy thoroughbreds had been reduced to a symbolic plater that could hardly see out the minimum trip, Sultan never lost heart.

In the thirty years since 1949, Sultan Buckrabhoy had dissipated a considerable inheritance. His father had left him a cinema chain (fifteen picture houses), a transport company (three hundred vehicles), two manganese mines, the prestigious Salsette Garage (pre-war distributors of Ehrhardts and Isotta-Fraschinis) and the mammoth Swastika Film Corporation of Bombay. But Sultan Buckrabhoy spent considerably more than the income these once vigorous and profitable companies generated. He was not a greedy man nor an unpleasant one. He had few enemies. He never gave himself airs and was well respected for his good manners and simple courtesies towards the most humble person. In general, Sultan Buckrabhoy was a cheerful fellow, who enjoyed sharing his shrinking portion with his many friends and acquaintances. But at fifty-nine years of age, Sultan had kept smiling through more bad times than good.

He had, of course, weaknesses. The first was his adoration of pretty women to the point of feverish insanity; the second was an addiction to booze – in the early days only pink champagne; and the third, his capacity for losing vast

sums of money on horse-races. Not even the most gro-
tesque losing sequence alarmed him; nor did the steady
liquidation of capital it had taken his family five generations to accumulate cause him to lose five minutes' sleep.

He had his detractors. His chief accountant, Iyengar,
whom he paid at least three times as much as the market
rate, despised him. Iyengar brooded upon the thought that
had Sultan's fortune been his, he would have increased
rather than diminished it. He would have invested the
loose change in a carp farm at Ootycamund, a multi-storied
roller-skating rink at Thousand Lights and a hotel in Vepery
that catered for the better class of commercial traveller. He
would have purchased for his son a pepper plantation, as a
hedge against the corruption of the rupee. Iyengar believed
in the future of pepper. He was a sound man. A Tamil. He
did not smoke, drink alcohol or waste his money on
racehorses. Iyengar had no time for useless dreams. Numbers, for him, were the seeds of reason, and reason lay at
the core of the cosmic scrotum.

Sultan's wife, Khurshid, also did not care greatly for him.
She used to shut her eyes and grind her teeth when Sultan
mounted her; she cared little for his silky words of endear-
ment or freakishly sexual predilections.

'I would rather not take it in my mouth,' she advised
him solemnly, when they had been married a few days,
'nor am I happy with you sniffing about between my
thighs like a pariah dog.'

Her words wounded Sultan deeply. She was the daughter of a famous imam, and had been raised in a pious and
highly respectable household. The walls had been covered
with morally elevating verses from the Koran, and each of
the large white rooms were graced by devotional mats
from Bokhara, Samarkand and Swat. Khurshid recalled
that her girlhood was filled with sunshine, trays of peaches,
figs and pistachios; the comforting sussuration of constant
prayer, and the crackle of joints as her father and nine
brothers energetically abased themselves in worship.

174

When they married, Sultan feared that his eccentricities would be reported to her father and that he in turn would broadcast them to the entire community. At an official reception given for Aly Khan when he visited Bombay, Sultan detected a dismissive coolness when he was presented to the great man. Had the prince, Sultan wondered uneasily, heard something disreputable about him from the imam?

Sultan and Khurshid had been married for several months when he discovered that from certain angles she looked remarkably like her father. It was possibly her nose which, although well constructed, was masculine. She also had the imam's small, light brown eyes set close together; and her articulation of vowel sounds had the same accoustical quality as his: sounds which had been shaped by the utterance of prayers in open spaces. The apprehension of these similarities sometimes invaded his consciousness as he lay with her, resulting in an immediate and profound detumescence. Sultan believed this to be an important factor in the deterioration of their marriage. Khurshid, on the other hand, suspected that this lack of virility was the result of his debauchery. She was dimly aware of the dancing girls and actresses in his life. Secretly this pleased her, for she derived little pleasure from his carnal attentions. One day, after persistent abdominal pains, she consulted her doctor, convinced that Sultan had infected her with a disease of the streets. This was not so.

'You have', the physician informed her sadly, 'a form of colonic cancer. The prognosis is not good.'

Sultan and Khurshid had no children.

Sultan's younger brother, Aziz, refused to speak to him. A prosperous taxation lawyer, Aziz prayed daily that his brother would be crushed beneath the wheels of a locomotive before the family fortune disappeared altogether. It was not that Aziz wanted the money for himself. He merely considered that the family wealth and position bestowed upon them social and charitable obligations which they

175

would not be able to discharge if Sultan squandered everything. He would have been quite content had the Buckrabhoy millions been donated to a worthwhile cause instead of being used to sustain a dissolute lifestyle. Whenever Sultan's name came up in casual conversation with friends, Aziz had to leave the room, unable to contain his trembling rage. He had even burnt all photographs, correspondence and documents relating to his brother. There were times in the stillness of the night when he wondered why Allah had placed this terrible burden on his shoulders.

Sultan dreamed of children. He sometimes wondered whether he had fathered any. It was possible, but unlikely. Anyhow, it was the substance that he needed. Somebody he could set his eyes upon. A small person he could pat on the head and whisk off for fast drives in his Invicta tourer. In earlier years, he had thought of visiting a fertility clinic, but when the time came, the prospect unnerved him. He decided that he could not live with the certainty that he would never be a father.

When he was twenty-five, Sultan had visited London. The year was 1946. He fell in love with the grey damp city that he discovered. He examined with wonder the devastation of the recent war; he stood in awe before the soaring blackened timbers of ancient churches, the shells of devastated buildings, huge bomb craters, the peaceful rectangles of stinging nettles and wildflowers between occupied habitations. He was captivated by the cheerful friendliness of Londoners. He learned to enjoy fish and chips, weak lukewarm tea and sharp brown sauce. He found his way around the pubs nearest the small hotel in Bayswater where he stayed. Seated in a leather chair in the saloon bar of The Lancaster Arms, by a grate piled a yard high with incandescent red coke, Sultan found the sweet acrid taste of the fumes in his mouth as much a part of his pleasure as the smell of fresh furniture polish, cigarette smoke and the milky bitterness of the Guinness he sipped.

At this period of his life, Sultan looked remarkably like Ronald Colman; darker perhaps, but Colman, nevertheless. He had the moustache, the felt hat and the Colman mannerism of tilting his head. What was also extraordinary was that he had the Colman walk. Jaunty, debonair and quite uncontrived. Sometimes, when he looked in the bathroom mirror, he could scarcely believe his eyes. He wondered whether, in some capricious way, they possessed a common ancestor. A medieval Anatolian, perhaps, whose bifurcate seed flowed down the separate tributaries of European and Asiatic dispensations, swirling to an end as Ronald Colman in Hollywood and Sultan Buckrabhoy in Bombay.

The idea had a magical plausibility about it. He even invested his mythical forbear with a name. *Abba*. An acronym for Abdul Abulbul Amir, after the crazy song. He visualised Abba as a dapper little Turk wearing billowing silk pantaloons and a turban set at a rakish angle, wielding his scimitar with Colman-like insouciance. Abba, Sultan imagined, probably raped many beautiful women. And, as he was a Turk, most of the victims must have been Christians. Armenians, probably. Come to think of it, Colman could pass for an Armenian. But Sultan felt that he had inherited his seed legitimately. He was certain that none of the women in his family had been interfered with by outsiders. This disappointed him. The Buckrabhoys had always been morbidly restrictive with their womenfolk. But Armenians . . . well. Christians had much more flexible standards, anyway. Most of the girls who attended Sultan's private beach parties in Bombay were Christians. Goanese, Anglo-Indians, the occasional European. True, there were a few Parsees, Jewesses and, sometimes, a Hindu. But the few Moslem girls who came were irretrievably lost: members of the *demi-monde*, actresses, dancers, sexual anarchists

177

or high-class whores. How Sultan loved Christians. Christian girls were brought up dancing close to men. It was their way of life. They understood the meaning of a man's stiff flesh pressed against them when slow-foxtrotting around a crowded floor. They accepted the pressure of a stranger's hand on their arses as they shuffled about in semi-darkness. And it was a matter of empirical truth that as kissers Christians were far superior to mere Hindus or Moslems. They had wonderful harlots' mouths, instinctive and sly from pubescence, opening to take tongues, caressing, sucking, nibbling and licking. My word, what a religion.

Sultan knew that old Abba was probably circumcised, like himself. Women preferred it with circumcised men. Sultan had researched the subject extensively. He had directed the question to many girls who had experienced both sorts of partners and the answer was invariably the same. He was convinced that it was the uncovered ridge that gave them a more emphatic sensation. The supremacy of circumcision, he had long decided, was beyond rational dispute.

In London, Sultan made friends with many people. And he had more success than he believed possible with the young ladies of Bayswater. They were taken by his charm and extremely impressed by his ability to buy them expensive presents. There was one girl, however, who was different. She was pretty and Irish. Her name was Veena O'Brien. Veena was small, with curled auburn hair and green eyes. She had a voluptuous pixy mouth that turned up at the ends, and strong white teeth, with a gap in front. At the tip of her small nose was the hint of a cleft, and she had deep flirty dimples, extravagantly evident when she smiled.

They went dancing twice a week and to the cinema ' every Saturday. Veena took Sultan to the Victoria Palace to see the Crazy Gang, and to the Palladium. He purchased a one-and-a-half-litre 1938 Riley, with a British racing-green body and black mudguards. They went everywhere together in it. There was always a hamper basket in the back for their trips to Newmarket, Goodwood and Sandown Park. Sultan introduced her to pink champagne and she showed him how to drink whisky macs. Veena drank lots of whisky macs. He moved out of his hotel in Bayswater and rented a large flat in Belsize Park. Before Veena moved in they visited Bond Street, where he bought her a glittering engagement ring and one that was just a plain golden band. Sultan felt that it looked more respectable, if they were to live together.

It was fun to be with Veena. Sometimes he forgot about Khurshid for entire days. Veena giggled when the cleaning lady called her Mrs Buckrabhoy, but Sultan felt proud. He wished that she was, and that he could spend the rest of his days with Veena in their Belsize Park home. In bed, they often ended up laughing when they talked about the possiblity of her returning with him to Bombay. He told her that life lived openly together in Bombay would be sadly improbable. He would have to install her in an apartment and his visits would be necessarily clandestine. The prospect of Sultan's calling on her in disguise had them both convulsed with laughter. They had a great deal of childlike fun, discussing big hats, false beards, wigs and comic teeth. But afterwards, when they stopped laughing, the thought of parting became a gloomy reality.

'We've only got six weeks,' she said one afternoon, as she nestled on his shoulder.

'Well if you don't come to Bombay, I'll return to England for another holiday.'

'When?'

'Next year.'

'But how will I manage to live without you?' she asked, not really expecting a reply.

Sultan looked thoughtful. 'I'll buy you heaps of games,' he decided solemnly, 'heaps of games.'

'Games?'

'Yes. Cards, ludo, carroms, snakes and ladders, chess, backgammon, even ping-pong if we can fit a table into the living room. We will go to Harrods tomorrow and order every bloody game in the shop.'

She looked at him for a moment, then placed her hand over her mouth.

'What's the matter?'

Veena giggled. And the more Sultan shook her to discover what she found so funny, the more she laughed, which made Sultan laugh as well. In revenge, he tickled her under the armpits and smothered her mouth with kisses. Then he took her in his arms and they made love.

One day, when he was with Veena at Euston market, Sultan saw an unusual postcard of a very splendid and fierce Turk. It was a reproduction of a painting by the eighteenth-century French painter Lagillière and depicted Bayezid (1481–1512). Sultan purchased it for a penny. Across the back he wrote *Abba*. Then he slid it carefully into his wallet. It was an investment in his invented past. Veena gave him a curious smile.

'What have you written?' she enquired.

Sultan told her the story of the ancestor he imagined he shared with Ronald Colman. She listened with that beautiful wonder not uncommon in the Irish.

'And why not indeed?' she asked, squeezing his hand and receiving his kiss on her cold cheek with happiness. They passed through a throng of shoppers on the grey October afternoon. It was cool and beginning to rain. Veena smelled the smoke of winter in the air and saw a portent of the summer's end in the dull antimonial sky. They walked towards the fading halo of the setting sun, almost lost in the blur of the early street lights along Tottenham Court Road. They had a coffee and a buttered bun apiece, then hurried across the road, taking shelter in the comfort of a cinema. Veena snuggled against him in the dark. Years later, she remembered the faint smell of camphor from the damp wool of his suit and the sweetness of the brilliantine in his hair. The film was *Les Enfants du paradis*.

The Swastika Film Corporation of Bombay made long and noisy musicals, specialising in colourful and energetic dancing. It was their house style to fill the screen with movement, pretty faces and as many catchy tunes as they could pack into three and a half hours of soundtrack. Sultan usually arrived during the last half of the working day.

'Keep smiling,' he'd shout provocatively to Iyengar, who was always waiting for him with a folder of several dozen cheques to be signed. By the 1970s the financial situation was already cheerless. The cinema chain had been sold. All the racehorses, with the exception of Dream Time, had gone. The transport company was in the hands of a liquidator appointed by the creditors. The Salsette Garage had sublet most of the workshop to a battery manufacturer whose activities filled the air with yellow smoke and sulphurous fumes. Sultan could not walk past the premises without streaming eyes. On that account alone he was thankful that his father, Hussein, was dead. The old man had spent most of his working life in a circular office over the showroom. It was considered avant-garde in the early twenties, with chunky white furniture, a zebra-striped floor and an illuminated aquarium built into one wall. The glass mobiles and the enlarged photographs of the great marques his company distributed were now in a dusty storeroom. But the yellow potted cacti, in silver barrels chased with intricate designs of snakes, chinar leaves and naked houris, still stood in the corridor. The sinuous houris were the delight of old Hussein. 'They're utterly decadent,' he used to laugh with delighted embarrassment when they were scrutinised too closely by visitors. It was the laughter of innocence.

The office looked out across a sable strand filled with nets and glittering fish drying in the sun. When Sultan was a boy, he enjoyed watching the koli women on the beach, from his father's window. He remembered the cheeks of their hard, muscled buttocks, tight in wet saris, breasts hardly contained in skimpy cholis. They were working women, strong, proud and aware of their sexuality. During the school holidays, when he was twelve, Sultan told his servant, Akbar, that he was ready for a girl. That afternoon, Akbar took him to a room at the back of the house, adjacent to the servants' quarters. A bright-eyed young woman of about eighteen was standing there. Sultan recognised her as one of the girls who sold fruit. She usually sat under a tree at the end of the avenue where they lived. She had nice lips and a gold stud in her nose. Akbar undid her choli, exposing firm, pointed breasts. Then he unfastened her sari, so that she stood completely naked before Sultan. He noticed that her pubic hair had been shaven and that she had floral tattoos around her muscular thighs. Akbar withdrew. Sultan dropped his loose trousers and, grubby with pubescent lust, went to the girl without the slightest trepidation. They settled down on a thin mattress on the floor. She held him as he fumbled over her, lifting her thighs to help him. When he found her warm wet fob, he entered her quickly and concluded with hardly a second stroke. He recalled her amusement when he kissed her on the mouth. It was something he had learned from American films. Afterwards, he asked Akbar how much he should give her.

'Two rupees is more than enough,' his servant advised.

Sultan gave her twenty. The girl was clearly astonished and apprehensive. He insisted. And, kissing her again, asked her name.

'Shanti,' she said.

When she had gone, Sultan told Akbar that he wanted to see the girl every afternoon. This Akbar arranged with discretion. Before the school holidays ended, Sultan found his love-making had improved. He had learned to suck her nipples and hold himself still inside her for minutes at a time.

One day, during Indian history, when they were studying the Peshwas of Maharashtra (it was the same time in the afternoon as his holiday couplings with Shanti) Sultan had a huge erection. He confessed to his best friend, Salim, who sat beside him, that he thought he might be in love.

Sultan divided his time between the Turf Club bar and his air-conditioned suite which overlooked the Swastika front gate. On Friday evenings, he usually invited the principal performers and the executive production staff for a drink and a chat in the Hospitality Suite adjacent to his rooms.

After Khurshid's death, he was less inclined to take pretty young dancers to his Marbleshwar retreat for the weekend. It was not that he had ever loved Khurshid. He had not. But, for a while, he felt that the daughter of the dreaded imam was watching him from the beyond. He knew that her life with him had been desperately unhappy and that she had been miserable for every single day of their marriage. She had needed a pious man and he could not supply that need. He had wanted a merry sensual girl, and that want was well beyond poor Khurshid. Sometimes, when he was in bed with another woman, he talked to her in his mind.

'Shut your eyes, Khurshid, if all this jig-jig upsets you.'

But Khurshid never answered.

'It's all bloody madness,' he told Salim. 'Our parents imagine that marriage is merely a conjunction of sexual organs. One fitting into the other. It is not so. Marriage is a conjunction of minds. And mine couldn't fit into Khurshid's.'

Ten years after he'd returned from London, Sultan was conscious of only one serious error of judgement. He should never have parted from Veena. As time passed, he thought of her more and more. He sensed that it was not

183

wasting life that mattered, but wasting life without Veena. Indeed life, like money and booze, was there to be wasted. But it was nicer wasting it with the right person. When he told Salim this, his friend scolded him for being self-indulgent. Veena, Salim told him, was only important because she coincided with a happy phase of his life in London. If it hadn't been Veena it would have been somebody else. The world was filled with Veenas waiting to run on stage. Veena, Salim said, was just a romantic dream. Worse: brooding about her was sentimentalism. If Sultan had married Veena, it would never have worked. Apart from the serious cultural improbability of their union, two romantics rarely make a sound match.

'Who told you that?' demanded Sultan.

'That's my opinion,' said Salim.

Veena and Sultan had exchanged letters about once a week for seven years. He did not return to England for the promised holiday. The illness of his father, followed by involved litigation relating to the liquidation of the transport company, had taken much of his time. There were tax problems and, at one point, a likelihood of serious charges being preferred against him. Leaving the country presented him with significant difficulties. He sent Veena a sum of money for her air fare to Bombay, but just before she was due to join him she wired Sultan to say that her mother had had a mental breakdown. Sultan told her to spend the money he had sent her on private medical attention. Then he sent considerably more. It was in Swiss franc drafts, secreted in the scooped-out inside of *The Life of Aurangzeb*. In the end, nothing seemed to happen for them. After seven years, he sensed that it might not be the same as it had been. At least not for her. He just suspected this. A friend who was visiting England called on Veena with a present from Sultan. It was a platinum pendant watch, with her name inscribed on the back. When the man returned to Bombay, Sultan questioned him closely. Reluctantly, he confessed that the meeting with Veena had not been pleasant.

'What was the matter?' asked Sultan.

'She was drunk.'

Sultan wrote Veena a long letter about drinking too much. After he posted it, he realised that he had been unforgivably pompous. He wrote four more letters in two days, apologising for his first indiscretion. He asked her to telephone him and reverse the charges. He was abject. But he did not hear from her again for three years.

One morning, he received an invitation to her wedding. He wore a black tie that day. After dinner, he sat by himself on the veranda, listening to Hutch singing 'Lovely Week-end'. It reminded him of an evening with her at Quaglino's. He wondered what her husband Mellish looked like and whether they laughed a lot together. In the early morning, shuffling back to his bed from the lavatory, he remembered with sudden despair the satin softness of her inner thighs. He lay in the darkness, thinking. Weary, he drowsed into first light and then, opening his eyes, was diverted by a lubricious prospect. He would fall in love with a nice young girl. An unspoiled young girl who would please him. He would marry again. The thought consoled him immensely and he slid back into a profound sleep. But on waking in the morning sunlight, all he could imagine was Veena, lying in the arms of her husband. Before he went to the club, he undid the packet of her letters and photographs which he kept in his wardrobe drawer. Opening a pink envelope with blue heart motifs, that still smelled faintly of lavender, he shook the fine whiskers of crisp red hair onto his open palm. And he recalled the sunlit morning in their Belsize flat when she had culled that souvenir for him. They had just showered and dried themselves together. Laughter. Sultan passed like a ghost through remembered rooms.

Later that day, after many phone calls, Sultan arranged for a pair of Georgian silver champagne-coolers, purchased privately from Southeby's list, to be delivered to the council estate in Peckham where Veena was to live with her

185

husband. When asked if there was any message, he informed the salesman that he could not think of a more appropriate felicitation for the accompanying card than 'Keep Smiling'.

The year was 1957.

More than twenty years later, Sultan Buckrabhoy had still not been swept away by the tide of his own improvidence.

'The situation is at crisis point, Mr Buckrabhoy,' Iyengar said. It seemed as though Sultan had been listening to Iyengar's apocalyptic voice for as long as he could remember. He did not like it. He liked Iyengar even less.

'Yes, of course,' Sultan murmured, looking out through his window at a cream-complexioned young girl with a hennaed pony tail and the fluent pantherine movements of a dancer. She had well-muscled calves and long lean thighs.

'We will need additional support within the next month or two.'

Sultan directed one of his soft doe-like looks at Iyengar.

'I'm grateful for all you've done for me, Iyengar.'

Iyengar wasn't even marginally interested in Sultan Buckrabhoy's gratitude. He had for some time been making his own long-term plans.

'The Japanese bank I spoke to you about has hinted at a larger facility than our present arrangements,' Iyengar said.

'Unsecured, you said.'

'There was talk about your family house. Is it still unencumbered?'

'I may have to talk to Aziz.'

'We could offer them a share of *Bhagwan ki Beti.*'

Sultan frowned. He stared out again at the young girl. Something about her style evoked old memories. He admired the arch of her back and her strong elegant neck. He took a pair of binoculars from his drawer and examined her closely. He focused on her face, turned towards the building away from the evening sun. He saw that she had luminous blue eyes and an attractive mouth. She was chewing gum. Iyengar seemed irritated by Sultan's preoccupation with the young girl at the gate. He cleared his throat.

'Do you mind if I talk to them?' Iyengar asked.

'Who?' Sultan asked absent-mindedly, lowering the focus to the young girl's breasts. The blouse was not very revealing. He decided that they were not big. Dancer's breasts rarely were.

'The Japanese, Mr Buckrabhoy.'

Sultan gave Iyengar a defensive glance.

'Use your discretion, Iyengar.'

Iyengar shrugged and withdrew. Walking back to his office, he seethed with inward rage. He was now certain that Sultan Buckrabhoy was more than slightly touched. He was, Iyengar concluded, cunt-struck.

When the chief accountant had gone, Sultan picked up the phone and dialled Mrs Hyacinth D'Mello. Mrs D'Mello, who managed Dance Casting and Contracts, had an office on the floor below him.

'Hyacinth?'

'Mr Buckrabhoy?'

'Look out of your window.'

'Yes?'

'The young girl in the red shirt and white polka dots. The one with a pony tail.'

'Poppy?'

'Ah.'

'She's Anglo-Indian . . . and very young. One of our three temple dancers in the finale.'

'Ah.'

'Do you want to meet her?'

'Bring her around to the Hospitality Suite for some champagne in a few minutes.'

'Tea, not champagne, Mr Buckrabhoy. Or Vimto, perhaps. She's fourteen, a child.'

187

'Whatever she wants.'

'Would you like to meet her mother?'

'Why should I?'

'Because that's the way it is, Mr Buckrabhoy. Her mother drives her to work and picks her up when she's finished.'

'Good God, Hyacinth. I only wanted to talk to the girl.'

Mrs Hyacinth D'Mello sniggered offensively before she replaced the receiver. Sultan found her response unpleasant. The world, he reflected, was becoming rather an ugly place.

Sultan's friend Salim owned a pickle factory in Borivli. He had a thriving domestic and export business. Unlike Sultan, Salim had never married. This was an eccentricity his family could not understand. But as he was the youngest of seven brothers, he managed to retain his bachelor status without too much fuss. For many years, he had conducted an affair with the Parsee lady who ran the Pimpri Pinjrapole animal shelter. Maneck also played the cello with the Bombay Philharmonic. Her husband, Jehangir, a paraplegic, was an accomplished guitarist, sometimes referred to as the Segovia of Bombay. Salim's relationship with Maneck had been tender but infused with a sad guilt as Salim admired Jehangir enormously. Like Sultan, they had been class mates. What complicated matters was that Jehangir considered Salim beyond reproach. 'A prince among men,' he'd cry, whenever Salim's name was mentioned.

Salim and Maneck spent one afternoon a week together at Salim's flat. Maneck visited him in a hired victoria and arrived at two.

'Why don't you come by taxi? It's quicker,' Salim complained, looking at his watch.

'The clip-clop of the victoria settles me,' she explained. 'By the time I arrive, I feel ripe and ready.'

Maneck liked to wear her spectacles when they made

love, even though they steamed up. She was self conscious of the ridges on her nose caused by the wire frames.

'Don't be a goose. I love them,' Salim assured her, taking her glasses off and kissing the marks. But as soon as she was able, she would set the spectacles back on her nose.

Their afternoons became a structured event, as these affairs often do. It started and ended with tea. After the second cup and a small sweet biscuit, Maneck rose and said that it was time she had a wash. This really meant that she was ready to undress. In the bathroom, she took off her street clothes, hanging them carefully on the shower rail. Then she changed into a light homespun dressing gown which she kept at Salim's flat. In her handbag she carried a toothbrush, a tube of Pepsodent and a bottle of Listerine. Maneck brushed her teeth and rinsed her mouth before going into the bedroom, where she disrobed and covered herself with a sheet. When she was ready for him, she would call his name. Salim came to her, naked.

'Why have you no trousers on?' she'd reprove, as he climbed into bed beside her.

'Because you have none on either,' he'd reply, pulling away the sheet and sliding his slim hairy body between her substantial thighs. They made love twice within the hour, then lay blissfully together. When the clock struck four, Maneck would sit up.

'It's time for me to go.'

At this point they made love for the third time, allowing themselves just a minute or two to relax before hot showers and getting dressed.

'Hope you have time for a cup of tea,' Salim would say.

'Just one.'

They would drink their tea, Maneck sitting primly on the edge of the seat, while Salim phoned for a taxi. And that was the pattern of their encounters. They both found the arrangement extremely congenial and the relationship continued until they were in their early fifties. Then

Maneck had a stroke. She was bedridden. On the afternoons of their former assignations, Salim called at the house, sitting with her for the two hours they had previously spent making love. Jehangir was deeply moved by Salim's solicitude. One day, when Salim was leaving Maneck's bedside, Jehangir gripped his hand tightly and drew him closer to the wheelchair. He kissed him on the lips. Salim found the contact wet and unpleasant.

'You are my true friend, Salim,' Jehangir said. 'My poor Maneck has had nothing in her life. How I wish you had been her lover before she was struck down.'

Salim did not reply.

Entering the house began to depress him. It reeked of decay and despair. One day, Jehangir phoned him and told him that Maneck had died in her sleep. Salim was relieved that he did not have to go to the house again; the smell remained in his nostrils for a long time. But some months later, he confessed to Sultan that he had never realised how much he loved Maneck until after she had died.

'I wish I could bring her back for five minutes, to tell her that.'

'It's a terrible thing,' Sultan agreed, 'not to recognise love when it's lying there under the sheet beside you.'

'Do you still think of Veena?' Salim asked.

Sultan shivered. 'Sometimes I dream that my Veena is dead.'

On occasion, Sultan and Salim managed a laboured game of squash or a set or two of tennis. Sultan had put on fifty pounds in fifteen years and suffered slightly from shortness of breath and high blood pressure. His hair line was beginning to recede and he had resorted to dyeing the grey around his temples. He now had to wear glasses permanently. He was no longer easily mistaken for Ronald Colman. He had not worn well. Sometimes they went sailing in Salim's thirty-footer. The ice-box was always filled with masala chicken, and they rarely set off without a few bottles of pink champagne. They used a shelter Salim had erected on a small island, hardly fifty yards long, that lay about twelve miles off shore. The island had no fresh water, only sand, a spine of gneissic rock, half a dozen coconut palms and a copse of wild cane and grasses on a ridge at its centre. In the old days it was here that they had held many of their wild beach parties that lasted all night and at times, several days and nights. The debris consisted of champagne and Coke bottles, chicken bones, paper plates, serviettes and used french letters. Salim insisted that it would be imprudent to leave any french letters behind to be discovered by the fishermen who occasionally landed there. At one New Year's party, the servant, Akbar, informed Sultan that he had collected one hundred and seven french letters. Of course there were eight couples on the island, and the party had lasted two days and nights.

'Those were the days,' sighed Sultan.

'I suppose so,' said Salim.

Now, just the two of them came to the island. They wired a record player to the accumulator on the boat and played music. Sultan's favourite was Elvis Presley's 'Are You Lonesome Tonight?' They sat at the water's edge by a calor-gas lantern, chatting about old times, sipping champagne from a cooler placed in the sea, and munching drumsticks of masala chicken.

'This is the life,' observed Sultan.

'I suppose so,' said Salim.

They chucked their bones into the darkness of the water. Salim leaned forward and, fishing a bottle out of the sea, filled their glasses by the lantern. Sultan toasted Salim. The shadow of his raised arm looked like a sea serpent. For a few moments, they were diverted by the distractions of their forms behind the lantern, and contrived ducks, fishes and giant spiders.

'Keep smiling,' shouted Sultan, his voice rolling across the whispering sea. Then they drank in silence, under the starlit canopy of the cloudless sky, watching the small red light of a passing ship disappearing over the horizon. Only the soft lapping of the water against the rocks disturbed the stillness.

'What about Poppy?'

Sultan coughed. The phlegm rattled in his chest. He rose and spat into the darkness.

'Poppy's mother, Mrs Milligan, is very tricky indeed. She guards her daughter like a bloody tigress.'

'I approve of that,' said Salim, 'particularly with old lechers like you sniffing around.'

'She's far too young for me,' Sultan brooded.

'But you're going to have a try?' Salim mocked.

'Who knows?'

'I do,' Salim answered, slapping Sultan on the back.

Sultan had invited Poppy and her mother to dinner. He had asked Salim as well, to make up a foursome. He had found Mrs Milligan to be an unusually shrewd woman when they first met in the Hospitality Suite. She had a hard edge to her, that comes with fighting for survival. She knew her own worth and that of her pretty daughter. Men, Sultan suspected, were not Vicki Milligan's favourite species. She was a tall slim woman of about forty, with silky brown hair. Her grey eyes, aquiline nose and long upper lip, marked by a small mole, gave her a cool, fastidious look. She had a well-maintained mouth, just a glint of a gold molar, and elegant manicured fingers. She was dressed in a white linen dress which showed a galaxy of freckles above its neckline. Her supple movements made apparent the athleticism of her body. Her white shoes were simple and neat. She smelled rather nice as well.

'You have had unfortunate experiences,' Sultan suggested, eyeing Mrs Milligan cautiously. The remark had been in response to a coarse observation of such lethal cynicism that his heart missed a beat. She regarded him with amusement, but behind the even smile he sensed there was an intimidating intelligence.

'No more than most women have had throughout history,' she replied. 'I don't suppose that I would be here, drinking champagne, if Poppy was a crow. You, Mr Buckrabhoy, are clearly lusting after my daughter. You can hardly breathe when she is close to you.'

'Any man would find Poppy attractive,' said Sultan defensively, 'but I also think that she is a very talented dancer.'

Vicki Milligan laughed loudly and derisively at that.

'I don't mind dirty old men, Mr Buckrabhoy,' she said cheerfully, 'but dirty old bullshitters I can do without.'

Sultan was hurt, but he did not show it.

'I would like,' he said softly, 'for Poppy and you to be my friends. Let me start by inviting you both to dinner. An old friend of mine will also be there.'

That was how the Milligans came to be invited to Sultan Buckrabhoy's house. Just before Vicki Milligan left the Hospitality Suite with Poppy, she embarrassed Sultan in a wholly unexpected way.

'Has anyone ever told you', she said, 'that you look vaguely like Ronald Colman?'

'No,' he laughed, 'no.' But when he saw them off at the entrance, he consciously drew in his slack belly at least three inches.

The bankers had suddenly become intolerant. Two of them advised him that they would be calling in his overdrafts at the end of the month. A third suggested that Swastika's facility might have to be underpinned by more substantial guarantees. There were rumours in the city that Buckrabhoy was going to the wall. There had been rumours before but the difficulties had been satisfactorily resolved. Iyengar was still optimistic about the Japanese money men. They were clearly interested in *Bhagwan ki Beti*, which was nearing completion at Swastika and which, it was felt, would be a great success. Iyengar had arranged an important meeting for the late afternoon. Sultan remembered that he had invited Vicki and Poppy to dinner on that evening. He suspected the bloody Japanese might delay him.

'I'm sure you can do without me, Iyengar,' he said. This was true. Sultan's contributions to the financial details of banking and leasing transactions were minimal. He had always felt in the way. His strength was on the marketing side. Entertaining the distributors, talking to the press, being pleasant to the critics. He enjoyed all that enormously. But finance was not his bag. Iyengar looked disappointed. He expressed concern that Sultan might not be there. The Japanese, he pointed out, were hot on protocol. Having the managing director present would give the meeting much greater significance, from their perspective.

'You handle it, Krishna,' Sultan said finally. It was the first time he had called the chief accountant by his given name. Iyengar was surprised, but not impressed. His hatred for Buckrabhoy was now so overwhelming that he found each confrontation more difficult to endure than the previous one. He suspected the managing director had probably planned an afternoon in bed with some whore, dribbling champagne into her mouth in between fucks.

'May I appeal to you, Mr Buckrabhoy? Just this once.'

Sultan shook his head stubbornly. 'Iyengar,' he muttered thickly, his eyes on two young Sindhi girls strolling past his window. Sultan enjoyed the movement of women. He liked the swing of their hips and the wobble of their bottoms.

'Mr Buckrabhoy?'

Sultan aimed a crushed memo into the wicker basket beyond his desk.

'Iyengar, finance bores me.'

'Bores you, Mr Buckrabhoy?' the chief accountant

194

repeated softly. Iyengar could not understand. Iyengar did not want to understand.

When Captain Toddyvala, trainer of the Buckrabhoy horses for forty years, died, Salim suggested Sultan try Nelson Pinto, a young trainer who was sweeping everything before him. But Mr Pinto was not enthusiastic.

'Quite frankly, Mr Buckrabhoy, that horse of yours is dog meat.'

'My Dream Time?'

'To call that animal a racehorse is a travesty of the term.'

'My God. He only lost by two short heads last month. A little more luck and who knows?'

'I'll consider training the animal, on one condition.'

'What's that?'

'No interference.'

Sultan laughed. 'I'm not the interfering type, Mr Pinto.'

'I'll try to slot him into a race he can manage.'

'Thank you, Mr Pinto.'

Nelson Pinto phoned Sultan the next day. He informed him that Dream Time was being sent to Poona. He proposed to run him in the Ratnagiri Cup, a mile and a half handicap.

'That's next week.'

'Correct.'

'But Dream Time is a sprinter.'

'We'll see.'

'He's well below handicap class.'

'We'll see.'

Later, Sultan told Salim that he thought Pinto was crazy and an arrogant son of a bitch.

'The horse will win,' prophesised Salim. 'Pinto is a genius.'

'I suspect', said Sultan, 'that my Dream Time has emotional problems. He was probably in love with a nice young

195

filly before I had him gelded. His losing sequence could be an act of revenge.'

'Perhaps if you had been gelded instead,' Salim observed, 'things might have turned out better for the Buckrabhoy enterprises.'

Of course, Sultan knew that Salim was only joking.

After dinner, Salim devoted himself to entertaining Poppy, while Sultan talked to her mother. When offered champagne, Vicki Milligan indicated her preference for a large Bloody Mary.

'Would you care to dance?' Sultan asked.

She accompanied him to the terrace from where the sound of some old-fashioned Glenn Miller music emanated. Salim and Poppy were already dancing on the frangipani-covered veranda. Poppy appeared to be enjoying herself with Salim, who was quite an accomplished dancer. Sultan kept his eyes on Poppy, admiring her fluent movements and the bobbing of her ochre-tinted hair. Her glazed expression might have passed for ecstasy but for the high-speed mastication of bubble gum.

'You can't keep your eyes off her, can you?' asked Vicki, laying her cheek against Sultan's as they danced.

'What's the use of pretending?' asked Sultan.

'I'd like to talk to you about Poppy,' Vicki whispered.

'All right.'

'Tomorrow afternoon?'

'I'll send the car around for you.'

Sultan managed to have several dances with Poppy before the Milligans left. She preferred jiving, bouncing adroitly around while he provided her with an anchor, performing a simple spaced square as she danced in and out from him. He inhaled her freshness and the smell of strawberry from her mouth as their faces came together. Whenever he made brief body contact, he felt the contours of her springy young breasts against his arm and chest, and the slenderness of her waist that slid down to the swelling curve of her swivelling hips as she surrendered to and then evaded his hands. Sometimes she smiled at him, a knowing beyond her years in her blue eyes, panting softly through slightly parted lips. Sultan started to wheeze with his exertions. He noticed patches of wet under Poppy's arms. Tiny beads of perspiration on her upper lip gleamed in the lamplight. He restrained a mad impulse to lick the salty moisture off her face as they went into the final flourish of the dance. Their faces touched, her wetness mingling with his. The music stopped and they laughed.

'You're terrific,' said Poppy, genuinely impressed.

Sultan wiped his face. As he tucked away his handkerchief, he found himself trembling with a kind of excitement he had not experienced for many years. Later he had a slight but troublesome pain in his chest and felt that perhaps it had been imprudent to show off.

Vicki Milligan turned up next day in a salmon trouser suit and open sandals. Her toe nails were painted to match. She drank three Bloody Marys and talked about Poppy's father.

'Never trust an Irishman,' she said.

'I've always found them to be charming people,' Sultan replied.

'They're romantics. They treat life like a dream and dreams like reality.'

'I'm a romantic myself,' Sultan grinned.

'God help you.'

Vicki inserted a cigarette in an ivory holder, lit it and, moving her long lean throat back, blew the smoke ceilingwards.

'You like Poppy?' she asked, raising her pencilled brows.

Sultan looked serious and misty eyed.

'Very much.'

She got up and paced the room. She stopped and stood before Sultan, one leg forward and one elegant hand on a tilted hip. She waved her cigarette holder before her like a conductor's baton.

'What do you know about us, Sultan?' she asked.

He shrugged. 'That you are a beautiful and desirable woman. And that you have a beautiful and desirable daughter. Need any man know more?'

Vicki Milligan smiled. 'When I was very young,' she said, 'I fell in love several times. Let us not over-dramatise my circumstances, beyond recounting that love did very little for my health, wealth or happiness. So I became a whore.'

Sultan's eyes opened. He lifted the champagne out of the bucket and tilted a measure into his glass.

'I thought you ran a dancing school?'

'It's easier to advertise that way. Men who are reluctant to visit a brothel have no qualms about enrolling at a dancing school. As the managing director of the Apollo Institute of Dance, I am the equivalent of a madam.'

'Do you still practice, yourself?' he asked with interest.

'You make it sound as though I played a musical instrument.' She glanced down at her empty glass and allowed him to fix her another drink. 'Business is lousy,' she complained. 'The police are the problem. They are aware of what I'm up to. I'm paying more in bribes than I can take in fees.'

'Our police are notoriously greedy,' Sultan agreed.

'So Poppy and I have had Bombay up to here.' Vicki indicated with a flat palm a level midway up her forehead.

'What do you want?'

'Basically, two plane tickets to London and ten thousand rupees to see us on our way.'

Sultan regarded her owlishly. 'Where do I fit in?'

Vicki took another puff at her cigarette. She realised that she would have to be more explicit. Sultan Buckrabhoy was not helping her.

'It'll take a month before we can fly out of this place. And we're being evicted from our flat tomorrow.'

'Why?'

198

'Many things. But ten months rent arrears is the official reason.'

'Move in here,' Sultan suggested genially. He touched the knee of her trouser suit.

Vicki kissed him on the cheek. 'That's sweet.' She looked at him reflectively, then half-smiled as she lowered her head. 'The plane tickets and ten thousand rupees?'

Sultan blew out his cheeks with air and hunched his shoulders. 'Are you proposing something?'

'Poppy?'

There was a long silence before Sultan spoke.

'You'll sell your daughter for two tickets and ten thousand rupees?'

'I'm not *selling* anything. She's loaning herself to you for a few days. After that, we're on our way.'

'Does Poppy know?'

'We've given the matter a great deal of thought.'

'I see.'

'There's nothing likely to happen to her that won't happen anyway. And we might as well get what we really need out of the transaction.'

Sultan rose from his chair. He poured himself another glass of champagne.

'I'll have to talk to my chief accountant about the cash,' he said. He frowned as he thought of Iyengar. Normally he would have used his private entertainment account, but recently he had agreed to allow Iyengar to countersign all cheques drawn on it.

'Accountant,' Vicki sneered. 'You spend more on booze in three months than the sum I've suggested.'

'Times have changed,' Sultan sighed. 'I have six cases of champagne left. And then that is that. The stuff is contraband, anyway. It costs twice the market price. A friend smuggles my supplies in from Goa. Unfortunately, it's a pleasure I will soon have to forgo.'

'Don't you want Poppy?' Vicki asked.

Sultan looked unhappy. 'I never imagined that it would be . . . quite this sort of arrangement.'

She snorted with laughter. 'What other arrangement could there possibly be? You're an old man, Sultan Buckrabhoy. You don't really imagine you're going to deflower my little girl for nothing, do you? You've been buying women all your bloody life, one way or another. This is hardly the time to have silly reservations.'

Sultan held up a hand. 'Please, Vicki.'

'Forget the "please, Vicki". What's it to be, Sultan? Yes or no?'

He stood up, reached out and held her shoulder. 'Buckrabhoy always finds a way. Rely on me.'

'You sure, you old bastard?'

'Keep smiling.'

Vicki looked relieved. She moved closer, kissing him on the cheek. Then, laying the still-burning cigarette and holder on the drinks trolley, she placed her right hand on his cock. She unzipped his gaberdine trousers and moved inside his briefs. He started when her long nails scratched his plushy cone but sighed deeply as her expert fingers gentled his stiffening flesh.

'The servants,' he warned softly.

She ran the tip of her tongue along his ear lobe.

'You'll have to take me somewhere private, then,' she drawled.

Sultan rented a large house for the Poona season. He only travelled up for the races and usually slept there on the night of the meeting, following the Buckrabhoy party, an event he no longer had to organise. It happened; people arrived, music played. Dancers scraped around a courtyard illuminated by Chinese lanterns. Food and drink were served to chattering friends in the crowded lounge. Doors to the ten guest bedrooms opened and closed all night. Eventually, some people began to depart. Others, stretched

200

out on the floor, slept in the garden, hunched up on the stairs. A few waited to eat breakfast, while one or two stayed for lunch. In time, nobody remembered to thank the man who paid the bill; more than half of those present did not even know who he was. One young girl thought he was Sultan Buckrabhoy's father; another imagined him to be the proprietor of a well known tandoori resturant in town, while several of them put it about that he was the Aga Khan's private secretary's chauffeur.

If Vicki and Poppy Milligan had not expressed such enthusiasm for going to Poona to see Dream Time run in the Ratnagiri Cup, Sultan might not have travelled to the meeting at all. Ever since he had jived with Poppy, he had felt unwell. At first, it was no more than a vague feeling of malaise, general lassitude, shortness of breath and slight twinges in his left arm. But an untypical depression had begun to overwhelm him. He had kept away from doctors; he could not bear to hear unpleasant news. Quite recently, the suspicion that he was an old man had started to haunt him. Although he had tried to avoid considering the implication of his abject performance in bed with Vicki Milligan, there was little doubt in his mind that there had been more artifice than authentic ardour in her responses.

'You were terrific, darling,' she said afterwards.

He was certain that was untrue. Vicki, he felt, had faked every spasm and moan. He had merely used the services of a high-class harlot. For the first time, Sultan saw himself as a victim. He shuddered as he imagined Vicki's laughter after they had parted. And now Poppy. The prospect that had excited him until he was almost deranged with lust, now alarmed him. His self-esteen had generally required some assurance that the women to whom he made love did not find the experience wholly repugnant. That assurance, Sultan feared, would be difficult to sustain in any conjugation with the young and beautiful Poppy Milligan. Even dreams that had been paid for needed some kind of inner reality. Sultan Buckrabhoy regarded his bloated face and slack obesity in the mirror after his morning shower and knew that he saw the reflection of an elderly buffoon.

Dream Time was backed down from fifty to one, to sixes, before the off. Sultan put five hundred rupees on, for both Vicki and Poppy at tens. The sheer magnitude of the market moves for his horse astonished him.

'I've hardly got anything on, myself,' he compained to Salim, who had backed Dream Time at twenties.

'What the hell is happening?' he asked Nelson Pinto in the paddock.

'I've got the horse very fit,' the trainer said smugly.

The race was a formality. Dream Time went to the front and, coming around the last bend, was six lengths clear. It went past the post, hard-held by four lengths.

'I don't believe it,' muttered Sultan.

Vicki was pleased. Poppy kept squealing with delight. They had cleared five thousand apiece. After Sultan had led Dream Time in and been presented with the trophy, he cornered Nelson Pinto.

'This is quite incredible. How did you manage it?'

Nelson Pinto looked at him with amusement. 'How do you think? The bloody horse was doped.'

'But what about the blood, urine and saliva tests?' Sultan asked in anguish.

'Simply a matter of astute management,' Pinto laughed.

Sultan Buckrabhoy was gloomy. Winning had become meaningless. He felt sorry for himself. And as he watched the blanketed hindquarters of his horse as it was led back to the stable, he felt even sorrier for Dream Time.

Sultan managed a slow-foxtrot with Poppy late in the evening. She chattered with excitement about the race. Sultan quoted Nelson Pinto. 'Simply a matter of astute management,' he said.

There were more people at the party than usual. The Ratnagiri Cup stood on the sideboard and the photographer posed Sultan before it with groups of people he had never seen. They stood around him, glasses raised, smiling happily, as the photographer flashed away. Sultan tried to escape again and again. He danced with Vicki. Poppy was already on the floor. As the music quickened, Sultan led Vicki towards some empty chairs on the terrace. He felt as though he was wading through glue. Everything seemed to dissolve before him. He sighted a smiling Salim and endeavoured to reach him. An unbearable pain travelled up his arm and across his chest. He tried to grasp Salim. Mentally, he called for help but no sound came from his lips. He fell, crashing across a tray of drinks. Sultan Buckrabhoy had just had a heart attack.

Just before they flew to England, the Milligans visited Sultan in hospital.

'Thank you for everything,' Vicki said, squeezing his hand.

'Try and write,' he said, not even half-believing she would. He knew they were just words, polite sounds to fill the emptiness between them.

'Of course,' said Vicki, 'of course.'

'I intend to visit England myself next year,' promised Sultan.

'I'll let you have our address as soon as we've settled in somewhere.'

Sultan nodded. He looked across at Poppy. She was chewing gum and staring out of the window. Already her mind had left Bombay. She looked pretty but bored. What a wonderful body, he thought. Sultan knew that when they walked out of the hospital he would never see them again. They seemed restive. He held out a hand to Poppy. She took it and squeezed it amiably.

'Goodbye, Sultan.'

'Keep smiling, darling,' he replied, turning his face to the wall to avoid watching them trip quickly across the ward and out of his life.

*

When the Swastika Film Corporation of Bombay was sold to a consortium, the deal was funded by the Japanese bank, introduced by Krishna Iyengar. He became the new managing director. The other Buckrabhoy interests were liquidated at the same time. Dream Time was disposed of over coffee at the Turf Club. The new owner was a lively Iranian lady who draped her silky black hair over her right eye and cheek. Sultan eyed her wrinkled cleavage with tired interest as he sucked an olive.

'How much do you really want for him?' she demanded with a grin, after Sultan had made a slightly improper suggestion.

'He did win the Ratnagiri Cup last year,' Sultan said.

'He was doped,' the lady shrieked, 'everybody in Bombay knows that.'

'You're not implying that Nelson Pinto – '

'He's a crook,' the lady laughed, beating the table with the flat of her palm.

'What about a kiss?' Sulta suggested hopefully.

'You're an absolute rotter, Buckrabhoy. A scoundrel of the first water.'

'Twenty years ago,' Sultan boasted, 'a kiss from Buckrabhoy would have clinched the deal.'

She squinted at her Longines fob pendant. Her sight was obviously poor.

'It's half-past nine,' Sultan said.

'This bloody watch is almost useless. The numerals are so tiny.' She rattled her jewelled fingers impatiently on the table, bobbing her head to allow the hair to fall away from her eye.

'Well?' she asked.

Sultan flicked open an empty cigarette case. He noticed that she had an unopened tin of State Express in the string bag that hung on the back of her chair.

'That tin of State Express,' he suggested, pointing to the bag.

He watched her eyes slit momentarily with greed. She

knew that Sultan Buckrabhoy was a man for eccentric gestures. His crazy impulses were woven into innumerable apocryphal and improbable stories.

'Done,' she shouted, reaching across and shaking his hand. He picked the cigarettes out of her bag and rose to leave.

'I'll send you the papers after lunch,' he promised, ambling slowly off to the car park. His legs felt leaden and his feet swelled if he walked too far. His diet of pink champagne had been replaced by local gin. His eyes were permanently bloodshot and his flatulence had become an embarrassment in company. He paused below a date palm and, seeing that he was alone, farted loudly several times, before continuing his slow journey to the Cadillac. It was dented along one side, where he had run it against a bullock cart. The rust was beginning to edge the fretted metal along the lower sill. He had been thinking about getting it repaired and painted for months. He intended to get some sort of price for it before he left for England.

Sultan found Bayswater had not changed as much as he feared. He recognised many of the streets. Adjacency to the park gave it a simple reference. Many of the buildings had been upgraded; some had vanished. There were more foreigners walking around than he would have believed possible, and the cheerful Londoners seemed to have disappeared completely. He drank his first Guinness in the saloon bar of The Lancaster Arms. The pub had been substantially redesigned. The piano had gone, along with the old public bar. Instead, there were two flashy fruit machines and a juke box. They served lasagne, taramasalata, ratatouille, spaghetti bolognaise, beefburgers and bhuna chicken. It was very busy. Nobody returned his smile.

Sultan found a Mellish in the telephone directory at Veena's Peckham address. He made sure that he had a

205

large number of coins available before he tried the number, but trembled when he heard the ringing tone. It was ringing in Veena's home. She was probably hearing the same sound as he was. He let it ring seventy-five times. There was no answer. In a way he was relieved that she had not answered. He could not imagine what he would have said had he heard her voice. He tried to compose his mind, to prepare himself for a conversation. Veena was fifty-seven years of age. Sultan wondered how time had dealt with her. Perhaps she was dead. Then he remembered her body, her face and her magical laughter and hoped that she was not only alive, but well and miraculously unchanged. He returned to the saloon and drank another two glasses of Guinness. He felt light-headed and more optimistic.

Sultan went out to the lavatory. As he washed his hands, he noticed the reflection of two young men staring at him as they zipped their denims. They appeared to be no more than eighteen. He imagined he heard the word 'Paki' as they went out laughing at some private joke, and he knew that they intended to be unpleasant. When he stood at the bar again, he sensed for the first time several white faces staring blankly in his direction. Sultan waited to be served then decided against another drink. He left, vaguely uneasy and hailed a taxi, directing it to Sussex Gardens where a friend of Salim's owned a restaurant. He decided to ring Veena after lunch.

When Sultan rang at three, he let the phone ring one hundred and fifty times. Nobody answered. He went into an off-licence and purchased a bottle of Black Label on his way back to the hotel. He walked the mile or so very slowly, stopping to examine the shops and restaurants along Edgware Road. When he got back to his room he unlaced his brogues and peeled his socks off. The size of his feet alarmed him. He poured himself a large scotch and lay quietly on his bed. Sultan Buckrabhoy sensed that he was

206

on his last lap. He tried Veena's number at seven. It scarcely rang. Somebody had snatched up the receiver.

'Hallo.' The female voice was young, cockney and abrasive.

'I would like to speak to Mrs Veena Mellish, please.'

There was a long pause.

'Who?'

'Mrs Veena Mellish. She used to be Veena O'Brien.'

There was another silence.

'That's my mother's name,' the voice said. 'She's been dead ten years.'

'Oh.'

The sense of loss Sultan experienced was physical and centred around his diaphragm, inhibiting his breathing.

'Who are you?'

'My name is Sultan Buckrabhoy. I knew your mother many years ago. I've just arrived from Bombay. I only called to say hallo.'

'She often spoke about you,' the girl replied. 'She said you were a Paki millionaire.'

Sultan laughed uneasily.

'I used to have money, in the old days. But I am not a Pakistani. I have always been an Indian National.'

'Oh. My mother said that you were a Paki.'

'Well it's easy to get confused. We were all one until 1947.'

There was a further hiatus in the conversation.

'I'm devastated by the news of her death,' Sultan said.

'Cancer. She was riddled with it. My aunt went the same way.'

A name from the past came back to Sultan. A name that he thought he had forgotten.

'Philomena?'

'That's right.'

'May I call on you?' Sultan asked.

He regretted the question the moment he asked it. There

was no point to anything, without Veena. The girl on the phone was a stranger. She did not even sound like Veena.

'It's not convenient right now. Next week, perhaps. Sunday would be best, after dinner . . . say, three.'

Sultan opened his mouth to speak, but the girl had put the receiver down. He did not even know her name.

On the Sunday of his appointment with Veena's daughter, Sultan arrived at the Peckham council estate in a taxi. He carried a bouquet of yellow roses, Veena's favourite colour, and a giant box of chocolates. The area was more dreadful than anything he could have imagined. Groups of black and white teenagers sat on a broken wall outside garages that appeared to have been gutted by fire. A rusting Ford Capri, upholstery knife-ripped, and glass shattered, rested on its axles, leaking oil at the entrance to the building. A mocking cry of 'Paki, Paki', was directed at him by a spindly black boy, and he heard catcalls and derisive laughter behind him as he entered with his conspicuous gifts. The lift stank of urine, excrement was smeared over the plastic panels and the graffiti was preponderantly racist: 'Pakis are fucking dog meat', was one that impressed itself on his consciousness. This was certainly different from the London of the late forties. The feeling in the air in those days was one of tolerance and hope. All he felt now was fear, defeat and a mind-numbing despair. By the time he arrived at the twelfth floor, Sultan wondered whether he would be able to leave the estate in safety. He pressed the bell-button at number 124. He could hardly believe his eyes. The young girl who answered the door was a reincarnation of his beloved Veena.

Veena's daughter's name was Sharon. She lived with a tall, well-muscled, blond skinhead called Roy, who never spoke to Sultan during the hour he spent in the flat. Roy sat drinking canned lager and watching television while Sharon and Sultan talked. Their exchange of words was fatuous. She was not interested in what he had to say about Veena and the old days, while he found it difficult to understand her obsession with motor-bikes. Roy, she told him, was a genius with motor-bikes and ran a small business from the flat, repairing and tuning machines. Sultan noticed a carburettor on the lavatory floor and a chassis shell propped up against the kitchen table.

Sharon's similarity to Veena ended with the astonishing physical resemblance. She did not possess her mother's memorable charm and sense of fun. A coarse and sullen girl, Sharon reflected the nihilism of her unpleasant environment. Roy frightened Sultan. He addressed several remarks to the young man, who did not even bother to respond.

'He never talks much,' Sharon said, as though they were discussing an exotic animal. 'He only understands three things: biking, telly and beer.' She paused, then crinkled her nose, as Veena would have done. 'And sex,' she added, 'the old bugger loves his oats.'

As Sultan escaped in a taxi, he lit a cigarette with a trembling hand and resolved never to return. He was certain that he would never see or communicate with Sharon and Roy again.

So he was more than surprised when Sharon rang him a few days later.

'Roy has a business proposition for you,' she said in a little-girl voice he hardly recognised.

'Roy?' Sultan could hardly conceal his contempt.

'Yeah, you know, my feller. He wants to take a lease on this shop at Deptford. Open a bike-tuning and repair service. He's looking for a sleeping partner. There won't be anything to do, except collect the profits.' She laughed. It was a metallic, humourless sound.

'I'm afraid, Sharon, I don't have any spare cash.'

She seemed shocked by his revelation.

'I don't think he needs all that much,' she said unctuously.

209

'Anything will be too much.'

'Can we come and see you?' she asked.

Sultan sighed. 'If you like,' he said, 'but I suspect that you're wasting your time.'

When they came to see him at his hotel, he was astonished at the change. Sharon was bright and communicative, and Roy spoke eloquently about the business potential of a good motor-bike specialist shop in south London. When he was talking motor-cycles, he was almost messianic in his fervour. Sultan told him about the old Salsette Motor Company. He remembered that they were once the Western India distributors for Harley Davidson. That fact impressed Roy more than anything else he had said. Sultan learned that Roy stammered when talking about anything other than motor-cycles; that he was dyslexic and, at twenty-seven, could hardly read or write.

'I help him with that side of things,' Sharon said. When animated, her resemblance to Veena was extraordinary.

'You see,' Sultan confessed, before they left, 'I don't have a great deal of money. Just enough to keep the engine ticking over.'

In the end, he was sorry to see them go and regretted that he could not help them. Before they left, Sharon gave him a manila envelope. When Sultan opened it in his bedroom, his eyes lit up. She had given him photographs of Veena. They were of Veena as an infant, a schoolgirl and the beautiful woman he remembered. He laid them out on the bed, directing a table light over them, bending his head as close as possible so that he could scrutinise every detail of the old pictures through his reading glasses. His favourite was one of Veena as a twelve-year-old, with an arm around a donkey. It was inscribed, 'Tipperary, 1936', in large, childish writing. Veena, he remembered, was born in Tipperary.

Ten days after Sharon and Roy's visit, Sultan collapsed in his bath. When the water flowed under the bedroom door into the corridor, the hotel staff found and rescued him. He was taken to hospital in an ambulance. The specialist was frank with him as he lay in his private room.

'If it were only a cardiac problem, Mr Buckrabhoy, things wouldn't be too bad. But you've got emphysema and a chronic liver condition. It goes without saying that drinking and smoking are inadvisable.'

'How long have I got?' asked Sultan, winking cheerfully.

'Wrapped in cotton wool, you could last another year.'

Sultan whistled. 'I'm a goner, then?'

The specialist smiled ruefully. 'What can I say?' he asked.

'Keep smiling,' Sultan replied.

Sultan discharged himself after a week.

'I've never been able to stay in bed too long without a woman beside me,' he joked to his pretty young nurse.

He drew five thousand pounds from his deposit account at the bank, taking the money in fifty-pound notes and tucking them carefully into his wallet. Then he bought a bottle of pink champagne with a pink ribbon tied around the neck, and took a taxi to Sharon and Roy's place. The thought of seeing Veena's reincarnation again lifted his spirits.

Sharon was in her dressing gown and surprised to see him.

'I should have rung,' he apologised. He stood at the door, wheezing.

'Didn't think we'd see you again,' she said, leading him into the living room which was littered with oily motor-cycle parts.

'Where's Roy?' Sultan asked, looking around.

'He's not expected back until seven.'

'You'd better chill the bubbly then,' Sultan said, handing her the pink champagne. She put the bottle in the refrigerator, then came back into the room, switched off the television and reclined on the couch in front of Sultan. He could not help noticing the inside of her bare thighs as the dressing gown slid over her knees. He looked discreetly away. Fishing for his cigarette case, he offered her one, lighting it and another for himself. Her breasts, he sensed, were larger than Veena's.

'Thank you for those wonderful photographs of your mother. I've brought them back with me.'

'Keep them,' she said, kicking a leg aimlessly before her.

'If you have a bucket and some ice, I could chill the champagne in the way it should be done,' he suggested.

She found him an old biscuit tin. Sultan took off his coat. He packed the tin with cubes of ice from the refrigerator, then nestled the bottle in the improvised cooler. He was already panting from his simple exertion.

'Roy was very disappointed you couldn't help him,' she said, blowing smoke up in the air.

'Perhaps I can,' Sultan smiled, putting a finger to his lips.

'God, how I wish you would,' she said. She rose and came across to him, slipping an arm around his thick waist. Her sudden familiarity surprised him.

'We'd be ever so grateful, Sultan,' she said, squeezing the roll of fat above his hip line. He stared down at her. For a moment the years rolled back, to a flat in Belsize Park, thirty-five years before. Sharon laid her head against his shoulder.

'Did you ever . . . have my mother?' she asked quietly.

At first, because of the quick way she used words, he could not comprehend the meaning of the verb she used. When he did, he was shocked. He hated her for daring to ask the question. The sense of defeat and despair he felt when he first visited the estate returned. It was reinforced by a repugnance for this young woman who wore the mask of Veena over her grubby personality. He moved away from her. He could not conceal his distaste.

'I don't think', he said tersely, 'that's any of your business.'

The moment he saw her eyes he knew that he should not have spoken so sharply. Sharon, taken aback, was immediately combative. She laughed maliciously. Brittle and mocking.

'Don't think that you were the only bugger pushing it into her,' she sneered. 'She was putting it about before and after you. My mother was on the bleeding game for most of her fucking life.'

'Shut up,' Sultan shouted.

'Who the hell do you think you're talking to, Paki shit?' Sharon screamed. She had gone completely mad. Sultan felt icy cold and apprehensive. He fumbled for his coat and struggled into it. Sharon barred his way. He knew that she had lost control of herself and sensed that this was not an unusual experience for her.

'You and your bloody Veena make me sick. I've got something far better between my legs, good as anything she had . . . better . . . a fucking sight better.' She struck him with her fists on the chest. She was weeping with a kind of hopeless and ominous melancholy. All Sultan wanted to do was escape. Words had lost their meaning.

'Please control yourself,' he pleaded, trying to open the door. It was opened for him. Roy stood there, hands behind his back, regarding him through his reflecting glasses. The tilt of Roy's head, away from Sultan as though he was trying to avoid contamination, evoked terrible menace.

'It had to happen, didn't it?' Roy snarled.

'Nothing has happened. Sharon just got upset.'

Roy gripped him roughly by the arm. He sent Sultan spinning towards the centre of the room.

'Knew you'd be back, sniffing around Sharon's twat. Knew it. You f-fucking Pakis are all the same.'

Sultan faced him with resolution. His voice trembled.

'I came here to help you,' he said quietly. 'You see, I'm not a well man.'

But as he spoke, he sensed that these two young people were insane. It was the same insanity he had glimpsed in

213

other eyes since he had returned to London. An insanity that seemed to have been shaped and made respectable by people in the highest places. He smelled evil.

'So, you're not a well man, eh?' Roy derided, imitating the singsong rhythms of Sultan's speech. 'I'll teach you w-what not well is.'

Sultan turned in dismay to Sharon, hoping that some-how she would intervene, to save him from Roy. But through the prasine eyes of Veena, all he could see was hatred. Roy pulled the bottle of pink champagne out of the biscuit tin.

'Here,' he shouted, swinging it at Sultan, who tried to duck. The bottle caught him at the side of his mouth, breaking teeth and bursting his lower lip. Roy pushed Sultan against the wall, extracting his wallet. He tore out the wad of fifty-pound notes.

'Just look at the loose change Pakis carry around!' he called.

He pinioned Sultan, ripping off his watch and diamond ring.

'Came here to s-stick it up my old lady, did you?' he hissed.

Pulling Sultan up towards him, he struck him across the nose with a steel-hard forehead. Sultan felt a bone crack and the warm gush of blood flood into his mouth.

'Please God, spare me,' he sobbed, staggering for the door.

Sultan reached the door before Roy. He ran on un-certain legs into the gloom of the landing. He pressed himself into a shaft that housed the garbage chute. Roy ran past. Sultan waited. He felt his heart flutter like a dying bird in his chest. Blood poured from his damaged face, dripping onto the stone floor. It was Sharon who found him.

'He's here,' she screamed down the stairwell to Roy. He returned, his fists clenched. Sultan urinated and fell to his knees, reaching out with a gesture of importunation to

214

Roy, who now stood above him. Sultan raised his head and saw Sharon's face, electric with excitement. Then Sultan prayed. But as he did, Roy moved in with his steel-capped boots. And broke Sultan Buckrabhoy up.

Nets

• • •

Every afternoon at four, Adi Shroff, also known as Techni-colour because his face was marked by leucoderma, would report for nets. While most of the boys at Kalachowki Cricket Club wanted to bat, Adi only wanted to bowl. Since he was considered a very good bowler – it was an accomplishment to survive ten balls against him without being either leg-before or clean bowled – Adi had plenty of practice. Sometimes, a few of the first eleven batsmen condescended to receive an over or two from him. Although they were more inclined to equivocate over the leg-before than the boys, Adi enjoyed their frustration and annoyance when they were unable to play him with any degree of adequacy. He was careful, however, not to let anyone discover the nature of his genius, for the power of that secret gave him pleasure of such intensity that he had lost consciousness on several occasions when the joy of his private knowledge became too exquisite to bear. Adi believed that once people knew the truth about him, he would be as diminished as the shorn Samson. His mother, who suspected that Adi's fainting spells were the result of excessive self-abuse, took him to the clinic, where old Dr Nariman concurred with her diagnosis. A tonic with soporific qualities was prescribed, which Mrs Shroff administered at bedtime. And every day she diligently examined his undergarments and sheets, but failed to find the slightest evidence for her suspicions. Adi, who realised that his mother had become obsessively watchful of him, imagined that she considered he was crazy. He attributed her fears for his sanity to the fact that his father had ended his life by jumping into a well, and that his uncle Jehangir, who

219

had kept wicket for the Parsees in the old Bombay Pentangular Tournaments, had to be restrained in a sisal harness during the full moon.

What Adi's mother did not know was that her son had the power to levitate. True, it was no more than two inches for about three seconds, but it meant that he could leap from great heights without injuring himself. Adi's real secret was that at fifteen years and nine months of age, he was the greatest spin bowler in the world.

Only one other person on earth could have suspected the truth. This was Miss Shireen Gazdar, the well-known Manipuri dancer, who shared his birthday but was two years older than himself. Although they were distantly related (she was his second cousin's nephew's half-sister) they had only met once. Seven years previously, their families had occupied adjoining bungalows at Matheran during the summer vacation. It was before Adi's father had dived into the well, and when they could afford the extravagance of a holiday.

The Gazdars had money, being big in rawolfia serpentina and chinchona bark. Adi remembered them arriving in a chauffeur-driven maroon Lancia, with a silver snaky supercharger and a studded toolbox on the running board. Mrs Gazdar had a pet mongoose with a pink nose, which Adi was allowed to take for walks on a lead.

Shireen had brown luxuriant hair that spread out like a cape over her shoulders and down her back. She had dark aqueous eyes and a proud face. She was resolute and fearless. Adi adored her, following her around like a pet animal. He loved the smell of the lavender powder with which she dusted herself after morning baths and the odour of dentifrice she exhaled when her face was close to his.

One morning, they went into the forest together. They made their way down a sunless avenue of broken twigs and dried leaves, below a canopy of trees that obscured most of the light. Here and there, through breaks in the

220

greenery, streamed columns of sunshine, illuminating patches of the ground they trod. They walked along this gloomy tunnel for about half an hour, penetrating deep enough into the forest to see a variety of animals – monkeys, deer, wild boar and two beautiful cobras. They heard strange sounds: the bell-like tonks of nilghai and a rasping which Adi imagined was wood being sawn but which Shireen assured him, with big eyes, was a leopard. Within a few paces, they startled a gathering of bloodsuckers and saw an emerald-green snake unfurl itself from a branch above. Adi was afraid but because of Shireen he said nothing.

Suddenly they heard an unusual bleating sound. It came from a bush to their right. As they approached the bush, the bleating grew louder. Shireen sprang forward, parting the branches to look into the clearing. There, embedded up to his chest in a pool of black slime, was a very old man. He had hoar-white hair that frizzed up above his head like a halo and his eyes were bright blue. When Adi and Shireen rushed forward to help him, he waved them away.

'Please,' he implored them, 'do not assist me. I have immersed myself in this pool of treacherous mud on purpose. I am a yogi and I have the power to release myself from this quagmire by the use of secret arts.'

'May we watch?' asked Shireen, seating herself on a stone at the edge of the bog. Adi stood beside her, his arm protectively around her shoulder. They stared at the tiny yogi as once again he began bleating strange words. He turned a half-inch with every bleat and, before their eyes, moved three hundred and sixty degrees in the mud. Then, the circle completed, he uttered a cry shriller than those he had articulated before and popped up from the bog onto the bank beside them. Apart from the fact that he was slightly out of breath and stank of the foul substance from which he had escaped, he seemed quite untroubled. They noticed he was naked. He possessed breasts like a woman

221

and an infantile male organ the size of a peanut. He told them that he was a holy hermaphrodite, slightly more male than female, but that he hoped to progress to a state of perfect balance before his next incarnation.

'But tell us how you managed to leap out of the bog,' Shireen demanded, excited and thrilled by the performance.

'I am an adept in the art of levitation,' he explained.

'Can you show me how it's done?' asked Shireen.

'Well,' said the yogi, 'nothing is for nothing. Like all difficult things in life, a price has to be paid.'

'We have no money,' Adi said, turning out his pockets.

The yogi smiled. 'The price, alas, is beyond the purse of even the wealthiest person.'

Shireen and Adi looked disappointed.

'Listen,' the little yogi said, 'do you know what innocence is?'

They shook their heads.

'It is', he said, 'being like little children forever.'

'But you're an old man,' Adi declared.

The yogi laughed with delight. He beckoned them nearer as his voice had cracked with all his shouting in the bog. He smelled dreadfully.

'Put simply,' he said, 'innocence is to be selfless in all you do, always truthful, trusting and loving. And you must believe that nothing is impossible.' He turned to Adi. 'Do you like her?' he asked.

Adi nodded shyly. The yogi addressed Shireen.

'Do you like him?'

'Oh yes,' she said genially.

'Then that', said the yogi, 'is how it should remain.'

'Forever?' asked Shireen.

'Forever,' replied the yogi, 'although you will have many temptations in life because you are a beautiful jewel. Men will not let you rest. Your path will be more difficult than his.'

'Will you show us how to levitate?' asked Adi.

'The power is already within you,' said the yogi, 'and will remain with you as long as selfless love endures in your hearts.'

When he had said this, the little yogi disappeared before their very eyes. Adi was terrified and, gripping Shireen's hand, rushed back along the path that had brought them to the bog. When they arrived home, Shireen told Adi that they should not discuss their experience with anyone.

'But is that an innocent thing to do?' asked Adi, who was a wise owl.

'I'm not sure,' frowned Shireen. 'Perhaps the little yogi will give us a sign.'

That evening, before twilight, they went to the sandpit near their bungalows and practised what Shireen called 'Nijinsky leaps'. When they stopped to get their breath back, Shireen confided to Adi, 'I saw your face turn into that of the little yogi.'

'I'm afraid,' said Adi.

'Did you feel a snakelike shiver down your spine, between your thighs and around your legs?' she asked.

'I feel dizzy,' sighed Adi.

'So do I,' she said.

'And I still can't levitate,' grumbled Adi.

'Perhaps', Shireen reflected, 'we should try our Nijinsky leaps naked, like the hermaphrodite yogi.'

'My mother will kill me,' said Adi.

'We could go back into the forest where nobody can see us,' suggested Shireen.

'Isn't that being deceitful?' asked Adi, his eyes filled with concern.

'I'm not sure,' said Shireen. 'I'm not sure of anything any more.'

She led him back along the path they had explored earlier that day. It was now quite dark. Shireen took off her skirt and blouse, then pulled down her cotton drawers. Adi undressed.

'Let us try our Nijinsky leaps holding one another,' she said.

Adi's teeth began to chatter. It was quite cool in the forest. But he faced Shireen and encircled her rounded bottom with his thin arms, clasping her soft body to him. They jumped. They seemed to soar higher than they had before. Then it happened. They remained high above the ground for several seconds and floated down through the darkness as slowly as two feathers. They held each other tightly as they did it again and again, melting into each other in wonder at their miraculous discovery. They only stopped when they heard distant voices calling them for the evening meal. As they walked back, holding hands, Shireen kissed Adi on his cheek, above his patch of leucoderma.

Later that night, there was a commotion because Adi's father cut his wrists and had to be taken to hospital in a tonga. The next morning, the Shroff family left Matheran for Bombay. Adi's father looked very pale and sat in a corner of the compartment with his uncle Jehangir. Adi's mother and his aunt Suki sat some distance away.

'Your father has not been well,' his mother confided. 'He must not be disturbed on any account.'

Adi stared at his father, who had a strange smile on his face.

'Is Daddy mad, Mama?' he asked quietly.

His mother looked at him sadly, then pressed him to her breast. Adi endured the convulsive heaves of her body with fortitude.

'The family is cursed,' she whispered in despair.

Locked in his mother's arms, Adi performed little Nijinsky leaps with her in his mind. He experienced the same snakelike tremor as he had with Shireen. Anchoring himself to his mother, he gritted his teeth and elevated slightly. His eyes fluttered in ecstasy, then suddenly all was darkness. When he came to, he was supine on the seat.

'You fainted,' his mother explained. 'Your father has been a great tribulation.'

But as he lay there, Adi allowed his right hand, and then his arm, to become weightless. It was at that moment that Adi knew he had opened a door few ever open.

One of the reasons why Adi was a poor scholar was that he thought of little else but spin bowling. He bowled imaginary balls on his way to and from school. If he could not persuade anybody to bat for him, he would bowl his ball against a wall, practising his spin on every type of surface. Sometimes, he imagined he heard the ball whisper to him before a delivery and modified the trajectory to take account of its message. His ability to levitate, however, was the crucial ingredient in his genius, enabling him to toss balls at batsmen from unconsidered angles. At the Kala-chowki Cricket Club, the geometry of his bowling, almost imperceptible from that of other bowlers, was sufficient to make him, when he so determined, quite unplayable. Of course, Adi did not try to take a wicket with every delivery. That would have let the cat out of the bag. Worse. It would have given him little satisfaction. If he enjoyed a particular batsman's leg glance, he would produce a ball that would encourage that stroke. If a batsman was hitting the ball with indiscrimate arrogance, Adi would beat the bat several times without taking the wicket before forcing the player to make an inelegant thick edge, shooting the ball vertically into the air for the simplest of catches. In some of his most extraordinary exhibitions of bowling, Adi did not take a single wicket but had everyone on their feet with excitement as he devised a heart-stopping succession of near misses. Averages were something about which he cared little. He secretly despised cricketers who were obsessed with the statistics rather than with the magic of the game.

Although Adi was the greatest spin bowler in the world

at fifteen years and nine months, nobody but he was aware of the fact. Shireen, however, was already being acclaimed as the most exciting exponent of Manipuri dancing among the younger dancers. Adi followed her career with enthusiasm. His room was decorated with her posters and whenever she danced in Bombay he attended every performance. He alone was aware that at certain moments of concentrated expression, she levitated. But even the most experienced critics of Manipuri dancing failed to perceive how Shireen Gazdar was different from all other dancers.

Adi addressed a series of letters to her. For the most part, they were of a serious technical nature, dealing with energy centres and etheric fluids. On occasion, he reminded her of their Nijinksy leaps at Matheran, seven years previously. He also reported his own metamorphosis from an ordinary youth cricketer to one of considerable ability. He felt that it might be imprudent to confide in her at that stage that he was the greatest spin bowler in the world. One day, he sent her a bouquet of jasmine, marigold and ferns, wrapped in silver foil and sprinkled with rose-water; also a box of halva, with his name inscribed on a pink card strapped to the cardboard lid. The fact that she did not acknowledge his gift did not make him unduly despondent. Indeed, he would have been surprised had she felt impelled to respond to someone who, despite the fact that they were distantly related and had played briefly together as children, was basically, a stranger.

Shireen Gazdar was at first amused by the letters.

'He is an ugly little wretch called Technicolour,' she once observed cruelly, passing the letters around for the other young dancers' entertainment.

'Such big words,' they giggled, for they were for the most part uneducated and irretrievably shallow.

'His loony father dived down a well,' Shireen informed them.

Everyone in the company found that remark extremely

226

funny and it confirmed Shireen's reputation for drollery. Eventually, she found the never-ending stream of letters tiresome. She never glanced at them, just passed them around for the pleasure of her friends. One day, one of her most ardent admirers, Superintendent Fatty Contractor of the Bombay City Police, happened to read one of Adi's letters. He was outraged by its audacity.

'The dirty little blighter makes an impertinent reference to your chastity in this passage,' he seethed.

'It's meant to be poetic,' Shireen explained with a bored smile.

'I'll teach the bastard a thing or two about poetry,' the vengeful superintendent snarled.

The young dancers, who knew Superintendent Fatty Contractor was madly in love with Shireen and pathologically jealous of all other males in her life, whether they were real men, Hollywood filmstars or mythological figures, clapped their hands with excitement.

'Poor little Technicolour,' they cried heartlessly. 'Fatty is going to pulp him beyond recognition.'

Superintendent Fatty Contractor was very useful to Shireen. Not only did he intimidate people she did not want to see, like debt collectors, salesmen and the crazier fans, but she and her friends had immunity from traffic violations and other minor offences. Fatty could provide motor-cycle escorts or even a wailing police ambulance when they were in a desperate hurry. And minor irritants, like Adi Shroff, were no problem.

The irony of Fatty Contractor's jealousy was that Shireen Gazdar, whom the ingenuous superintendent had been led to believe was a virgin, was being regularly mounted by: Bapu Babakhan, the film producer; Krishnagopalchari, the Kathakali dancer; Sami Sonavala, the racehorse owner; Urban Braganza, the property tycoon; and other less-celebrated pokers. But her capricious lust excluded obese men like Superintendent Fatty Contractor. They made her physically ill.

'Several physicians have advised me that I am much too small to admit a male organ,' she confided to Fatty. 'Besides my Dance Coach feels that some of my subtler movements could be impaired by sexual intercourse. Perhaps after I retire I may place myself in the hands of an international surgeon who will be able to enlarge my vagina sufficiently for me to accommodate a husband. I am informed that there are clinics in Switzerland that specialise in vaginal sculpture.'

'Go abroad,' agreed Fatty. 'Don't let these local butchers lay a scalpel on that precious jewel.'

'I appreciate your solicitude,' she sighed, tenderly patting one of his powerful paws.

'If you married the right guy,' he cajoled, 'maybe he would be prepared to take his time. You know, easy . . . easy.'

'Oh, Fatty.'

'May I kiss you?' he asked.

'Now what's the point of getting me all itchy, darling?' she sniffed.

'Don't cry, Shireen. Don't cry.'

Adi's cricketing career was beginning to take shape. Major Khambatta, the club secretary, was extremely pleased with the young lad's dedication. More than anything else, Adi enjoyed nets. He was now strong enough to bowl for an hour or more without rest, troubling the best batsmen in the club with his deception, changes of pace and flight. On his début for the second eleven, he allowed himself to take seven for eighteen, despite being dropped five times.

Adi was given a full column in the evening paper: SHROFF'S DEADLY BOWLING, it read. He cut it out and sent it to Shireen Gazdar.

A week later, a very large and hairy superintendent of the Bombay City police called to see Adi's mother.

'Your son', he said grimly, placing a pile of envelopes on

the kitchen table, 'has been making a nuisance of himself. Miss Shireen Gazdar, the celebrated dancer, has filed a complaint.' He tapped the letters with his baton. 'As a matter of fact, Mrs Shroff, some of these communications are slightly indecent and could, if Miss Gazdar wished to proceed, form the basis of a serious prosecution.'

'He's only sixteen,' wailed Mrs Shroff, drying her hands and looking out of the window for Adi, who was expected home. And just at that moment the key turned in the lock and Adi appeared.

'Adi, why did you refer indelicately to Miss Shireen Gazdar's chastity?' cried Mrs Shroff.

'I'm sure that Shireen understood the reference was not meant to be improper,' said Adi, a little loftily, which was significantly out of character.

'Now, listen to me, young fellow,' Superintendent Fatty Contractor shouted, 'we can't have a whippersnapper like you wasting the time of important people.'

'It's none of your business,' said Adi. 'If Shireen wishes to complain about my behaviour, I have made no secret of my whereabouts.'

'You little swine,' cried Superintendent Contractor, reaching for Adi.

'Don't touch him! He has brittle bones,' screamed Mrs Shroff.

Adi moved adroitly around the table.

'Besides,' he observed insolently, 'I'm deeply in love with Shireen and I intend, when I am of a suitable age, to consummate my passion.'

'Bastard,' roared the superintendent, lunging at him once again.

At this point, Adi dived head first out of the fifth-floor window. His mother fainted and Superintendent Contractor went weak at the knees. He rushed to the balcony in the next room and, looking down into the courtyard, saw Adi standing there unscathed.

'I'm going to arrest that technicoloured bugger,' he

229

vowed, blowing a whistle and bounding down the stairs. Police constables appeared from everywhere and by the time Mrs Shroff had recovered consciousness, Adi was in handcuffs.

After the police had whacked Adi across the testicles with a light cane and inserted two cones of ice up his anus, he confessed to assaulting three police officers, threatening to kill Miss Shireen Gazdar and burning down a Chinese restaurant – a case the superintendent had kept unsolved for just such an emergency. Adi was also quietly advised that if he was imprudent enough to be acquitted, his mother would be blinded with hydrochloric acid.

When Adi's case came to trial, he was found guilty of all three offences, but insane. He was committed for psychiatric care at the Thana Madhouse.

'The family is cursed,' Mrs Shroff shrieked, running sorrowfully out of the courtroom.

After he had been at the madhouse for almost five years, Dr Desai said to him, 'You know, Shroff, you're hardly mad at all.'

Adi nodded and told the doctor about Superintendent Fatty Contractor.

'We need a decent spin bowler for the madhouse team,' Dr Desai reflected, 'but it's tricky to wangle that level of freedom so soon after certification. In the meanwhile, I'll arrange for you to get some net practice.'

So every day, Adi bowled to a succession of batsmen for an hour at a time. The standard was not very high at the Thana Madhouse and a few of the players got extremely excited if they were bowled. Adi had to be careful. Some of the inmates could turn nasty without any provocation. One or two of the madmen had played club cricket at a fairly respectable level. Premchand, an elderly accountant, who was there for hacking his wife to pieces, had learned all the classical strokes from an old textbook by Victor Trumper, while Dost Khan, a middle-aged surgeon who had strangled several nurses, once opened for Kandahar.

One day, Dr Desai brought Adi good news.

'If you give an undertaking to behave yourself, you may represent the Thana Madhouse against an Indian Air Force Eleven.'

Adi asked whether, now that he was a certified lunatic, he would be expected to bowl like one. Dr Desai, who wore an MCC tie-pin, was not amused.

The Thana Madhouse batted first and were all out for nine runs. Adi spoke to Dr Desai, who was the captain.

'You must let me bowl first,' he pleaded. 'I'll get the lot of them out for under nine.'

'I thought Premchand and I could trundle on with some of our quick stuff,' Dr Desai observed. 'I mean, it's hardly on to open with a spinner.'

'I'm a very high-class fast bowler as well,' Adi lied. 'Please allow me to have the first crack at them.'

Dr Desai called Premchand over. Premchand was the acknowledged expert on field strategy. After a lengthy discussion, Dr Desai tossed the ball to Adi.

'We expect at least a fifteen-pace run up,' Premchand warned.

Adi ran the seam against his cheek and loped leisurely towards the first batsman. He floated the ball towards the Air Force striker, who flashed at it and missed completely, the late break taking the off and middle stumps. The second ball was a shade quicker and kept low, just nudging the off stump down. The third looked short but sailed on, tipping middle out of the ground. The fourth and fifth went to vicious breaks, shooting the off stumps well beyond the keeper, while the sixth ball was played on. Dr Desai was delirious with delight.

'Six for nought,' he crowed, jumping around the pitch. 'Let me finish them off.'

'Do you really think you can get the last four wickets?' Adi demanded.

Premchand ran up to Dr Desai and grabbed the ball.

231

'Let us be sensible,' he shouted. 'I can pin them down with seamers until Shroff returns.'

Dr Desai and Premchand argued angrily for several minutes before Dr Desai reluctantly allowed Premchand to keep the ball.

The grey-haired and portly Premchand bowled three good-length balls. The fourth was short and whacked for two. The fifth was overpitched and was touched away for a leg side single. The sixth was a full toss and was crashed up in the air towards the boundary. Mercifully, the ball dropped two yards short and rolled across the line for four. It was seven for six. Adi Shroff was on again. He yorked the seventh wicket with a ball that appeared to hang in the air. The eighth played on. The ninth batsman missed the flight completely as Adi's ball stopped and came again, taking the off stump. The tenth lost his middle stump, going for a winning thwack. Ten for six. Adi Shroff's figures were ten for nought, all bowled.

When he produced the same figures against St Xavier's College the following Saturday, the phones never stopped ringing. Major Khambatta, the secretary of Adi Shroff's old club, saw the chief minister of Bombay State.

'We've got to get Adi Shroff out of the madhouse,' he said. 'This could be a matter of national importance.'

Two weeks later, Adi was released. His mother prepared a chicken dansat for him.

'I hear Shireen is dancing at the Cowasji Jehangir Hall,' he said.

'My God,' Mrs Shroff screamed. 'Why can't you forget all that nonsense? You are on the verge of playing for a Parsee Eleven, perhaps Bombay State before the season is out. Then, who knows? Even India. Adi, my son, soon you could be a celebrity. Forget this woman who has brought you nothing but trouble.'

Adi did not answer. The next evening, he bought a seat in the front stalls at the Cowasji Jehangir hall. As soon as Shireen Gazdar danced, he realised that she had lost the magic they once shared. The applause was tumultuous but Adi knew that Shireen was struggling, anchored to the stage like every other dancer. He wondered whether he could persuade her to honour her promise to the little yogi and was even prepared to transfer his own power to her, if that were possible. He felt that if she would allow him to speak to her for ten minutes there was a chance that she could be saved.

Later that night, Adi walked to the tall apartment block where she lived on the fifteenth floor. For more than an hour, he agonised over what he should do. He suspected that she would not see him if he called at the front door. So in the darkness he climbed quickly up the side of the building. When one can levitate, climbing does not present the usual difficulties. Eventually he reached Shireen's apartment. Opening a window, he slid in. There was a light shining from underneath a door. Adi walked towards it. He entered the room. He saw Shireen in bed with an elderly bald-headed man. They were both naked.

'Technicolour!' Shireen screamed.

'Who the hell are you?' cried the man, jumping out of bed. Adi noticed that he was built like a horse. He had never seen genitalia of that size. He wondered for a moment whether they were made of black foam rubber but saw to his astonishment that they were real. He felt depressed.

'What have you done with your precious gift?' he enquired, in a weak, despondent voice. She didn't appear to be interested in his question. 'Throw the crazy shit out,' she cried, tucking the end of the sheet between her thighs and covering her breasts with a pillow.

The naked man was on his knees searching for his trousers. Two servants rushed into the room in response to Shireen Gazdar's screams.

'Throw that madman out,' she repeated hysterically.

They gripped Adi's arms and frog-marched him to the door.

'No,' Shireen shouted, 'no – over the balcony!'

The servants looked startled. But they pulled Adi out onto the balcony. They turned back to Shireen for instructions, stupefied by her command yet subject to her will.

'My God, Shireen,' the naked man protested. 'This is the fifteenth floor.' A senior minister in the central government, he felt it would be morally appropriate at that stage to disassociate himself from Shireen's impetuous directive.

'Over!' she howled, jumping out of bed and pummelling the servants' backs.

Before they tossed Adi into the dark night air, his eyes met Shireen's. It was just for a spasm of time but he realised instantly that the Shireen he once knew was no longer there. Her spirit no longer occupied that body. Instead, peering at him through her eyes was a terrible demon filled with suffocating hatred. Where, he supposed, had his Shireen gone? Had she been consumed by the beast lurking in that body? Or had she been sucked back into the great reservoir of eternal goodness that lies at the heart of the universe? Adi sailed down, slowly as a feather, pondering these questions. Between the fifth and fourth floors, he was suddenly aware of the little yogi's presence. Then he was overwhelmed by the smell of crushed marigolds and burning sandalwood. This, he knew, was Shireen's innocence drifting away into eternity. Her precious gift was now just smoke. He accepted the inevitable. And Shireen Gazdar faded from Adi's mind forever.

He landed lightly on the drive. He heard a faint cry. Looking up, he saw four dark blobs peering down at him from a distant balcony. He continued on his way. On the ground before him he saw a green coconut, no larger than a cricket ball. It had been shaken down by the strong monsoon wind. Picking it up, Adi loped into his easy bowling stride, aiming at a milk bottle twenty yards ahead. He bent his wrist back and curled his cunning fingers around the coconut, tossing it up artfully into the night. The coconut pitched three yards to the right of the bottle, breaking at an extravagant angle to strike the base of the target, transforming it into a shower of jagged white fragments that glittered like diamonds under a nearby street light. So Adi Shroff passed on his way, dreaming of tomorrow's nets, the inter-state tournament and the glorious possibility of being selected for the Nawab of Pataudi's tour of England.

Bismarck

. . .

The Victoria Watch Company of Bombay was located in a portable teak box. It was sufficiently capacious to accommodate a fairly small but not unduly restless manager, provided he was able to sit cross-legged throughout the working day. The space was organised to display a selection of wristwatches, arranged in descending order of prices. They were suspended against a blue fluted mirror upon which remained the faded trace of a water transfer. Close inspection revealed this to be the bloated physiognomy of the eponymous monarch on a Union Jack. There was also a number of alarm clocks on three retractable shelves, and a polished work surface across which the manager dealt with his customers. This was also the area on which he placed the work tray where he carried out the repairs that were the substance of the business.

The previous manager, Kapadia (1896–1946), was barely five feet tall and weighed not much more than eighty-five pounds. Bismarck Mann, who applied for the job when old Kapadia's eyesight was no longer capable of carrying out repairs to the smaller wristwatches, was one inch taller and fifteen pounds heavier. Mr Anklesaria, the proprietor, was doubtful about Bismarck's suitability.

'We were looking for a rather more compact manager, Mr Mann,' he said.

'I'm a small fellow, by any standards,' Bismarck replied, squatting instantly on the floor before Mr Anklesaria's desk and constricting himself into a square metre of space.

'You appear to have heavy haunches,' Mr Anklesaria declared, standing up and taking a critical step around the

239

compressed Bismarck, who looked up at Mr Anklesaria hopefully.

'To tell you the truth,' Mr Anklesaria admitted, 'we were really after a lighter-complexioned man. A Parsee, perhaps.'

'I get on famously with the Parsees,' Bismarck said earnestly. 'My younger sister, Heidi, is the live-in mistress of an extremely influential member of your great community. Furthermore, I'm not so very dark, in the sunlight.'

Mr Anklesaria looked doubtful. 'The Victoria Watch Company', he solemnly explained, 'is one of the oldest established watch businesses in the presidency.'

'I know,' replied Bismarck. 'It is almost as old as the Ticky-Tick-Tock Company where I was trained.'

'And we have important professional customers, senior people in the pharmaceutical and import-export trades.'

'I understand,' said Bismark, trying to follow Mr Anklesaria's movements around him.

'What we require, Mr Mann, is good manners and maturity.'

'That's me,' said Bismarck, 'and I have something else as well.'

'What's that?'

'Speed,' cried Bismarck. 'I am one of the fastest watch repairers in Bombay.'

Mr Anklesaria bent over Bismarck. 'Can you lower your haunches an inch or two?'

Bismarck did as he was told. Mr Anklesaria walked around him once more. Then he reached down, surprising Bismarck by grasping his hand and giving it a vigorous but amiable shake. The contract was sealed.

'I trust you will be able to meet the challenge, Mr Mann.'

Bismarck was stunned with joy. He sprang to his feet and, pressing the palms of his hands against the seams of his trousers, bowed respectfully to Mr Anklesaria. Bismarck could not imagine any dignity to which he could reasonably aspire greater than this one. It was the happiest day of his life. Bismarck was forty-eight years of age.

On his way home to his room in Sandhurst Road, Bismarck rang his sister, Heidi, who was fifteen years younger than he. Heidi did not hear from Bismarck very often, and that arrangement suited her.

'What do you think of my wonderful luck, Heidi?' he shouted down the phone.

'If that is what you want in life, Bismarck,' she replied in a cool and distant voice.

Heidi often wished that she didn't have brothers. Naval, her lover and protector, who had inherited a lucrative silk mill from his father, also disapproved of Bismarck. He had disapproved of Siegfried even more, but Siegfried was dead, and Naval was thankful for that.

'I warned you that bastard was unreliable,' he told Heidi, when they got the news that Siegfried had jumped from the fourth-floor window of the room he shared with Bismarck.

'What is more,' Naval added indignantly, 'he's not even properly dead.'

'What do you mean, not properly dead? Either one is dead or one isn't. My dear brother is lying desperately injured at the King Edward Memorial Hospital and you have the nerve to say he's not properly dead.'

This unexpected outburst of sororal solicitude astonished Naval. Heidi had never had a pleasant word for her brothers. She despised them as much as he did. He concluded that she was being self-indulgent. Feeling sorry for oneself when somebody else has to bear the pain, was a diversion he understood. He remembered how he had enjoyed being miserable when his mother had a gangrenous leg amputated. Naval wandered around for days with a tragic attitude, demonstrating to the world that he had psychic rights in the sundered limb. He decided to write

241

Siegfried off as quickly as possible, to deprive Heidi of her morbid and vicarious entertainment.

'Listen, my pigeon. Siegfried is kaput. Broken skull, legs, ribs and pelvis. And that is the good news. God knows what a mish-mash he is inside. Shit and pulp, guava jelly, plum jam, jungli pilau: all buggered up. Consider him a goner. And he has shown a regrettable lack of consideration for you, so why bother? This, my dear, is not the way for respectable people to die, on Sandhurst Road, before a crowd of goondas and whores.'

Heidi tried to hold onto her victim.

'If I can endure the pain, so can you,' she said, snivelling into a handkerchief.

'Weeping unnerves me,' Naval shouted. 'The next development in this farce will be the arrival of that black dwarf, Bismarck. I will not have him coming to these premises with his depressing nonsense.'

'He's not a dwarf,' Heidi protested. She did not like Bismarck but found it offensive that somebody who was a blood relative should be described as a dwarf.

'But, darling, he is almost certainly not your real brother. Your poor father must have been cuckolded. For God's sake, how can a German, even half a German, be two feet tall and black as an African?'

'Don't be stupid, Naval,' Heidi said. 'He must be a half-brother at least, even if Daddy was cuckolded. And furthermore, he's not two feet tall.'

'Anyhow,' grumbled Naval, 'he's a very short and unpleasant bastard. Not the sort of person I receive in the drawing room. He is no doubt full of bugs. And he stinks of rancid coconut oil. If he comes here, kindly speak to him in the compound.'

Heidi did not complain. She had no wish to encourage Bismarck to visit her. His obsequiousness made her ill.

'I'll tell you what, darling,' Naval said, squeezing a cheek of her arse affectionately, 'let us go to Damun for a few days, and give Siegfried a chance to die properly.'

242

Heidi nodded thoughtfully.

They left Bombay within the hour and stayed at Damun for a week. When they got back, Siegfried had been dead for three days. Heidi was informed by the chaprassi that Bismarck had stood outside the gate since their brother's death, waiting to see her.

'Where is he now?' Heidi asked irritably.

'Today', the chaprassi informed her, 'is the day of the funeral.'

'My God,' Naval cried, when she told him of Siegfried's death, 'what right has that blighter to annoy us, on the very day we return from holiday?'

Bismarck, Siegfried and Heidi were the children of a German father and a Tamil mother. Their mother, a tea picker called Rajkumari, conceived Bismarck when she was fourteen on an old mattress behind the boiler room at the sugar refinery at Kotagiri, not a mile from the plantation where she worked. Gunter Mann, a sixty-year-old retired ship's engineer from Bremen, was the boiler superintendent and found the mattress useful for casual sexual encounters. However he took a shine to little black Rajkumari and, when her belly started to balloon with Bismarck, he promoted her to the status of mistress. When he lost his job, through drink and belligerence, he took his child-cohabitee north, working as a steam roller maintenance fitter for the Bombay Port Trust, where the teutonic Siegfried was born. The family finally moved to Miraj, where Gunter Mann managed a small cotton gin-mill for an entrepreneur called Maruti, who had once been a multibillionaire but had lost almost everything trying to corner Broach cotton. Mann was seventy-five when Heidi arrived. He died from a coronary a few months later. Rajkumari could not bear the loss of her partner. She poured kerosene over herself and set a match to her saturated clothing. She died the next day.

The children were appropriated by friendly Jesuits and secured in a Catholic orphanage. Here they were fed, clothed, educated, beaten from time to time and taught to pray several times a day. Bismarck grew up to be a short dark man with a square face, a snub nose and crinkly hair, which he parted in the centre. When he was twenty he grew a moustache that turned down on either side of his full lips. He was apprenticed at the Ticky-Tick-Tock company when he was sixteen.

Siegfried, who was six feet tall and blond, was two years younger than Bismark and was trained as a refrigeration mechanic. He was quick-tempered and drank a great deal and he could never keep a job, for he would take time off and turn up late for work several times a week. He was successful with women and always had access to two or three married ladies at any period of his adult life. Then, quite inexplicably, he fell in love with a young Persian virgin called Hanousi, who was unable, and probably unwilling, to return his affection. One afternoon, after drinking tinctures of alcohol and soda water, he jumped, crazy and screaming, from the fourth floor to land at her feet as she was returning from school. Siegfried was forty-one.

Heidi was the cleverest. She believed that the only way to escape from her brothers, of whom she disapproved, was by an alliance with a wealthy man. This she achieved with little effort. Light complexioned, with long brown hair and grey eyes, she was a desirable female, much sought after when she was a girl. After completing her schooling at the orphanage, she became a shorthand typist. Naval was her first employer. She went to bed with him three days after the first dictation. They had lived together for fifteen years. Marriage was precluded for the first twelve of those years because of a threat of disinheritance from his father, and after the father's death they both observed the need to placate Naval's mother, an ailing octogenarian amputee whose early demise had been confidently

244

expected ten years previously. Eventually it became a case of 'since we've waited this long, a little longer would not matter'.

Naval's and Heidi's relationship was not narrowly sexual. They enjoyed dancing, swimming, playing badminton and going to the cinema together. They particularly liked technicoloured movies. The subject matter and the players were of little consequence; there was just one prerequisite: the film had to be in technicolour. Naval was unfaithful to Heidi once, but confessed almost immediately, humble with contrition. She had never even contemplated another affiliation, content with their post-tiffin engagements. Naval was partial to sunlit visibility when coupling and was particularly addicted to mirrors. Heidi, who had a slight propensity to narcissism, did not mind the most lascivious poses for Naval's immediate delectation, nor for his mon-ocular Leica that recorded the sweaty vibrancy of their love. The grainy enlargements were picked through later in the evening over iced cashew liquor and small salted plums dusted with chilli powder. Naval and Heidi never made love at night.

Since Siegfried's death, Bismarck had lived by himself. This suited him better. Once every six or seven weeks, he visited a brothel in Foras Road. If possible, he spent the night with a plump girl he particularly liked. She was Nepalese and jolly; when she laughed, her eyes were transformed into slits. She seemed as fond of him as it is possible for a hard-working whore to be fond of a regular customer. At forty-eight, Bismarck had only consorted with prostitutes. He would have found it difficult to approach a respectable woman. Once, his Nepalese whore gave him a clap, but generally she was reliable. Apart from that, Bismarck had been infected on only two occasions: by a banana woman whom he'd taken back to his room, and by a pretty whore he would have sworn was safe. After that, he felt that older plainer women were best, for the pretty young ones did twice the amount of business and so ran a greater risk of picking up a dose. As things went, he was fairly lucky with his encounters.

One night, on his way home, Bismarck was accosted by a young girl in a grubby short dress. She had a skinny body and legs, her nose was rather too long for her solemn, old face and she had the largest black eyes he had seen. Her hair was short, sun-brown, and rough cut like a boy's.

'You've got owl's eyes,' he laughed.

She held out her hand. He found a rupee and gave it to her.

'Can I come with you?' she asked.

'Why me?'

'I've seen you many times,' she said.

'I work here,' he said, pointing to the alley and the shop where the teak box was secured every night in Anklesaria's Confectionary and Pharmacy.

'I can work for you,' she said.

'But I'm poor as a cockroach,' Bismarck laughed.

'I don't like rich people. They have no heart,' she said.

Bismarck thought that a very curious remark for a street girl to make. And there was something in her voice, which was rasping, husky and much deeper than one would have expected in such a fragile frame, that attracted him.

'Where do you sleep?'

She shrugged. 'Anywhere I can. On the pavements. Under those arches.' She pointed to the covered walkway across the road.

'Where are your mother and father?'

She showed her teeth, amused at his question. 'Who knows?'

'Have you lost them?'

'I've lost everything,' she said quietly.

'I hope things work out for you,' he said, suddenly depressed as he turned from her.

'Can I come with you?' she called, as he walked away.

He raised a hand and shook it, without looking back.

Bismarck tried not to think about the skinny girl as he travelled home. But the memory of her haunted him. He wondered what had attracted him to her. Perhaps she spoke like that to every man she met. What the hell could he do for her, anyway? She was miserably thin and far too unformed for his inclinations. Bombay was teeming with unwanted people, born on the streets to die on the streets. One could not walk ten yards without meeting derelicts, beggars and lost souls. He was glad that Heidi was living in a posh house on Cumballa Hill with her rich boyfriend. Who would have believed it? His sister, a queen among women. He was grateful that she didn't have to sleep on the pavements. As for him, he liked his job and earned enough to live in his simple room. He suspected that he had outgrown wanting a woman on a permanent basis. Even with his Nepalese whore, one night once in a while was enough. And then he could hardly wait to slip his trousers on and bugger off. There was nothing Bismarck wanted other than for life to continue as it was until he died, as long as he went painlessly – preferably in bed, a peaceful end. He could not imagine what he would do if fortune had given him much more than he deserved. Some people – the lucky ones, Bismarck reflected – could manage to be happy with just enough. If that were not the case, my God, how the shit would fly. The world would be in turmoil indeed.

That day, Mr Anklesaria had called Bismarck in and told him that he was doing well. Then he had actually shaken his hand. Bismarck smiled at the thought of that, as the tram jolted and crashed towards Sandhurst Road.

Bismarck lived in a tenement building of four floors divided up into single rooms. In these rooms the tenants had to cook, sleep and wash themselves. There were communal latrines on the first and third floors. When he had first moved in with Siegfried, twenty years earlier, it was almost a respectable place. Now hoodlums slept in the passageways and on the stairs, large rats and cockroaches infested the garbage areas on each landing, and it was dangerous not to lock and bolt one's door at night. On the ground floor was a noisy all-night Irani restaurant, frequented by loafers and whores, a bhel-puri stall, a wrestling club, a black magician's consulting rooms, a barber's shop and a sugar-cane press that retailed thick glasses of grey-green juice, served with assorted syrups and ice. Stabbings, rapes and robberies were not uncommon occurrences. These generally happened late at night, but even in broad daylight there were terrible incidents. Unhappy wives set themselves alight, little boys were forcibly buggered, enemies were blinded with acid, and Pathan moneylenders beat defaulting debtors with metal-tipped staves.

But Bismarck had no trouble. He nodded to most of the troublemakers as he came and went, and they nodded back. They imagined that he was one of them, and he never gave them reason to question that assumption. When Siegfried jumped out of the window, this reinforced his neighbours' estimation that he was part of the inexorable cycle of death and violence which was normality in the area. And if Bismarck sometimes thought himself to be an outsider, nobody, fortunately, recognised him as one.

The next evening, Bismarck saw the skinny girl again. She greeted him cheerfully. 'Did you sleep well, last night?' she asked.

Bismarck frowned. 'What's that to do with you?'

'I was making conversation,' she said. 'I slept in there,' she added, pointing to a dark alley. Bismarck knew the place. It reeked of urine and rotting food.

'You could have found a better place than that,' he observed, with a look of disgust.

'There's a high ledge, halfway along, hidden from view.

I climb up there and make myself comfortable in a gunny-sack.' She was now walking beside him.

'What have your sleeping arrangements got to do with me?' Bismarck muttered.

'Do you live by yourself?' she asked.

Bismarck stopped. He shook the loose change in his pocket.

'I can only afford eight annas tonight. You can get a good meal with that.'

He handed her a coin.

'Can I come with you?' she asked.

'What earthly good am I to you?' he asked angrily. 'I'm not a talkative man and I am quite happy with my own company. As for the other thing, I am content with my present arrangements. Besides, you are far too young for me.'

'I can work for you,' she suggested simply.

Bismarck sighed and sucked a hollow tooth.

'Can you cook?' he asked.

'A little.'

'Well,' he said, glancing around to see if they were being observed, 'if you want to follow me home, you may do so. I'm not forcing you.'

He set off down the road, looking around every now and again to see if she was there. She was. And when he jumped on the tram, she climbed in as well, discreetly seating herself three seats behind him.

When Bismarck arrived back in his room with the girl, he saw that she was even more emaciated than he first suspected, and her scrawny neck was covered with blue marks.

'What's that?' he asked, pointing to the scars.

'I had a plague of boils,' she said quietly.

He had prepared lentils and rice that morning on his metal charcoal stove. He motioned her to sit on the bed beside him as he shared out the portions on the long walnut table Siegfried had made several years ago. It was

249

far too elegant for the humble room. Since Siegfried's death, Bismarck had eaten with his hands. He felt slightly guilty about this, but as long as he was alone and unobserved he thought this more convenient. Siegfried had insisted on cutlery and Bismarck never argued with him. But secretly he disliked the metal smell of the spoons they used. He once mentioned this to Siegfried but his brother didn't appear to understand Bismarck's aversion. He sniffed the spoons but did not appear to be unduly concerned with the smell.

'What we need', Siegfried had said, in his usual, grand way, 'is a set of silver cutlery.'

'Silver?' Bismarck had asked, daunted by the prospect.

'Silver doesn't smell. That's why the big bugs use it,' Siegfried had advised him. Siegfried appeared to know more about the high life than he did. Shortly after that conversation, Bismarck remembered stopping at a jeweller's on the way home to enquire about the price of silver cutlery. The salesman regarded him with a supercilious smile.

'We can do you a set of half a dozen E.P.N.S. knives, forks and spoons, that is, table, dessert and tea. All in a blue velvet-lined presentation box.'

'All I need', Bismarck told the man, softly, 'is two silver spoons and two silver forks. As for the package, well, a paper bag will do. At a pinch, I could stick them in my trouser pocket.'

The salesman shepherded Bismarck out of the shop. He even laid a palm on his back. 'I'm afraid we don't do that sort of business here, sir.' His use of the word 'sir' had a malicious edge to it. That annoyed Bismarck but he could not think of anything clever to say and just walked away, as quickly as possible. After that experience, Bismarck never tried to buy silver cutlery again. Nor did he tell Siegfried about the nasty salesman: Siegfried was quite capable of causing a terrible fuss.

Now Bismarck turned to his skinny guest.

'Do you want a spoon?' he asked, offering her the best one he possessed.

She shook her head and, making a ball of rice with her fingers, dipped it in the lentils and put it in her mouth. They ate in silence for a while. Bismarck eyed her carefully.

'How old are you?'

She shrugged. 'I don't know,' she said.

'Do you have periods?' he asked.

'Sometimes,' she said.

They finished the meal without saying anything more. Then they washed their hands and gargled in the drain area. He wiped his hands and handed her the small towel. After he had cleaned the plates and utensils, he filled two glasses of water from the tap. He watched her drink the water noisily, her neck lean, veinous and taut with intensity.

'Have you got those marks all over your body?' he asked.

She nodded. 'Would you like to have a look?' she enquired, lifting the corner of her dress.

Bismarck lit a Charminar. He blew the smoke down between his feet.

'No,' he said, frowning as he regarded her owlish questioning eyes. 'There is no need for you to show me your body.'

Later, Bismarck showed her where the latrine was on the next landing and told her that she could urinate in the drain during the night.

'Take care to wash everything away,' he said, 'and if you need to do the other thing, I'll accompany you to the latrine. This is not a nice building for young girls.'

Then he arranged a thin mattress on the floor for her and an old counterpane, torn along one side. He gave her a hard cushion that had belonged to Siegfried. She stood beside the bed he had arranged and appeared to wait for his order.

'That's for you,' he said.

She kneeled on the floor, then wriggled fully clothed

251

under the counterpane. She looked up at him and smiled. The invitation was clear.

'I have no desire to share your bed,' Bismarck informed her. He put out the light, and made his way to his own bed. He lay there for some time, listening to her settling down.

'What is your name?' he asked.

'Tara,' she said huskily.

'Do you know what that means?'

'Star,' she replied.

'And who gave you that name?' he murmured drowsily, after some time.

But Bismarck was asleep before her answer reached him.

The next morning, Bismarck gave Tara instructions to prepare rice, lentils and spinach. He put two rupees in her hand.

'Bring a chicken from the bazaar,' he said.

'A chicken?'

'Yes. You can kill it in the drain there.'

'How?'

Bismarck showed her a large knife he kept in the tin box under the bed. He mimed the action of slitting a chicken's throat. Tara shivered unhappily.

'There's nothing to it. If you clean it, I'll cook it for us when I get back from work. But don't kill it before four o'clock, otherwise it may go bad.'

'I can't do it,' she said with feeling.

Bismarck smiled. 'Well bring the chicken anyway. I'll kill it when I get back.'

'I don't eat meat,' she said miserably.

'Don't worry,' he said. 'I'll eat it myself.'

On his way home, Bismarck bought three cotton dresses and knickers. He was tempted to buy Tara some plimsolls but was uncertain about the size of her feet. When he got in, she was sitting huddled in the corner, crying.

'What's the matter?' he asked.

Tara pointed to a small black cockerel under the bed. Bismarck dragged it out by the hessian string attached to its scaly yellow leg and examined it critically, particularly the green smudge below its tail feathers.

'It's sick,' he declared, lifting the bird up in the air and squeezing its fevered body. Tara was silent.

'I can't eat this,' he said finally.

'I'm sorry,' she said, weeping and sniffing.

Bismarck opened the door and shooed the black cockerel away. Then he wet a cloth and cleaned the shit under his bed. Before the evening meal, he gave her the clothes.

'Have you washed yourself today?'

Tara nodded, drying her eyes with the back of her hand.

'Then change into something clean.'

Without hesitation, she took off her old dress. She did not, Bismarck noticed, have any breasts, only long black nipples. But for that, she might have been a boy. Then she pulled down her drawers. She had a small black tuft of hair at the junction of her spindly legs and her body was covered in blue spots. Bismarck estimated that she might be twelve, thirteen perhaps. She pulled on her new knickers proudly, smiling at Bismarck. Then she slipped on one of the dresses he had bought for her, a pink one with white diamonds. It was at least a size too large.

'You'll have to take it in,' Bismarck declared.

Tara grinned self-consciously. 'I don't know how,' she said.

'I'll show you,' Bismarck smiled.

When she was ready, she served him lentils, rice and spinach. She had also cooked a curry of okra and onions, which tasted rather nice.

'This is good,' Bismarck said appreciatively.

Tara laughed. He noticed for the first time that she had strong, unflawed white teeth.

*

When Bismarck prepared for his visit to the brothel, he worried about Tara. She had been with him for six weeks and had made his life much easier. She had even put on a little flesh and her hair had grown well below her ears. He had bought her ribbons and a celluloid comb.

'I won't be home all night,' he said.

She looked at him anxiously.

'I am going', he advised her, 'to a brothel at Foras Road.'

She seemed miserable. She would have to learn, he decided, to manage the odd night without him. After all, she had lived by herself on the pavements of Bombay, so she should be used to solitude. Besides, he had never given her the slightest indication that he was interested in her body. But despite these thoughts, Bismarck felt ashamed of himself. And he did not like the feeling.

'I have a Nepalese whore whom I see from time to time,' he explained, grinning sheepishly.

'I understand,' she murmured.

'Lock the door. And for God's sake, don't go wandering off to the latrine during the night.'

She bit her lip apprehensively. Bismarck gave her two annas.

'Buy yourself some sugar-cane juice but be up here before seven.'

Tara took the coin and stared gloomily at him.

'I'll see you in the morning,' he promised. He went out, looking very smart in his cream silk shirt and grey drill trousers. And he was wearing new brown-and-white leather shoes.

At the brothel Bismarck told his Nepalese whore about his new companion.

'A street girl, you say?'

'Very young, about twelve.'

The Nepalese whore laughed. Bismarck shook her roughly by one melon-sized breast. 'What's the matter?' he asked.

'That girl of yours. She has had many men.'

'She's a child, hardly formed,' Bismarck said, pinching the Nepalese whore's nipple. She squeezed his cock in reprisal.

'Eunuch,' she cursed.

'Slack slit,' he swore.

They wrestled playfully, rolling around each other. Bismarck tickled her until she was helpless with laughter. He slapped her arse to bring her to her senses but she laughed even more. Bismarck felt in his pocket and gave her a cigarette. He took one himself and lit both.

'In Bombay', the Nepalese whore said, 'it is impossible for an unprotected girl to survive a night on the streets without some mad beast mounting her. That is the way of this city.'

Bismarck was silent. He puffed at his Charminar. The Nepalese poked him in the ribs.

'Have you come here to fuck me or to talk about your little street girl?'

Bismarck looked at his watch. It was two in the morning. He got out of bed and put on his trousers.

'I'm going home,' he announced.

'At this hour?'

'I'll get a victoria.'

'You've paid me for another four hours,' the Nepalese whore complained.

'I know,' Bismarck said, slipping on his shoes.

She sat up and stared at him in disbelief.

'Can I take another customer?' she asked, frowning.

Bismarck shrugged.

'I won't be back tonight.'

When Bismarck returned to his room in Sandhurst Road, it was nearly four o'clock. He opened the door and found that Tara had gone. He searched all the cubicles in the latrines. He went downstairs. He called her name several times. Then he came back to his room. Her bed had not been slept in, and folded on the table were the three dresses and three pairs of knickers he had bought her.

255

Bismarck lay on his bed, wondering why she had disappeared without warning. He was resentful that she hadn't warned him that she was unhappy with their arrangement. But after he had spent some time considering the cause of her disappearance, he became resigned, and finally relieved, that she had gone. Tara was far too young for him. She was a child. He closed his eyes. When he awoke, he looked at her empty bed and felt like a sick animal. He wondered where she could be.

Every evening, on the way home, Bismarck looked out for Tara. There was nobody he could talk to about his problem. He had no friends; he had been a loner all his life. He thought of going to see the Nepalese whore but suspected that she might make fun of him. He wished he could speak to Heidi. She was such a wise person. But Bismarck felt that the subject might cause her offence. Certainly Naval wouldn't approve of Heidi's brother living with a street girl.

Then, six months after Tara had left him, he saw her. She was with a tall young man, possibly a Moslem, sitting on the Apollo Bunder wall. She was dressed in a saffron sari and her hair was oiled, pinned neatly in a bun, with a circlet of jasmine around it. The man and Tara were sitting close together. Bismarck approached them cautiously.

'Hallo, Tara,' he said.

She looked up at him but did not register surprise. She had a smudge of rouge on each cheek and her lips were painted red.

'Hallo, Bismarck,' she said, in the same husky voice.

'Why did you leave me?' he asked. His voice was quiet. Even the implied rebuke was tender. The tall young man laughed at him. Tara got up and led Bismarck aside.

'Go away,' she said, 'I'll come tomorrow. Please don't make trouble with this guy. He's a knifer.'

Bismarck outstared the young man with ferocity. He had never experienced such rage. He was quite prepared to rip the man's windpipe out with his fingers.

Tara caught his trembling hand. 'Tomorrow,' she said, 'I promise you. Go away now.'

As Bismarck walked away he was conscious that the young man was mocking him. He quickened his steps so that he would not have to endure any further humiliation.

When Bismarck got home from work next day, Tara was waiting outside the door. She was in the same saffron sari. She was still painted and smelled of cheap perfume. Her fingers and toes had been dipped in henna and she wore silver sandals. She looked at least five years older than she had six months ago. Bismarck let her in. He stood awkwardly, looking at her, searching for a change in her big owlish eyes.

'Who was that man?' he asked.

'A predator,' Tara answered.

'You slept with him?' Bismarck demanded.

Tara nodded. 'Of course. That's the way things are with me.'

'You're just a child,' Bismarck shouted.

'I'm a woman,' Tara said simply.

'Why did you leave me?' he asked.

Tara hung her head. 'I'm no good for you. I have an illness.'

He moved his face closer to hers, to search for an answer. 'What illness?'

Tara rubbed the side of her neck with the end of her sari. He saw a dark brown stain on the cloth. She pointed to a small greyish-pink circle on her neck, from where she had removed the pigment. Her eyes filled with tears.

'Can you see?' she asked hoarsely, arching her neck for his inspection.

'What is it?' Bismarck demanded, staring at the strange mark.

'I'm a leper,' Tara said quietly.

Bismarck took Tara downstairs to the Irani restaurant for a cup of tea, a bowl of keema and some bread. Nobody

257

paid much attention to them. That was where the local men brought their whores. Bismarck poured his tea into the saucer, blew on it and sipped it noisily.

'Do you want to stay with me?' he asked finally.

Tara shook her head.

'You'd rather sleep on the pavements?' he demanded.

Tara shrugged.

'Listen,' Bismarck said, 'you must have treatment. The illness you have is curable. We'll go together. It's my day off tomorrow.'

Tara stared at him. 'What's the use of it all? I may as well earn some money on the streets before things get too bad.'

'Are you completely crazy?' Bismarck screamed. The other customers in the shop looked up, expecting him to strike her. Men often beat their whores in this restaurant. Bismarck squeezed Tara's arm with passion. She did not respond to his anger but finished her meal in silence.

Tara did many things to please Bismarck in the ensuing months. She never wore the saffron sari again, which she knew he detested; she never used rouge or lip paint, nor did she dab herself with the cheap perfume. She wore simple cotton dresses, white socks and plimsolls. And she never failed to attend the leper hospital at the appointed times. Bismarck was reassured by the doctor about their occupation of the same room, the preparation of food, and the degrees of possible contagion. He bought her a spring bed, a wall mirror, a golden crucifix, rosary beads, a picture of the Sacred Heart, glass bangles, two ivory clips for her hair, a parasol, a brush and comb set, a red plastic belt with a black buckle, a depilatory razor, perfumed soap, talcum powder, and a mackintosh for the monsoon season. On the evening of the day on which Tara received her final negative test result, Bismarck took her to French Bridge for a kulfi, to Chowpatty Beach for bhel-puri and finally to the Metro cinema to see an American musical.

Bismarck expressed mock astonishment that after three years Tara's breasts had still not developed. When he occasionally saw her bathe under the tap in the corner of their room, he would ask her with a laugh, 'When are you going to grow some breasts?'

'Breasts', Tara would scoff, 'are for babies, not for grown men.'

This, Bismarck knew, was a sly dig at the Nepalese whore, whom he still visited. But the reproach was always oblique, and avoided reference to the fact that Bismarck had never tried to sleep with her. Tara suspected that although he wanted to, Bismarck was afraid. Sometimes in the early morning, when the sheet fell away from his body, she could see that he was having priapic dreams. She hoped that they were about her. Tara often dreamed about Bismarck coming to her at night, taking her silently then returning to his bed. For this, she waited.

'Next week', Bismarck informed Tara, 'is Christmas. And as this has been a special year for both of us, I'll take you to the cathedral at Bandra for the midnight mass.'

He tried to explain to her what it would be like.

'Is it like a circus?' she asked. She had once had a sweeping job in a circus and had never forgotten it. She could not imagine anything more wonderful than a circus.

'There are no elephants or horses, but it is something like a circus,' Bismarck agreed.

'Will we exchange presents there?'

'Not there, but when we return home,' he said.

The thought of the mass excited her. She spoke about it continually.

'This Christmas,' Tara proposed, 'I'd like to give your sister a present.'

Bismarck looked doubtful.

'She may', he reflected, 'consider that an impertinence.'

Bismarck phoned Heidi on the morning of Christmas Eve.

'Oh it's you, Bismarck. Thank you for the card. I couldn't decipher the other name.'

'Tara,' he said.

'You've got yourself a girlfriend at last. It's about time. Naval thought that you might have been the other way.'

'She's just a simple girl,' Bismarck muttered evasively.

'I hope she's not living with you in that dreadful room.'

'This is all we can afford, Heidi.'

'It's time you bettered yourself,' she yawned.

Bismarck took a deep breath. He wished he could make Heidi understand that it would be difficult for him to do better. She never seemed to appreciate that he was not as clever as she was.

'Tara and I would like to give you our presents.'

Heidi made a clicking noise with her tongue.

'Afraid it's out of the question, Bismarck. Naval and I are off to Goa tonight.'

'We didn't intend to come to the house, of course,' Bismarck said.

Heidi hummed thoughtfully. 'I'm going shopping shortly. If you could rush down here by, say, eleven, I could see you outside the pharmacy at the bottom of my hill.'

'Thank you, Heidi.'

'And don't be late.'

Heidi asked the chauffeur to turn off the main road. She intended to walk the fifty yards back to the pharmacy, greet Bismarck briefly and receive his dreadful gifts. It had taken all morning to stiffen her resolve to see the squalid business to a conclusion.

She was shocked by Bismarck's skinny black girlfriend. Tara was in a blue-and-white dress, three-quarter socks and sandals. Jesus Christ, Heidi thought, what the hell has the mad bugger picked up?

'She's very beautiful,' Tara whispered to Bismarck.

'Tara thinks that you're very beautiful,' Bismarck grinned.

260

Heidi half smiled, dropping their two small gifts into her shopping bag.

'I'll send you a cheque when we get back from Goa,' she promised Bismarck.

They stood before her on the pavement, grateful that she had made time to receive them. Heidi was dressed in shimmering white sharkskin, her brown hair, streaked with auburn, pinned up on her head and secured by a silver clasp. Her long nails were iridescent pearly-pink, and her suntanned skin gleamed with well-being. Tara inhaled the mysterious and subtle perfume Heidi's body seemed to exude. In her white kid high heels, Heidi was at least nine inches taller than Bismarck and Tara.

'Didn't I tell you', said Bismarck, 'that my sister was a queen?'

'I have never seen lips so wet and red,' whispered Tara in awe.

'It's a wonderful thing to see on Christmas Eve,' reflected Bismarck, as they watched Heidi swing elegantly through the sunlight to her limousine.

Bismarck and Tara arrived at the road leading up Mount Mary to the great cathedral. Already the concourse was jammed with struggling celebrants; the choir, sweating in gold and scarlet vestments; jigging blue stars of Bethlehem; and a throned effigy of the Virgin and Child, swaying precariously above reverent heads towards the vaulted entrance. Inside the building, Tara was subdued by a luxuriance of statuary, fat votive candles, rococo flourishes along the nave and the aureate ostentation of the sacrarium. She watched the thurifers corrupt the air with frankincense, and trembled when the resonance of the organ, tingling through the pews, supported the glottal swell of *Gloria in Excelsis* swirling up to the clerestory. The princes of the church, in purple, mitred and splendid as seraphim, commanded a procession up the aisle. Everywhere people prayed. Bismarck fell to his knees, hands clenched, eyes closed, as he mumbled half-remembered words. He had not been a man to observe his obligations.

'Can I pray?' Tara asked Bismarck.

'Of course,' he said.

'What shall I pray for?' she asked, as they kneeled side by side. He did not reply but smiled vacuously, as though the excitement had been too much for him.

'What shall I pray for?' Tara repeated, poking him wildly with her elbow.

He looked startled as he tried to comprehend the question. But no sooner had he understood than the answer came from his lips.

'Happiness,' Bismarck whispered. 'Just happiness.'

Tara shut her eyes and lowered her head, lost in the mystical madness that engulfed them. Bismarck turned and saw the circular greyish-pink blemish on her arched neck. Now benign, it would always mark her. He placed his mouth against Tara's neck. Then kissed the fateful lesion, in answer to the prayers that bound their destinies together.

Plage de Pampelonne
October 1988